The

Virus

II

Searching for people and looking for a
new home

RON SAINT

ACKNOWLEDGMENTS

To all my friends who encouraged me to complete this book.

The virus started one year ago. At first, the news reported that it came from a market in Wuhan, China. The only truth about the news was it did come from China. It just did not start in a market. It was developed in a lab and escaped making its way to the rest of the world.

Six months after the virus hit America, the pharmaceutical industry put out a vaccine, and it was protecting anyone who received the shot. But by then, eighty percent of the people in the world had died.

John Carstairs had taken his wife, children and grandkids to Florida and was staying at his younger daughter's house when the country was told to hunker down in place.

When John and his family drove to the facility to get their shot, they were told to board a truck, and they would be driven to another location. John, and Anna, his six-year-old granddaughter, who speaks beyond her years, climbed on the back of one of the trucks. His son-in-law, Donald handed his eighteen-month-old grandson, Ben, up to him. A National Guardsman told them the truck was full. They thought they would meet at the dispensary when they got the shot.

John was concerned when the truck his family members had gotten on turned in a different direction and he had a reason to be. Every other truck went to a different location. One went to Jacksonville, and one went to Pensacola.

It was a hot day in July when John left Pensacola pushing his two grandchildren in a double stroller. He hoped he would find transportation. Cars and trucks were plentiful, cars and trucks with gas were nonexistent. There was one thing for sure. They were going to make it home if he had to walk every step. John was not the type of person who would complain about having to walk home. He looked at having the choice to walk home as a gift. He was a, the glass is half full person.

During his search for his family, he met Ralph who was a math whiz and former college professor. He saved John and his grand kids from two men who was going to kill John and to take Anna and Ben to their farm and make them work.

Later the two of them had a friendly encounter with two men who John later saved from a death by bullets. The two men helped them save a doctor and his wife. During the process they locked two men in a morgue.

Before parting company, the two men invited the doctor and his wife to come live in their town. He told John and Ralph they and their families were welcome. John told him he would take him up on his offer after he found his family. Ralph said he would be delighted.

Not far up the road after parting company, John and Ralph found Betty, who was the women's national rifle shooting champion and had appeared on the cover of many magazines. She was left in a house with her seven-year-old son Jammie. After feeding the woman and her son she told them about her husband and his friends leaving them.

She turned out to be the wife of one of the men John had locked away in that hospital morgue. She told them she did not want to know where he was.

Betty told them she had an aunt who lived in

Brunswick, Georgia. If she and Jammie could get to her, they could live with her.

The next morning after staying in a motel and having breakfast in the parking lot they set out to find a car for her to make the trip to South Georgia. Two hours later they gave up on finding transportation for her. They headed to a town where a woman Betty knew lived. After finding the woman and her husband dead, Betty decided to remain with Ralph and John.

After finding his family, the group had to battle a group of South American drug dealers to get his son-n-law's truck back.

On their way home, they helped a Mexican man named Juan Garcia and his pretty wife, Maria. They helped obtain medicine for their young son, Miguel, by flushing four bad guys out of a drugstore. They found out that days earlier two of the guys had raped and killed a young girl. Two of the boys were teenagers and they said had been forced to take part in the rape but had not helped kill the girl. John believed them and he sent the two on their way. Only to meet them two days later when the boys dropped off food at Juan's house. The next time he saw them was when he spotted their vehicle in the parking lot of a small church. He eased inside and heard the boys praying.

He saw them for the last time the day he and everyone were leaving for Roswell. He gave them some gas and left their guns on the side of the road for them to pick up.

John found out Juan and his family were on their way to Atlanta and had set up residences in the town because they were afraid to go any further.

Juan invited John and the others to rest for a few

days at a house they had moved into. When the Carstairs left, Juan and his family went with them.

They later found out Juan was a professional wrestler, and his wife was his manager. Donald said he recognized Juan and his wife from seeing them on television.

After spending three days in the house Juan and his family were living in, the caravan set out for John's family home in Roswell, Georgia.

John thought, just a few days ago I was pushing my two grandchildren in a stroller not knowing if I would live to see my family again. Now here we are all with several new friends headed home. He looked at his wife. "Ain't life great."

Millie smiled. "It is. But it has been greater."

What was waiting for them at home was not a peaceful and quiet home. One of the neighbors they found still there was Bill, who had once been a guest of the state prison system. He had formed a committee and appointed himself the head honcho. Not long after John returned home Bill revealed what he wanted John to do.

After lying to Bill about going along with his plan, John had to kill him. Only to later find out Bill and his army of drug addicts had killed all of John's neighbors and their kids when they tried to leave his committee.

And that wasn't all, Bill had planned to use his army and an insider to take over a town in North Georgia. It turned out to be the town the two men John saved from being shot in the back had invited them to make their home in.

The Army's leaders kidnap Anna to keep John

from going to the town and warning them about the takeover.

A childless couple, William and his wife, Debra were lucky enough to escape the neighborhood with John and his family. William's brother, who has struggled with addiction for years, used his education in history to decipher a clue and saved Anna only seconds away from being blown up in a historical house.

After securing the town and settling in and thinking the fighting is over. That notion is put to rest when two men from a summer retreat inhabited by released prisoners slipped into the town and molested a woman and her daughter. The team that fought so hard for a chance at peace had to swing into action one more time.

They brought the men back to the town for an abridged version of a trial.

Keeping the men in jail would have meant a loss of food and man hours they did not have to spare. A firing squad conducted their punishment shortly after if found guilty. Swift justice would work as a deterrent for anyone else.

The North Atlanta community

The area had been a water treatment plant before the virus. Now twenty-two families have made it their home. With them, they brought food, clothes and several useful items that had been salvaged. The items such as tools are used and brought back for the next person who will need them. The food section is used as a huge pantry for everyone. No one takes more or less than what their family needs. The system works well enough that there is no one holding anyone accountable.

There are thirty-seven kids and teens from the age of two to eighteen years old. The rest are adults. two men and two women are single parents. Five married couples had no kids. In all, eighty-three people are living in the community. They moved into the apartments and houses close to the ponds that supply the water. The water is dipped up into buckets and taken to the family's yard and boiled. There is an area where the entire community could boil water when the fields were being worked. They cooked a meal for everyone to save time by not having to go to their home and cook. It was better to wash their hands and face together because it saved time. And occasionally the entire group would have a cookout after work.

The members met as they moved around looking for a place to live. Within a month, people had gathered from Dekalb, Gwinnett and Fulton County.

Ten in the group had grown up farming. They were the ones who suggested they turn as much of the land as they could into gardens. Thanks to them the people would have food. Vegetables anyway.

One of the farm girls named Jennie stood. She was five foot five inches tall and weighed one hundred and five pounds with black hair and dark eyes. Her skin was light brown. She had a five-year-old daughter. Her husband died from the virus. "My family owned one of the black operated farms in South Georgia," she told them. "We will have to locate seeds, fertilizer and tools."

Among the group were six pick-ups and three cars.

A search turned up in a community directory book. with a listing of businesses in three counties around them. Each driver received a written list of places to look for what they needed. First on the list of the search was gas. Two men in the group said they had worked at the gas storage facility, and they knew how to get gas and diesel fuel.

Since there was no gas in any of the trucks, they would have to walk to the storage tanks and bring back the gas. Everyone who was old enough except for the women who had kids to watch, went on an expedition to bring gas back to power the vehicles. Each person had two gas containers that held two and a half gallons each. Better to distribute the weight to each hand than have a five-gallon can in one hand. After their first trip they managed to scrounge up four fifty-five-gallon drums. They loaded them on the trucks and brought back two hundred and twenty gallons of gas.

They found one flatbed wrecker and it used to transport two tractors and attachments from a dealer to the community.

Two days later they had everything they needed to start getting the ground ready to plant.

Jennie was thinking ahead and told everyone to gather all the vinegar and canning jars they could find and bring it back. When someone asked her what it was for, she explained that the food would rot if it wasn't canned.

After the tractors plowed the land, Jennie and the others went about getting the weeds out and setting in the seeds. It was challenging work, but no one complained. They were thankful for the opportunity not to starve.

People in the group were amazed at how hard the members who grew up on a farm worked. And they made the work look easy.

On the day, the gardens were all planted, everyone stood beside the field admiring their work. One person commented on how beautiful it was. Another admitted he hadn't believed they could do it.

When it was time to harvest, not all gardens produced as well as others. Four had failed to produce a crop at all. But in the end, there was enough food to last until next year. Then the people repeated the process.

One of the single moms admitted it was depressing to think that would be her life from now on. Year after year planting seeds, so she could live. She commented how she wished she could find a man.

The Middle Georgia Community

Everyone working in the fields stopped and stared at five pickup trucks stopped on the road beside the field. The bed of each truck loaded with men and women. They stepped off the trucks and looked around. Each holding a weapon in their hands. A man about six-foot five inches, thick chest, wide shoulders raised a huge arm and pointed a finger at the women. His long dark bushy hair caught a gust of wind from his back, and it looked like he had a bonnet on his head. He scratched his chin under his long dark beard and spit. The group took off after the man and walked across the field slowly.

One of the workers stopped and leaned on the handle of the tool he was using to chop weeds. He stared at the group as they closed in on the workers. "Welcome, I am in charge here," he said to the big man. "My name is Jason."

"Is that right." Then he said back to Jason in a deep voice. "Now I don't remember asking who is in charge or anyone's name. You know why? Because I don't give a damn."

"I just want to welcome newcomers to our community."

"That's downright friendly of you. What are you growing in this field?"

"Beans here." Jason pointed. "Corn over there. If you don't have any place to stay you are welcome to join us. All we need is that everyone must work in the fields and do other chores. That way we will all have enough to eat. There is an empty field you can have to grow your food."

"Work, in the dirt you said. I got a better idea. You folks do the work while we watch. And we will still eat."

"Another field hand piped up. "It doesn't work that way. You don't work you don't eat."

The big man scratched his beard. "Says who."

"I for one just did."

"Well." The leader raised his pistol and shot the man between his eyes.

"Daddy," a girl yelled out. She ran to the man on the ground and knelt beside him.

Everyone stood wide-eyed.

"Now, anybody else feel the way that fellow did?"

Nobody said a word.

"I didn't think anyone else would object." He looked around. "I think we have found a place to stay." He pushed the girl kneeling beside her daddy over as he walked off. On his way to his truck, he grabbed a young girl's hair. "You're mine." He turned around. "This town belongs to me and my friends now. You all work for me."

The gang cheered as they walked to their vehicles. After reaching their trucks two men climbed in the bed of a new looking Ford and pulled bottles of whiskey from boxes that were in the back. The men opened several bottles and passed them around. The members would turn the bottles up, pull them down and hand them to someone else. One of the bottles emptied of its content went flying across the road after five men drank from it.

The imbibing went on for two hours before the gang drove to the town.

The gang settled in and made their presence known by walking around threatening to shoot anyone who didn't do as they say. The leader told the men if he shoots, one of them, their woman becomes his.

The first night, the gang members went into all the houses and gathered up all the weapons and women.

Two days after the takeover of the town a field hand decided he had had enough. He dropped his hoe and ran toward a line of trees to escape.

"Look at that fool," a gang member standing watch over the town's people said. "He thinks he is going somewhere. I'll give the poor bastard some hope. Just a little farther." He raised his rifle and waited until the runner reached the trees before he fired, hitting the man in his back. "I bet he thought he was going to get away. Nothing like giving someone hope."

The Rangers

Jes Crier eased out of bed, snatched his pants up, pulled them on and buckled them around his thirty-six-inch waist. Next, he picked up his shirt and ran his finger over the curved patch stitched on the left sleeve with the word RANGER on it. Under it was the patch reading AIRBORNE. On each sleeve were three stripes pointing up resting on three rockers, in the center was a star. He slid his arms that measured eighteen inches around in the sleeves. After bending and straightening his fingers a few times and buttoning his shirt on his forty-eight-inch chest he tucked the tail in his trousers and fastened his belt.

Jes turned to the mirror and looked at his six-foot four, two-hundred-and-fifty-pound image staring back at him while singing. "I want to be an Airborne Ranger; I want to live a life of danger. But just not to be killed by a virus, he said to himself." He thought, back eighteen years. He had been the best tackle his high school had ever had. That put him on his way to LSU when school started back. But things changed because of a night of celebrating with friends. He had not meant to get into a scuffle with the three police officers. But one of the officers got in his face and was yelling at him for underaged drinking. That sent him off into a rage.

The judge delayed his trial because one of the officers had to heal from the bruises on his face.

The judge said if he would enter into the army, he could avoid jail time. With that went his chance of becoming a professional football player.

A knock on the door pulled him away from his thoughts.

"Come in only if you have good news."

The door opened and in stepped a man wearing a shirt with the same patches Jes had on his. The only difference was the stripes on his sleeve rested on two rockers. His name patch read West. He stood six-four and topped the scales at two hundred and thirty pounds, all muscle, and arms as big as his lead Sargent's. "The vehicles are ready, and the men are waiting on you to give the word to pull out, Sergeant Major."

"Well, let's get the hell out of here, Staff Sergeant."

The two men exited the room, walked to the street, and stared at three Hummers. Connected to the back of each vehicle were trailers loaded with supplies.

"We were lucky these were just gone over from top to bottom. We found plenty of tires mounted on rims. We loaded four extras for each."

"Good what other goodies are we taking?" Crier asked.

"Plenty of food and water and." West pulled back a tarp exposing six M4 Carbines. He lifted them one at a time from the back and handed one to each man. "We have six. One for each of you." He pointed at two small drums sitting in the middle of the trailer. "And fourteen thousand rounds for each Hummer."

"Lets have a pow wow," Jes walked and stood next to the second Hummer in line. "Men, we have no idea what is out there. We are prepared to deal with anything we might run across. Civilians anyway. We have the advantage with our Ranger training to manage anything. What we must look out for are large groups or gangs. West has been out scouting the area. He is going to fill us in on what he has observed."

The driver of the lead Hummer, whose name was Dawson Garvey, six foot two inches. Two hundred pounds could lay his hand upside a man's head before he knew what hit him. He knew several ways to kill a man. "I just want to know. Did you fulfill my request? If you did all's well?" Dawson said.

"I'll get to you last, ass. Now shut your pie hole and listen. There are not a lot of people out there. And there are only two types. The good and the bad. The good are particularly good and the bad are bad."

Dawson chimed in. "The good and the bad. Were there any ugly people? Or shall I say any pretty? Really, I could care less if they are pretty or not long as they are female. I have been couped up on this post with only you guys to talk to for a long time."

Dawson's gunner, Mike Hand, was six foot two hundred pounds fifth degree black belt. Sometimes when Mike got to fighting, he lost his stopping mechanism. He spoke up. "Yeah, he's tired of sleeping with his blow-up doll."

Dawson fisted Mike on the arm. "You are just jealous because she's prettier than yours."

"Bull. he got the ugliest one in the store, Sarge," Mike said.

"That's fine. You couldn't reach around yours."

"Alright ladies that's enough of the bull shit. Let's get down to business," Jes said.

"Women is business, Sarge," Dawson said.

"I got you something Dawson." West shoved his hand in his pocket as he walked to Dawson's Hummer. He pulled his hand from his pocket and ripped the wrapper off a candy bar. "Open wide." He pinched one of Dawson's breasts causing his mouth to open with a yelp. West shoved the candy bar in his friend's mouth and walked to where we had been standing.

West continued. "The good want food and water and will ask for help. Remember one thing, your survival comes first. The bad want what you have too. The difference is they won't ask for it. They will try to take it. Not just some, all of it. There is no reasoning with them. The only way to deal with them is to kill them. And don't hesitate because they are Americans."

I believe Seargeant Crier has some instructions to add."

"This is not like it was when we were fighting the war. We had to be careful and make sure we were shooting at the enemy they wanted us to shoot at. And the government wanted to Court Marshall your ass when you slipped up. That is not going to happen now. If you think some one is going to kill you. Blow the bastard to pieces first, then think about it later.

And one more thing. We must treat the gang members like the radicals we encountered in the war. There is no rehabilitating them. So, you know what to do with them. West has something for you."

West pulled two bags from his Hummer. "One more thing before I pass these out. Some of the people we encounter will be on there last leg and it is easy to fill sorry for them. But we don't know how long it will take us to get to our homes. And the time will come when we will be traveling on our own to get to where we are going. We have one hundred gallons of diesel in each trailer. That will take us at least fifteen hundred miles. Luckly we all live in the Southeast."

Crier spoke up. "I paired us up by where we lived. One man will drop the other off and drive on home. That is when you must be careful because you will not have a gunner. Dawson, your home being in Atlanta, I recommend that you figure out some other place to go. Atlanta like all the big cities is not safe."

"That is why I am going home with my gunner. I have no family to go to, so it worked out fine. Mike's family lives on a big farm in South Alabama. I am sure they will need all the protection they can get."

Carl, the driver of the second Hummer in line was five eleven and a lean mean fighting machine. Two at a time was his favorite way to go. Walker rides with Carl, he lives in Houston. Six two and two hundred and ten pounds is quiet and wastes no time taking care of business. Walker is going to stay with me and my family in South Georgia." Carl said.

"West and I both live in Monroe Louisiana. Our homes are not that far apart. One of us will drop the other off."

"Hey, sarge do you know where your brother, Les is?" Dawson asked.

"Last I heard he and Richard were going to Fort Stewart to see some friends. That was the same time we were leaving to come here. Wish I knew for sure."

"Man, what convenient names, Les and Jes. Is that a Louisiana thing." Carl said.

"Get with the program will you guys," Jes said.

"It sure is nice to be leaving here after a year." Virgle said.

The commander was right about people trying to loot the base," Mike said. "Especially the armory. He was right to request us six come here and guard it. I can only imagine the damage those weapons could do in the wrong hands. I just don't see why it took a year for them to be moved to a secure location."

Carl asked, "Do you know where they are taking them, Sergeant Major?"

Jes looked out over the base. "I wasn't privy to that information." He watched the men close and lock the doors of the armory.

"I guess they loaded everything all of them are leaving," West said as the men loaded into the trucks and drove off.

A staff car broke from the trucks and drove to where the six men were waiting. The car stopped and a Bird Colonel got out of the back seat. He walked over to the men with six envelopes in his hand. "As you were promised for spending an extra year guarding the weapons." He handed each man an envelope. "Your separation papers, gentlemen. Sorry, there is no separation pay. Just take what you men need and consider it a thank you." The officer got in the car and the driver pulled off.

"Sorry, for no separation pay," Dawson mocked the officer.

Jes looked at the envelope in the men's hands. He held his hand up. This represents eighteen years of service. No thank you, kiss my ass or anything."

West held his up. "Fifteen for me."

"Six for me," Dawson said.

Mike tapped his paper on his chin. "Six for me."

Virgle tossed his letter on the dash. "Eight years for me. How about you Walker?"

"Seven wonderful years. I was going for twenty,"

Walkes said.

"Do we get anything else for our service?" Carl said.

Yep, the colonel said for us to take anything we want." Jes said. "Follow me guys. I have a surprise for us."

They entered Criers quarters and came out with three m60 machine guns. After loading one in each Hummer, they spent thirty minutes wheeling out and loading twenty thousand rounds on ammo for each of the guns.

Mike spoke up. "Something that has been on my mind is how was that vaccine developed in four months. I was under the impression it took a couple of years or longer to develop something like that?"

"You are not wrong about that," Crier said. "I have a friend that somehow obtains information no one else has access to. He told me the pharmaceutical companies had been working on it for two and a half years before it came out. So, the government knew about the virus long before it hit."

"They knew China was developing it. In order to develop a vaccine, it would be necessary to have a sample of the virus. The government must have known it was going to be released on the world," Dawson said.

Crier nodded. "I believe you are right. But what we don't know why? Unless it was a test to see how much controlled we would let them have."

Mike shook his head. "They didn't think it through very well. The virus didn't leave much to control."

"That friend believes the Chinese set a different virus loose on us. It wasn't the one the vaccine was developed for."

"You can't trust those bastards as far as I can throw one of those Hummers," West said.

"Which bastards? The Chinese of ours," Dawson said.

"Both of them," Carl said.

West reached into his Hummer and pulled out three bags. "To many minds thinking got in the way of each other. Here you are, guys," he handed a bag to one man in each vehicle. "In that bag you will find one map, one GPS and a satellite phone for each man both with a charging cable. The satellite signal still works. And two radios with a good range. Last was peanut butter and jelly sandwiches and two Gatorades."

Dawson waved at West. "Did you forget one thing? My good friend.

West pulled on his bottom lip. "I don't recall anything else." He looked at the long face of the lead driver. "Oh, you must mean this." West pulled the tarp away from the front of the trailer showing six cases of beer. "For later men. Grab you a case each."

"Oh, yes," Dawson yelled. "I knew our friend wouldn't let us down."

The loud roar of an engine coming down the street got their attention. The car's pipes bellowed when the driver let off the gas and stopped next to the Men.

The driver shoved the transmission into park and revved the engine a couple of times and let it idle down. His head turned smiling at the six men.

"It's that civilian preacher from across town." Dawson said.

The driver opened his door and stepped out of the Chevrolet Impala. It was solid black with lots of chrome and looked like it had just come off the showroom floor. "Man, don't you just love that sound."

"Sure, is a pretty thang. What year is it?" West asked.

"1958, got a 348 engine with three factory two-barrel carburetors. It's one of the later ones that came with 315 horsepower. She's a beauty isn't she? I don't want to wear it out, so when I find a home I will park it and find something else to drive."

"Where did you get it," Mike asked.

"My granddaddy bought it brand new. He hardly ever drove it. When I told him I was going to become a preacher he handed me the keys and said. 'This is yours. It will outrun the devil.'

"Will it," Mike asked.

"Don't count on it. I see you gentlemen are ready to hit the road."

"Reverand, Allen Ball, what are you doing still here? I thought you were leaving when the weapon's convoy left," West said.

"The Colonel said I could stay as long as I choose to, and I can help myself to anything I care to take. He said his men had taken all they want. Nice of him to share the Army's stuff with a civilian."

"We all are civilians now. He gave us our walking papers. It must be a downsizing thing," West said.

Ball reached into the front seat of his car and pulled out a plate covered with a white towel. "I have something for you fellows. Like a parting gift. He handed the plate to Jes.

Jes put the covered dish to his nose. "That smells like fried chicken." He pulled the towel off. "Hell, it is chicken."

Ball said. "Hardly a way to address such a gift."

"So, preacher, where did you run across this?" Jes, reached up and pulled a feather off Ball's shoulder. "Is this from the chicken?"

"Where one finds chicken, they will find feathers. A little sacrifice from a friend's stock. Luckily I was raised on a farm. I have been feeding them for a year, so I could have eggs. Since I am leaving and cannot take them with me. I figured why not."

"Where are you going Ball?" West asks.

"Anywhere my Chevy and the Lord takes me."

"Well, we are headed to Georgia, Alabama and Louisiana," West told him. Good luck and thanks for the chicken."

Jes said. "Let's go to the armory and see if they left anything fellows."

"May our paths cross again." Ball got in the Chevy and drove off.

The Rangers stopped at the armory and went inside. "They cleaned it out, sarge," Mike said.

"Why would anybody paint that wall knowing we were leaving," Walker said.

"Because of this," Jes said and walked over and pulled a corner and one panel fell exposing four drums of ammo. "Fifty thousand rounds."

"For what?" Carl asked.

He pulled the other panel down. "For this."

"Wow, a Ma Deuce." Dawson said.

"I didn't trust the colonel to not search our rooms when we were out."

They loaded the gun and ammo and left the post.

CHAPTER 1

The Town

Juan Garcia, his wife Maria, and son Miguel were the first people to show up at John's house. Not long after, Ralph and Betty appeared and before the door closed, Donald, Julie, Anna, and Ben walked in followed by Peggy.

They were having a get together to celebrate six months of friendship and surviving one year of the virus.

John had a kerosene lantern burning but told them they were going to gather in the backyard around the wood burning fire pit. It would save them fuel, and they would have plenty of wood.

Fried peach and apple pies were going to be their treats tonight. Followed with a couple of drinks. John and some of the other residents ran across a liquor store a couple of months back. He made off with plenty of Millie's favorite which is scotch. And bourbon for himself.

John sat in the barber chair facing the street. The man standing behind him, working with a comb and scissors was Daniel Hawkins. Daniel had been the barber in the town thirty years before the virus took eighty percent of his customers away. During those years, he used electric clippers and had a machine that produced hot lather from soap. He still uses the white foam made by swishing a brush around on a cake of soap at the bottom of a thick cup and is not heated. Still a man can get a shave and a haircut.

Daniel had finished giving John a haircut and was laying the chair back to finish him off with a shave. The door opened and in walked a man in his early thirties. He ran his hand through his hair. Hop up pops, I need a haircut, and I am in a hurry."

"Wait your turn fellow," Daniel said.

The man picked up a razor. "Well, if he is not going to leave, I'll shave him. What do you think about that, fellow?"

John motioned the man over with a curling of his finger.

"Okay, I'll shave you."

"Put that razor down. You don't know how to use it," Hawkins said.

"No," The man moved next to John. "So, you going to leave, or do I get to shave you?"

"Neither option appeals to me," John said and caught the man with an upper cut under the chin.

The man straightened up and stumbled backward. Hawkins opened the door, and the man backed out, passing Dean who was standing on the sidewalk. He made it a few feet more and fell flat on his back.

Dean looked down at the man before he walked in the barbershop. "Walter was looking a little strange."

"Is that his name? He was acting sort of strange in here," John said.

"Do you know that man?" Hawkins asked.

Dean looked out the door at the stretched-out body. "He showed up two weeks ago with a younger woman and a little boy."

"Is he productive?" John asked.

"Somewhat. The girl is more."

"Probably not worth the trouble he might cause," John said.

Dean watched a young girl bend over and try lifting Walter off the sidewalk. "There's the girl now. I guess she takes care of him."

John turned to Dean. "What time is that meeting?"

"Let's head on over. It should be starting as soon as we get there," Dean told him.

The two men walked out the door and watched the girl struggle to get Walter to his feet. Neither offered any help. Even though people were more likely to lend a helping hand to someone now. This was a situation that was better left alone.

They reached the meeting after a couple of minutes. "Going by the number of people there, we must be the last to arrive," John said.

Dean glanced at his watch. "But we are on time."

"Now we can get started and on time for the first time ever." A man at the front of the room said.

Another man up front walked over and stood in front of a large map of Georgia hanging on the wall. It was one of those plastic maps that could be drawn on and erased.

The man standing in front of the crowd raised both hands. "If I can have everyone's attention we will get started. We need to be finished before it gets dark." The room went silent, and he proceeded.

"Listen up people. Does everyone know the reason for this meeting?"

Everyone gave a nod. Except for one man. He said, "To talk about relocating the town down south."

The man up front answered, "No not the town. Just the people who live here. Dean, do you want to explain what we have in mind? "I'm sure everyone knows Dean Martin, out chief of police."

Dean stood, walked to the front, and faced everyone. "Good morning, folks. I'll get right to the business at hand. What we have in mind is moving to South or Middle Georgia."

A man on the second row said, "For what reason."

"Very good question," Dean said. "For one, because the weather is warmer most of the year. And second there is more level land there to plant crops."

"We did well here this year. Didn't we?" a man asked.

A man stood in the back and walked to the front. He faced the people. "We did okay, but it wasn't enough to carry us. Most of our food came from crops we planted a good way off. A lot of the gardens were planted before the folks who planted them died. That was because the virus hit here later than it did in other areas."

A woman stood in the middle of the room. "What you are saying is we are going to have to plant more this coming season. Is that right?"

"That's right and we don't have enough level ground here to do that. Another thing I want you to think about. How much of your time is going into cutting and hauling wood for heat and cooking? By moving South, we can delay the onset of cold weather."

"Where are we going to go? I mean what town?" A man asked.

"We don't know yet. What we have in mind is to send a group to look for a suitable place." Dean turned to the map and carefully outlined an area with a red marker. "Around this area here." He had drawn a rectangle starting five miles West of Perry, South to the North of Tifton and East to Brunswick, North to Claxton and back to the starting point. He blocked out Valdosta and Albany, Waycross, and Brunswick with a black marker. He told them, "We would prefer staying away from towns that had large populations. Maybe look at the ones that had no more than eight to twelve thousand people before the virus. Gangs tend to form in these larger towns. And we don't want to impede on another community if there are others there."

"I used to get watermelons from Cordele," came from the back of the room.

Dean turned his attention to John to see his reaction.

John looked at Dean, raised his eyebrows and shook his head. He cut his eyes to the man who had spoken hoping he didn't see him.

Dean said, "That town is right on the Interstate, and it could draw the attention of any group passing by. John and I had an altercation with some fellows there six months ago. Doctor John Airs and his wife came from there. they had a terrible experience before they left." He didn't mention that he, John, Ralph, and Jerry Tilson left two men in drawers in the hospital morgue. And they were alive when they left them.

A woman in the back of the room stood. "I would

like to know about the schools in the areas."

"I don't believe that is an issue we will have to be concerned about," Dean said.

"Oh, of course not. I apologize," the woman said.

"Who will go on this seeking out expedition?" Came from a woman in the front row. "I am volunteering. I just have this burning desire to get out and see what is happening."

"Ruth, you are as of now first on the list, I have made up." Dean said. "I'll contact you. The ones I chose to be a part of the expedition are excellent shots and I know are capable and willing to protect themself and other members of the group. In other words, they must be willing to kill a person if the need arises."

"You think it will be that bad out there, Dean?" a man asked.

"I know how it was six months ago. I don't know if it is better or worse now. The bad folks have had more time to organize, and resources are scarce. That means whoever is out there will be desperate. Whoever goes will have to be prepared."

"So, you are picking who goes rather than asking for volunteers," The same man asked.

"I know which folks are good shots. I have a good idea who will be willing to kill if they must."

"You think Ruth would kill if she had to?" another man asked.

Dean reared his head back and looked high in the bleachers at the person. "I know damn well she will."

Three months ago, a man slipped into the town and broke into Ruth's house. He had gotten one leg in the window before she saw the knife in his hand. She didn't hesitate about shooting him in the head.

The meeting ended with three quarters of the people voting for the move. A few were against, some were undecided.

While walking back to Dean's office John asked him how many people he was going to send on the mission.

"I was thinking at least eight. What do you think?" Dean said.

Well, that should be enough. Four of us took out an entire gang in Cordele."

"And two of the four were police officers. Ralph is a damn good shot, and you are an experienced fighter. We were as good as eight. Anyway, I have a list of the ones I want to go to. They all would volunteer even if I didn't ask them." He handed John the list. "What do you think?"

John skimmed the names. "All are excellent. That means they will be gone the same time as Ralph and I."

"They will and that means ten of our best men will be absent. So, I may rethink the count."

The next morning after the meeting, Dean sat in the only café operating in the town. A few wood burning stoves were donated. The owner removed the gas pipes from underneath the other stoves to allow room for wood to be used to heat the ovens. People would bring their own food and cook it or prepare it at home. They would sit and eat in the booths and at the tables enjoying each other's company. It was a place where people could go back to a time that was lost forever.

Percolators were brought in for when someone

located a store that had not been looted. For a few days, the indulgers enjoyed the smell and taste of freshly brewed coffee while it lasted.

Wonda June, one of the women who keeps the tally of all the food in the food bank took a seat at the table next to Dean and Jerry.

"Wonda, how is that husband of yours doing? And why is he not here having coffee with us?" Jerry asked.

The woman stared briefly out the window, at a couple walking past. "Damn," she said and looked at the two men. "I hate to be the bearer of bad news, but our food is going missing."

Dean gave her a surprise look. "What do you mean?"

Wonda looked around the room to make sure the other people weren't hearing her. "I mean, someone is taking it without it being signed out."

"So, are you saying someone is stealing it?" Jerry asked.

"I noticed some canned peaches were missing from where I put them the day before. Wanting to be sure, I checked the books for the past few days. After that we did an inventory. There was more stuff gone than I had signed out."

"And you know this for a fact," Dean said.

I have been keeping books for thirty years and yes. At the start of every week, Jeff Redd and I do an inventory of the entire building.

"That must take a while," Jerry said.

"Not long as you would think. Jeff is good. He was a warehouse manager for years. He did everything there was to do in warehousing at one time or another. He organized everything in equal rows, and we would walk down the center of the room counting. You know ten, twenty, thirty. If a row had something missing, we could easily spot it. Not everything was in rows, but it was that easy.

Each day I write down who received what and at the end of the day I tally it and write the numbers on the bottom of the sheet. On Monday's I add the checked-out items on all the sheets. After we do our count what was signed out and what we have must add up to what we had the first of the week. Yesterday the numbers just did not match."

Dean rubbed his chin. "Can you tell what is missing?"

"Darn right I can. Here is a list." She handed Dean a piece of paper.

"Wow, I see twenty-five pounds of coffee here."

"Jeff and I could not tell where anybody had broken in. You and Jerry might can figure it out after you look around."

Dean turned his cup up, sipped the coffee and put it on the table. "We are headed that way when we leave here."

Wonda left the café with Jerry and Dean and walked two blocks to the food bank.

The bookkeeper unlocked the door and led the men inside.

Dean and Jerry checked every door and window and found them locked tight. Neither showed signs they had been forced open.

"I'll spend the night in here until I catch the culprit." Dean said. "Twenty-five pounds of coffee. Yep, you bet I will catch them."

The North Atlanta community

After the harvest, they ended up with corn, pole beans, snap beans, okra, squash and turnup greens. They also had potatoes. And added to the garden were watermelons.

At the end of the season, the large storage building resembled a farmers' market.

Jennie stood in the crowd looking at the food. She announced to them that it was the most important crop any farm had ever brought in.

They all cheered for each other.

What was noticeable after the harvest was something not seen for a long time. There were smiles on the faces of everyone.

The smell of vegetables cooking began to fill the air daily.

Hard work has a different meaning when it means the difference between life or death. No one says you worked hard today or good job when everyone is doing the same thing, and it is because they must. No one is looking for a pat on the back, just a plate of food.

It's January and the food supply is still holding up.

One of the guards came in and found the head of security talking to two men. "Jim, there are three men behind the last building in the row of apartments. They are a couple of hundred yards off. They have binoculars and rifles."

Jim told the two men. "You guys come with us. We'll get behind them. I want to find out what they are doing here without any shooting if we can."

They walked out the back of the storage building

and walked behind the buildings until they reached the corner of the building where the strangers were. Jim peered around the corner and spotted the men who were watching the supply building.

He heard one say. "Hell, yeah, that is enough food to feed our gang for some time."

Jim motioned for his men to step out. With all four men pointing rifles he yelled. "But you fellows will never know." He only saw two men.

The strangers turned and pointed rifles at them. Jim and his men fired, and the two men fell to the ground.

A shot rang out from across the field a hundred yards away. It hit the building just missing Jim's head. They looked at the other end of the field and saw a man pointing a rifle at them. The men fired back but the man moved an instant before they fired. They never saw the shooter fall or where he went.

"He can tell his friend what they'll run into if they come here," one of the men said.

Jim shouldered his gun. "But we don't want his friends knowing where we are," "Let's find him."

The tree line was only fifty yards wide. Jim and his men caught the man running across an open and chased after him. They caught the man as he ran into the trees and surrounded him.

Jim pulled the rifle off the man's shoulder. "What are you doing here?"

"Just looking for food," the man said.

"Your friends sounded like they wanted all if our food."

"Takes a lot to feed all of our friends."

Jim stared at the man. "Where are your friends?"

"I can't tell you anything."

"So, you are no use to us right."

"That's right," the man said.

"Well, I guess." Jim put the barrel of his weapon against the man's head and pulled the trigger. "I hate a useless piece of crap."

No one saw the fourth man watching behind a building. The waited until everyone was gone before he found his way back to his truck. "You just wait until the rest of us come back here," he said to himself.

CHAPTER 2

The Rangers

Jes and his crew decided to double back and see what the City of Augusta looked like. What they wanted was to find some food. The six pieces of chicken the preacher gave them didn't last. The mess hall food had run out a few months back and all they had was MREs.

Aside from seeing several burned-out buildings they made it in and out of the town without encountering any trouble. But the grocery stores had been emptied.

They went into a furniture store and found several mattresses that they laid on the floor and spent the night on. They took shifts pulling guard duty.

The next morning each had an MRE for breakfast. Instead of leaving the town they decided they would spend another day checking things out.

They slept in the furniture store again.

Before hitting the road, the next morning. They thought about the fried chicken while having an MRE for breakfast.

Not knowing what shape the Interstate would be in, they took Highway 278 from Augusta heading west toward Atlanta.

After searching a few farmhouses and finding nothing they gave up on the hunt for food and settled for the MREs.

They had not seen one person since leaving the base.

"This is depressing," Jes said over the two-way radio in the Hummer. "Not a single person for hours."

"Maybe things are worse than we were told," Carl said over the radio.

Dawson in the first Hummer radioed. "Pull over, guys. I see a person up ahead." Dawson eased to the edge of the road followed by the other two Hummers. "Somebody stepped from behind a tree up head and moved back out of sight." He told the others.

"I'll check it out," Mike said and stepped out on the ground. He unslung his M4 from his shoulder and eased into the woods.

After a few minutes Mike spotted a man standing next to a tree looking around at the Hummers. Mike scanned the area for others but didn't see anyone. "Hands up fellow. High as you can get them."

The man startled reached far as his arms would go. "I'll go back with you. Just don't shoot. I promise I won't leave again."

"No body is going to shoot you. Just step out into the road." Mike followed the man out in the open and motioned for the others to join him.

When the three Hummers stopped beside the two men. Walker was standing up resting his hands on the M60 attached to the Hummer.

Mike searched the man. Not finding anything he told him to put his hands down.

The man eased his arms to his sides and looked at

the men in the Hummers. "You guys' Army for real?"

The Rangers stepped out and circled the man.

Reaching up and scratching his three-inch beard the man eyed each of the soldiers one at a time. He checked out their uniforms. "You guys are Rangers."

Neither of the men said anything, they just stared at the scrubby looking man.

"I'm Dennis." His hand went out, but he got no response.

"You are the first person we have seen since leaving the Post. What are you doing out here?"

The man relaxed. "Then you guys are not part of those men who took over our camp."

"No, we are not with them," Jes said and asked. "You know where we can get some food."

"You mean you guys don't have any food? I know where there is plenty of food.

"We have Army food, but we want real food. Do you know where we can get some real food?"

"Sure, I do." The man looked around. "I haven't eaten in three days. Can I have one of your Army meals?"

"Sure, if you'll tell us where we can get that food you are talking about," Jes retrieved an MRE from his Hummer, handed it to the man. The Rangers watched Dennis tear the package open and dig into the contents.

After devouring his first meal in three days the man pulled a handkerchief from his pocket and wiped his beard.

"Okay, where is that real food you mentioned?" West asked.

"The man pointed. "Two miles up the road. It's

canned food. Meat, vegetables, and such. The kind of Stuff you used to buy at the grocery store. Come on lets drive up there and I'll show you."

After driving into the town of Thompson, the man said. "Stop here. You need to walk to that building and slip around back. You will see it. Don't let them see you."

"What do you mean? Don't let who see us?"

The men that took over my group. Thay came up on us one day and took over. Locked everybody in a room in the building. I escaped."

"You old fool you. What are you trying to get us into? You talk us into feeding you by telling us you have food and now you inform us we must fight for it."

"There is food, and it did belong to my group before those men took it."

"How many men are guarding it?" Jes asked.

"Twelve is all I could see. The leader is a big guy. They shouldn't be a match for six Rangers."

"Do you know who the men are?"

"No, they just showed up one day and took over," Dennis said.

Jes got out and walked to the first Hummer. "Dawson you and Mike check it out. The old man pulled a con on us. He said there are a dozen men guarding the place."

Five minutes later Dawson and Mike returned.

"We saw six men outside. We'll have to wait until dark to get close enough to see inside. Looks like they have 30-06s and shotguns. No match for what we have," Dawson said.

The town

A call Came from the front gate to Dean's radio. "Chief Dean there are two cars here wanting to gain entry. The driver of the first car said the Governor of Georgia is in the car behind him."

Dean keyed his radio. "What in the hell are you talking about. There is no Government, so how can we have a Governor? What is his name?"

"I'll check with the driver." The radio went silent for a few seconds. "Dean, the driver said it is Governor Roy Barnes." The guard said when he came back on the radio.

"Roy Barnes," Dean blurted out. "He hasn't been Governor in years. Hold them there, I'm coming up."

Dean turned to Jerry Tilson. "Did you catch that transmission?"

"Yeah, I did. I think it is a crock of bull. Let me go next door to the café. That fellow that came in last week is having coffee. I'll ask him if he heard anything about an election." Jerry got out of his seat. "Just when I was fixing to snooze off." He stood. "I'll be right back."

Dean called the gate. I'll be there in ten minutes. Don't let them in."

Jerry was back in four minutes with news from the newcomer. "That fellow said there is no Government of any sort. There is no way to hold an election. He said that same man tried to pull that line of bull in Atlanta two weeks ago.

"We don't have time for this crap fellow. The driver of the first car said and floored the accelerator pedal. The second car on his tail.

"Dean the drivers took off and they are on their way down there," the guard said over the radio.

Dean snatched the door open, rushed outside, pulled a whistle from his pocket, and gave it three short blasts.

The two cars parked across the street from the police station next to the park. Four men exited the lead vehicle, and four men got out of the second car. They all wore black suits, white shirts, and black ties except for one man from the second car. He was dressed in a blue suit and a red tie.

The man in the blue suit raised both arms and shouted, "People. I am Governor Barnes. I have selected your town as the home of the Governor's Mansion." Barnes motioned for someone to get out of the car. "This is my wife, Maree. Now who is in charge here?"

Dean stepped forward with Jerry at his side.

Barnes looked at the two men. "Which one of you gentlemen should I address as mayor?"

"Neither of us. We don't have a mayor," Dean said.

Barnes rubbed his hands together, "Well, that settles that. I'll just take charge of that duty. But first I need to be directed to a house that is suitable for the head of the state."

Dean put his hands up. "Hold on just a minute, Barnes. I know for a fact there has been no election for the position you are claiming to hold."

"I beg your pardon sir. But you are so very badly informed. An election was held three weeks ago."

Dean rested his hands on his gun but with no intention of drawing it. "Look fellow if you and your men want to stay here you will be welcomed. First, your cars will have to be searched."

"I take you putting your hand on that gun as a threat. Guards," Barned yelled.

All the men in black suits opened their coats exposing their weapons but making no attempt to remove them from their holsters.

"You will notice my men did not pull their weapons. I don't believe they need to. Do you?"

Dean pulled his whistle from his pocket. "No, and it is a good thing they did not draw them." Dean gave one quick blast from the whistle.

Ten men stepped out from behind trees, buildings and off park benches with rifles leveled at the men in the suits.

"Would you men please put your weapons on the ground," Dean ordered.

Maree put her hand on her forehead. "Oh, Roy I feel."

"Feel what," Barnes said.

"I am going to——." Her knees gave way, and she hit the asphalt.

"Oh, dear, are you all right. Look what you caused my wife to do."

Dean ignored Barnes and his wife who lay motionless on the ground. "Did you men hear me? I said put your guns on the ground." Seven pistols hit the asphalt faster than Maree had.

Dean looked at the weapons. "Now you men just stand right where you are."

Dean, Jerry and two other men gathered up the pistols. "What will I find when we search the cars?"

One of the men spoke up. "Rifles and ammo. We

had to have some protection."

"That is understandable," Dean said.

Two men searched the cars and removed the all the weapons from the trunk.

Dean walked over to Barnes. "Do any of your men have families?"

"Yes, they do. They are nine children, and each has a wife. They are waiting down the road in three cars."

"Can you raise them on a radio?" Dean asked.

"Yes, we can," Barnes said.

Dean keyed the mic on his radio. "Three cars will approach the gate in ten minutes. I will send three men to help you guys search them. "Hold on a second." Dean looked at the men. "Is there anything in those cars that you want to tell me about?"

"Yes, there are rifles and ammo in the trunks," one of the men answered.

Dean keyed the mic. There are weapons in the trunks. Remove them and send them down. Dean yelled out the names of three men and told them to report to the front gate. He yelled to the men with Barnes.

"Call them up, ever who has the radio."

One of the men called the waiting cars and ordered them to the gate and stop.

Jerry got the men's attention. "We have houses and apartments, gentlemen. We will send someone around with you to show you the available places you can pick from. That is the best we can do for you."

"But I am the former Governor of the state. Surely you can't expect me to live in a common house like everyone else. And I do prefer that you address me as Governor."

Dean gave the man a stone-faced look. "Governor, we are in a different time now where no one is above anyone. We are all equal. So, get used to it. Over and out.

Barnes, you might want to get your wife up now. You should have her checked out by our doctor."

Barnes looked at his wife lying at his feet. "Oh, Dear, I forgot about you. Can you get up?"

Maree pushed herself up to a sitting position and looked around. She got to her feet. "I can't believe we are reduced to common citizens."

Jerry motioned for two men. "Show these folks the living quarters. Preferable in the common people area of town. And leave the weapons. You will get them back later. After we are sure you, all have accepted our rules, and you want to stay."

Don't you mean laws?" Roy asked.

"Whatever you prefer to call them, just abide by them," Dean said. "But for now. Do not damage anything, harm anyone, steal, rob or kill. Do not deprive anyone of life, liberty, and their pursuit happiness. It's that simple. Good luck."

"You think life is that simple?" Barnes said.

"You will find out that it is since all the politicians are gone," Jerry said.

Barnes walked over to Dean. Where do the affluent folks live?"

Dean hesitated for a moment. "We don't have any here. Like I told you; everyone is the same."

"You had better choose a house while we still have some," Dean said.

Walter Hite entered his home at seven o'clock in the

evening, walked to the kitchen and stood looking around. He checked the other rooms. No one else was in the house. That never sits well with Walter. Lilly should have been home waiting for him with his dinner. He walked back to the kitchen. Where are you, bitch.

The front door opened and closed. Two sets of footsteps, one lighter than the other, crossed the foyer, went into the den, and stopped. Lilly opened a door and pulled two hangers out, wrapped their coats around them and hung the hangers on a bar.

Lilly told Tommy to wait on the sofa until she called him for dinner.

When she went into the kitchen Walter grabbed her by her shoulders. "Woman, you know when I get home, I want to see my dinner on the table. What should I do to you for making me wait?"

Lilly quietly turned, slowly, unbuttoned her blouse and let it fall to the floor.

Walter pulled his belt off.

Lilly hated the sound of the belt sliding through the loops on his pants. She knew exactly how long it would be before the first blow would slash across her back. Not wanting Tommy to hear her and come into the kitchen she winced but did not dare cry out. She could not bear him seeing what was happening to her. And he might do something to cause Walter to turn on him. That would be worse than the beatings she received.

After Walter finished beating her, she put her top back on, went out in the back yard to a pole sticking six feet out of the ground. It had a foot wide cone made from sheet metal wrapped around it to keep the animals from climbing it. She lowered the bag of ham tied to the pole she cooked earlier in the day. It was cold enough that meat would keep.

She had to help in the community store hanging meat and other items in the cellar to keep them cold. The men had brought ice off the mountain they had gotten from the streams and placed it inside the cellar to keep it cool.

She built a fire outside to heat enough water that Walter could wash off.

She laid his clothes out and next she started a fire in the living room fireplace, and she laid on the sofa on her side next to Tommy and fell asleep.

The next morning Dean Martin, the police chief, walked out of the community storage building with a hand on a man's shoulder. The man's hands were cuffed behind him. The two walked on the sidewalk so everyone to see. People stared and pointed.

"I see you got yourself one," one man said.

"Take a good look at him, folks. This is a thief. He was stealing our food." He reached the police station, opened the door, and pushed the man inside. As he closed the door he told the assistant Chief Jerry Tilson, "I caught the thief who had been stealing our food. He came before daybreak. I tied him up until it was light. I wanted people to see who has been stealing from us."

Jerry stood. "Well, I will be damned, it's Walter Hite. "I am not surprised," he said as he walked over and opened a door on one of the cells.

"When we search his house, we'll probably find the missing guns and ammo," Jerry said when he came from locking Walter up.

Dean, John, and Jerry showed up to search Walter's home. The young woman who helped get him off the sidewalk after John laid him out in front of the barber shop greeted them. Her three-year-old son held onto her dress. The woman was shocked that they were there. And more surprised when she heard the reason for their visit, but she put up no resistance. She backed out of the door, "You are welcome to come in and search," she said. And answered, "My name is Libby. I am Walter's live-in girlfriend." When Dean asked who she was.

The search in the house produced nothing. By all accounts they were living off the rations from the gardens the same as everyone else.

"There's a building out back let's check it," Dean said, and asked, Libby, "Is the building locked?"

Libby looked out the window at the structure. "I have no idea. I have never been near it. Walter told me to stay clear of it, or I would be sorry, so I did."

In the shed they found four rifles, two thousand rounds of ammunition and thirty cases of canned food. They also found the missing coffee. The guns and Ammo came from the armory and the food from the food bank building. They put it in the back of Dean's car and took it back to where it belonged.

Dean confronted the woman. "Libby, you mean you were never curious and looked in that building?"

"No, Sir, if Walter told me not to do something I knew better than do it.

"Well, Lilly you can say that but the people in this town might have a difficult time believing you."

"I will show you why I didn't go against his word.

And I am going to ask the people to do one thing for me, Chief." She turned around and pulled her shirt up showing the belt marks from the beatings he had delivered to her. "Kill the bastard."

"That, son of a bitch," Dean said.

Later that day Dean, John and Jerry contacted all the leaders of the community and told them there was an emergency meeting and they would need to gather twelve citizens to serve as the jury.

To be fair the town did a thorough but swift investigation.

They had a prosecutor and a defense attorney present. The trials happen quickly. Holding a person in pretrial meant they would be eating their food. They did not want to keep him locked up and feed him. Any person who eats must be a productive member of the community. If there was a chance the punishment could result in banishment, they were not going to waste food on them before a trial or after. They would escort the person to the gate and turn him loose. There were no appeals. When the defense attorney asked if Dean had a search warrant, the judge said, "There was no need for one. The defendant being caught in the building, was enough."

The attorney said, "I agree with you, judge."

In the case against Walter if guilty he was to leave town right then.

They could not bring themselves to kill him. So, he would receive ten lashes from a leather strap while chained to a utility pole in the center of town. He would remain chained for two days with a sign next to the pole telling everyone he was a thief and was being banished from the town. During that time, he would be fed bread and water.

After the two days were up, he would be given enough bread and water to last two days and ordered to leave town on his bicycle. If he had not had the bicycle, he would have had to walk.

Since this was not his first time being caught stealing, he did not try begging for another chance. This was his third time being found guilty. He was deemed a worthless citizen.

After two days he was sent on his way with orders to never return.

To Libby's credit the town's people testified that she worked hard. And they believed she had no hand in or knowledge about what Walter was doing. She could stay in town and work and take care of her son.

CHAPTER 3

The Rangers

When the sun disappeared, the Rangers walked around the building and located the six guards.

"All we want to do is disarm those guys. I'm not up to killing twelve men for food we don't know who it really belongs to," Jes said.

"Yeah, I feel the same," West said. "I don't want to end up being who the old man said those guys are." The others agreed with West and Jes.

Jes looked at his men. "Pick a man and remember all you want to do is disarm him. And bring them back here."

They picked a man each to approach. It was surprising haw easy it was to get next to the guards and take their weapons.

After questioning the men, they learned that there were six men inside and they did have people locked inside a room in the building.

Around the corner from the men was a set of double doors wide and high enough to drive one of the Hummers through.

Jes asked the men. "Can you get those doors open?"

"Sure, they aren't locked."

"Let's go and open the doors. Dawson, you get in your Hummer and after we get inside you drive in and hop up on the M60 like you are ready to cut loose."

The men walked to the doors and opened them. Jes and his men nudged the six men through the door. As soon as they were in and spotted the men in the loft pointed weapons at them the Rangers fired three rounds each over their heads.

"This is the United States Army, drop your weapons, gentlemen," West said.

"Army doesn't mean nothing anymore." One of the six men pointed their rifles at Jes and his men. He stood. "I suggest you men drop yours. We have six shotguns on you." He had a dark beard and was about six four and two hundred and thirty pounds.

They heard a diesel engine approaching the doors. The Hummer entered the building and stopped. Dawson jumped on the M60 and pointed it at the men.

"Drop your weapons, we are out gunned men." The man with the dark beard said.

The men eased their weapons to the floor.

"Come on down gentlemen. We need to have a little talk," Jes said.

"What's to talk about. The old bastard won."

"You talking about that old fart, Dennis?" Jes said. "He said you guys popped in here and took their food and locked everyone up."

"Yeah, he would say that. The old bastard. Would you step over there." The man pointed to a door about twenty feet away. "I want to explain something to you. My name is Walker, by the way."

Jes looked at the door. "I'm dying to find out what

Old Dennis has gotten us into."

The men eased to the door and Walker opened it and stuck his head inside. "Angie, would you come here please."

A pretty blonde appeared. "What was all the shooting about? It scared us almost to death in there."

"It's that daddy of yours. He's at it again. This time he sicked the army on us."

Jes looked through the door at all the people in the room and back to the girl. "How about you tell me what is going on here. We were told he had some food. Then he tells us we have to take away from a gang of hoodlums who took it over. On top of that he said that you guys had locked everybody up."

Walker threw his hand up. "That old rat. There is food here. And you guys can have some. After I tell you what is going on."

"Come in here," Angie said. "I'll show you everybody."

Jes followed Angie and Walker into the room full of people sitting at a long table eating.

Jes walked over to West and Mike came out of the room fifteen minutes later. West and Mike took off to fetch Dennis.

They found the old man sitting in one of the Hummers looking out a side window. The two men approach the vehicle. West slapped the door, startling Dennis, causing him to drop the bottle of water he was drinking from. "It's all taken care of old man. You can go back to your friends now. Those men won't bother anybody else." West told him.

"What do you mean. I heard gun fire, did you run them off."

"We are not in the business of running people off. We took care of them the right way. We killed them all."

Dennis's face went all twisted. "You killed them? Oh, my Lord what have I done?"

"You didn't do anything. We did it for you. We got your food back."

"My daughter is in there. Let me go to her. She will never forgive me." Dennis got out and hurried to the building and went inside. He stopped when he saw twelve bodies lying on the floor. "Angie I never meant for this to happen. I promise." He ran to his daughter and grabbed her. "I am so sorry."

"For what, Daddy?"

"For this." His words stopped when he saw the men get up from the floor. "What is going on here. I thought they were all dead?"

"They could have been if we were not trained soldiers. If you had come up on the wrong people, this could have been real. Walker and his men were guarding your food stash, so nobody would steal it. They were doing that in the hopes that you would let Walker and Angie get married."

"I don't want my daughter to marry a farmer. She needs to marry a lawyer or a banker," Dennis told him.

Jes shook his head. "You old goat you. Don't you realize we are living in a different time now? There is no law. And money is useless. Your daughter will be better off with the president of a food bank than she would be with the head of a money bank. And this looks like a good stash here."

The old man studied for a moment. "We don't have a minister. When my daughter ties the knot, the ceremony will have to be performed by a man of the cloth. Preferably a Baptist."

"You know we don't have a preacher in our group," Angie said.

Dennis looked at Jes. "Find a preacher then you will get my blessing. And we will give you fellows some food to take with you."

Jes and his men walked out of the building and stood next to the Hummers. "Where can we find a preacher?"

"With eighty percent of the people gone our chances are very slim." Dawson said.

"Listen, you guys hear that?" Jes said.

"Hear what?" Dawson said.

"I hear it. And it sounds like our slim chance has just widened." West said.

The roar of the engine got louder as it closed in on their location. The 1958 Chevy stopped next to the men.

Preacher Ball put his head out the window. "Howdy fellows. You guys haven't gotten very far."

Jes rubbed his hand together. "You are just the man we need. We have a situation that calls for a man of the cloth."

"This world has been in that fix for a year."

"What I mean is we need a real honest to goodness preacher here and now," Jes said.

"You talking about right now?" Preacher looked around. "All of you are still alive."

"Not for a funeral. A wedding," West said.

"A wedding. Which one of you want to get married?"

"It's not either of us. They are inside that

building."

"I uh don't know. That would take someone who has the authority to do that."

Jes rubbed his hands together. "That is why we are asking you.

Sorry, gentlemen but I gave that up some time back."

West took Ball by the shoulders. "Do you have anything that says you are a preacher?" West asked. "If you do and marry that couple these folks will give us some food to take with us."

"Food, for real. I just happen to have my certificate stating that I a genuine preacher."

Bring it on reverend. Do you have a bible," Jes asked.

"I have everything I keep in the trunk of my car. What denomination?"

Jes thought for a second. "He mentioned Baptist."

Ball shuffled through a stack of papers. "Catholic, Methodist, Presbyterian. I got it here somewhere. Here it is. And my coat and tie. Let's get some food."

By the time they entered the building Ball was dressed in a grey coat and blue tie over his white shirt.

The ceremony went off without a hitch Followed with a celebration that lasted into the night. There was more food than the men had seen in a year.

The Rangers decided to stay and leave the next morning. When they did leave the had enough food to last them a week.

CHAPTER 4

The Mission

Dean decided to send six persons instead of eight on the mission to middle Georgia and look for a new town. Two days after the meeting five men and one woman departed the town in a suburban. They were pulling a trailer loaded with gas, water, food, clothes, and room for any useful items they might come across. Not only was this trip to seek out a new town but also to find out what the virus left in the way of people.

Not wanting to leave the town short of protection Dean's decision came down to two highly trained ex-military men who had fought in the Gulf War. Each had experience in leading missions where the unexpected could happen. The group could break up into three person teams with one of the ex-military men accompanying each group.

One of the veterans was Les Crier. A former Army Ranger, trained in martial arts and is an expert shot with a rifle. He is a quick thinker.

Sitting next to Les in the driver's seat is Ruth Beal. A Utah girl who loves the outdoors, hiking, and rock climbing. And she holds a black belt.

Les had his eyes on Ruth and would like to get to know her better. But he is still dealing with a heart ache that he has not had time to get over. "Where are you from?" he asked Ruth.

"Moab, in the beautiful state of, Utah," she said. "I was visiting a friend in Atlanta when the shit hit the fan. Now I 'm stuck here."

Les bounced the stock of his M4 on the floor. "Damn, you are a long way from home, lady."

"Hell yes, I am and no damn way to get back."

"How did you get out of Atlanta and up to our town?"

"I knew what was coming to the cities when the food ran out and the shit bags figured out there would be no more. They would go postal. I went out and confiscated all the gas I could, got me a map of the state and studied it."

"Smart thinking. Brave too, not being from here and taking off like that. What about your friend, did she or he, come with you?"

"No, she thought she had enough friends to take care of her. Her brother was with her. I told them the food would run out and there would be chaos. 'We have grocery stores. They never run out of food,' she told me.

"I tried to convince them they were in for a rude awakening. But they were always taken care of through a trust fund and never worked."

"Where do you think she, and her brother are?" Les asked.

"If I had to guess. I would say they are dead. She was a pretty girl. She would have a hard time if the wrong man or men got to her. Her friends and that brother of hers are not survivors."

"I would bet you two pretty girls got your share of

looks when you were out," Les said.

"Thank you. I don't hear complements now days."

Looking out the windshield, Les turned the M4 rifle in his hands. "I guess people are absorbed with survival. They don't stop and admire the beauty in anything."

Ruth smiled. "Yep, this is going to be a great trip."

They pressed on down 575 until they reached the exit for Woodstock. Les motioned. "Pull over here. By mistake I put my thermos of coffee in the back. I need a cup. I need an eye opener."

"Only if you have enough for me, a cup," Ruth said as she slowed, veered off the road and stopped.

"I like the way you handle this vehicle. You are smooth with your stopping and maneuvering," Les told her.

"I did a lot of traveling back home and the places are far apart. So, I acquired plenty of driving practice. I guess I could have stopped on the road. Old habits. Used to be lots of traffic and now nothing."

"Those days are gone forever." Les said, opened the door, got out and walked to the back of the vehicle. "Cream and sugar, Ruth. How about the rest of you? You guys got your coffee?"

"Hand me that red container," said Richard Durant, a veteran who was in Crier's special forces unit. He stands six foot two inches and is muscular. Hands quicker than a rattlesnake's strike. Richard doesn't take anything serious other than surviving. His only goal in life is getting through whatever faces him at the time. If the situation calls for a Psychopath, he becomes one. He always made sure he had enough of what it was going to take to get the task done.

Les passed the two-quart container to his army buddy. "You think you brought enough coffee for today?"

"Yeah, I'll heat it up tomorrow and maybe the next day until I finish it. The older gets the stronger it gets. I take my coffee like my women. Sweet and strong." He asked Billy if he cared for a cup of coffee.

Billy Wilbanks is from North Georgia, owned a gun store and ran a shooting range before the virus. At six feet and one hundred and ninety pounds he is easy-going, quick, wiry, strong and has a good humor. He had no military experience, but he hunted in the woods all his life and studied survival since his teen years.

Les reached up and pulled the road atlas off the dash and opened it. After studying the section of Middle and South Georgia, closed it and threw the map back where he got it from.

Ruth said, "This state is full of small towns with so many roads to get there. It's confusing which one to take when you start out. Utah has twenty thousand more square miles and only a fourth of the people Georgia has. And there are not as many roads in Utah. How do you get anywhere in this state?"

Richard said from the back seat. "People used a GPS. Or now a map. You find where you want to go on the map and take the roads there."

Ruth unconsciously checked her side mirror. "In Georgia and all the Eastern states, you have to figure out how to get to a road that will take you to a road that will take you to another road then another. On and an on."

Richard reached over the seat. "Let me see that

road atlas."

Ruth picked the book up and passed it back. "You will see what I mean. And how confusing it is."

Bentley Lemont is a former owner operator truck driver from North Georgia. He is six feet four inches tall and spends three days a week pumping iron in the gym. from the back seat he spoke up. "She's right, I used to drive a truck. I've been all over this country. You get out west and the roads are few and far between compared to here."

Richard opened the atlas and studied two maps. "Damn, you are right. Not near the roads in your home state as Georgia for it to be as big as it is." He flipped to another page. Darn, Arizona is the same way. It's twice the size of Georgia with only two thirds the population as here. I would love to live in Arizona. I wonder how life is there now. You could probably go for a year and never see another person. Maybe you never would see another soul, gee whiz."

"You know, that's what John Carstairs was talking about. He has traveled everywhere," Les said.

"I love to park my ass behind the wheel and go," Ruth said. "I did a lot of traveling out west."

Les was staring out the door glass. "You don't like the Eastern side of the map?"

"Ah, it's okay. It's just crowded as shit. Give me the wide-open outdoors." She fluffed her shoulder length blonde hair a couple of times. "Where to?"

Billy from the back seat told her to get on 75 and go to 285.

Les said, "Yeah. And John said we should go west around Atlanta."

Jerry Tilson is a former Georgia State Trooper

with thirty-two years of service. He is the oldest in the group and from Middle Georgia but moved to North Georgia five years before the virus. "The other way goes to Sandy Springs and into Dekalb County and we should avoid Dekalb. The West side isn't going to be a picknick."

Ruth perked up and said, "Jerry, where did you say the other direction goes?" She picked up her speed on the highway.

"Over into Dekalb County."

"No, the first place you mentioned. Sandy Springs didn't you say?"

"That's right," Billy said. "It's across the river and a few exits to Roswell Road. I'm from up close to our town but I used to hang out with some guys and gals down here."

Ruth thought for a moment. "That road you mentioned is the exit to my friend's place. Just off 285. How far East is the Sandy Springs exit?"

"About five miles." Billy said.

Les saw her perk up only to swap it for a sad expression. "You want to check on your friends?"

"It's out of the way, isn't it?" Ruth said looking disappointed.

"Mission first," Les said. "It's tough. I know how you feel. If you don't find out, it will bother you from now on."

"You sound like a person who's missing someone." Ruth commented to Les.

Les didn't say anything, but Richard did. "He is."

Ruth looked across to Les like she was expecting a response from him. She reached across the wide space and put her fingers around his thick forearm. "Come on big boy. Let's hear who you long for. Is it a girl?"

Les shook his head. "Yeah, I'm from Louisiana. My mom my dad and one sister are there."

"And for real, no girlfriend?" Ruth questioned.

Les didn't answer, he just looked out the side window.

Ruth checked the rearview mirror. Richard shook his head and put a finger on his lips.

Ruth studied the road ahead. "We are all missing someone I guess."

Richard said, "I have family in Mississippi. Les and I left the service at the same time."

"I'm sorry for the both of you. Let me know if I can be of any help for you two getting home," Ruth said. "You guys must be having a tough time not knowing. I mean Angie and her brother are friends and I can't help worrying about them. I think often that I should have stayed to help."

When they reached the exit for 285 Ruth said, "Here is where we are supposed to go West."

"Go, East," Jerry said. "If it's okay with everyone. It's not that far to that exit. And there is a need for young people in the town. Part of the mission remember is to seek out other people. Her friends are possible recruits. And she needs to know how they are."

"Ahh, we must go where no man has ever gone and seek out other life," Richard said.

"Thank you, Jerry, and the rest of you." Ruth said and maneuvered into the East bound exit lane. "Sorry Horace Greeley." She had to swap lanes to keep from hitting a man on a bicycle. "Damn, no more people that there are, and I almost hit someone on a bicycle.

Should we stop?"

"No, I know that fellow. His name is Walter Hite," Jerry said. "He was caught stealing three times and was asked to leave the town. He beat his girlfriend with a belt."

"That is the fool I saw chained to a pole in the center of town and was lashed," Richard said.

"The whipping was for the beatings he gave his girlfriend with a belt. He was banished for stealing food," jerry said. "And twenty-five pounds of coffee."

That much coffee? We should have killed the SOB," Richard said.

"Didn't they used to do that to people years ago for breaking the law?" Ruth asked.

"Yeah, it might seem harsh, but it was not his first-time taking food," Les said.

His third time," Jerry said. "It wouldn't take many people stealing food to put the town into starvation."

CHAPTER 5

The Town

Two men from the community over the mountain that until recently was called, Con Town, sat talking to Dean. The name came from the residents being former prisoners who were released from county jails and work farms, city jails, State prison farms and a few from the state prison. The bad ones have been weeded out by the ones who wanted a place to live with their families. So, the town now is called Prosperity because the folks there have prospered well.

The visit from the men was for two reasons. One had to do with the food Walter Hite had stolen. Dean found out from Wonda that some items they found at his house did not belong to the town and Dean thought they could belong to Prosperity.

They were sitting in the café in town. Dean poured the men a cup of coffee each. Over the coffee Dean told the men about the food confiscated from the house that might be theirs.

"We keep a tally on everything, and we have missed seven cases of beans, five cases of corn and three cases of carrots," one of the men said.

"That's the stuff we have. You people returned our food to us six months back. I am glad to return the deed.

One of the men named, Leo Giddy was wide across the chest with big arms. His beard trimmed neatly under a handlebar mustache. He put his arms on the table. His voice was deep. "That is good for two reasons. We need food. The other. Nobody from our town took it."

"It's good to know your residents are honest. I believe all of ours are now," Dean said.

"What did you do with the thief?"

"Two days tied to a post in the center of town with a sign telling what he did." Dean didn't mention the ten lashes. "And he was put on his bicycle and sent packing. Just in case he shows up at your town, his name is Walter Hite."

They went out and stacked the food in the bed of Leo's pickup, and they left.

Dean was watching the men drive away when a voice came over his radio. "There is a fellow at the edge of the woods, Dean. He stepped back behind a tree when he saw me looking at him. He has a rifle."

"I'm on my way." Dean spotted John Carstairs, Ralph Bishop, and Betty Larkin. He motioned for them. Betty had her Winchester Classic Model 70. Ralph had an M4 hanging on his shoulder.

You three get in. Betty, I'm glad to see you got your Winchester. There's someone with a rifle in the woods across the field from the main gate.

Before they reached the top of the rise to the gate, Ralph said, "Let us out right here, Dean. Betty and I will slip around behind them."

Betty and Ralph crossed a clearing below where the man was spotted and went into a stand of pine and cedar trees. The evergreen trees supplied cover for them as they advanced on the man's position.

They were two men, and they gave no sign they noticed Betty and Ralph had stopped fifty feet behind them. Both were dirty with bushy hair and beards; their clothes were filthy and torn. Each had a rifle and were eyeing two women limping across a field toward the two guards. The men were talking loudly and sounded mad. Betty and Ralph eased toward the men. When they were within thirty feet of the men, they could understand them.

One said, "Jed, I told you to keep a hand around their wrist."

"Hell, I thought they were going to pee. They couldn't run far with their britches down," Jed said.

"If we can't stop them from crossing the field, we'll shoot them."

"Are you sure you want to shoot them? Cause if you do, we won't have any women," Jed said.

"If they get to those men up there, we'll lose them anyway. If we can't have them, no one is going to."

The men raised their rifles to their shoulders and pointed at the girls. They never got a shot off before Betty fired at Jed and he dropped. Ralph fired and the other man fell to the ground.

"I wonder who they were and where they came from," Betty said.

"I'll tell you who they were." Came from behind them. "You two just killed my brother and friend."

"They were going to kill those two women," Ralph said.

"Neither of those women are kin to me or is a friend. They are just companionship is all they are."

"We couldn't let those men shoot them," Ralph said.

"Well, you should have. Drop your guns and turn around. Might be I will kill you fellow and take the woman to replace them two hightailing across that field."

Betty and Ralph eased their rifles to the ground and turned around.

A big man stood pointing a rifle toward them. He had a scruffy beard; his clothes were dirty and torn like the two men they had just shot. He raised the rifle and took aim at Ralph. "Say bye, fellow."

A shot rang out, the man with the rifle stiffened and his eyes widened. Blood began to leak from his mouth as he stood still as a statue in a park.

Betty saw two big shoulders come up behind the bleeding man A foot went to his back and pushed him over. "Howdy, folks."

"Howdy, hell, thank you, Leo," Betty said. "Do you just walk around the woods saving people from bad guys?

"It's a hobby of mine. I started it just now."

"Thank, God you had no interest in toy trains," Betty said.

Ralph stared down at the guys lying on the ground. "Where do you think those butt wipes came from?"

Leo spit tobacco. "From the looks of them, I would say they came out of the ground. I have two shovels in my truck. I guess we should put them back in."

"Shovels, hell. We got a backhoe in town," Ralph said.

Leo gave them a thumbs up. "I'll leave the fun to you guys then," he started walking off. "Watch your backs from now on."

"Thank you, we will, Mister Getty," Betty said.

Leo had been doing time in the county jail for possession of stolen goods. That was not his first time in the joint. He was a career thief who was turned lose when his time was up. He went back to his old ways, stealing anything of value in this time.

Leo's turnaround happened one morning after he came upon a house with two chickens in a pen on the porch. He entered the house without knocking and saw a woman and two children sitting on a dirty sofa. The girl looked like she was about eight years old, and the boy looked like he was six years old. Leo went through the house and gathered all the food, took it out and put it in the back of his truck with the other food he had stolen.

The woman and kids didn't say a word. They just looked at him each time he passed through the living room from one room to another. The entire time he was in the house they didn't say a word. The little boy went out and stood on the porch watching Leo load the last scrap of food from the house onto his truck. But he wasn't finished. He walked upon the porch, picked up the chicken coop, went back to his truck and loaded it into the bed. He looked at the boy. "Tell your mom thanks." He got in to leave. When he reached for the key something caused him to turn his head. He saw the woman and girl standing on the porch next to the boy staring at him.

The boy's arms reached out and he said, "Please mister we're hungry."

He sat still for a moment looking at the family. His vision began to blur. He closed his eyes and when he opened them instead of seeing the woman and her kids, he saw his mother crying and pleading. The boy was him, in torn overalls, with no shirt and no shoes. The girl was his sister with stringy blonde hair, torn dress, and no shoes. He remembered they had gone without food for days. He turned his head and put his hands on his face.

Leo got out and put the chicken pen back, next he unloaded all the food and took it back inside the house. He left two extra cans of vegetables.

He spent the entire day delivering the food to the people he stole it from. That was the beginning of a new life for Leo Giddy. That was his last day as a thief. From that day on he never took anything from anyone that didn't offer it to him. After he finished giving everything back he began to think. He had always been a thief, but the last run in he had with the law before the virus hit. It had nothing to do with stealing. It was a scorching summer day and Leo had spent it putting pipe in the ground for a sewer line. All day he had wanted a cold beer so bad he could taste it. That afternoon after work he stopped at a neighborhood bar in the area he was working in.

The bartender was a short slim man with a mustache and short red hair. "What'll you have," He asked as Leo approached the bar.

Leo leaned on the bar. "The coldest longneck you got."

The bartender put a napkin in front of Leo. "They are all cold, what brand you want."

"Miller. "Hey Bud, what's the deal on them boiled

eggs down there?"

"If you are drinking they free. Just put the shells in the garbage. My name's not Bud. It's Red."

"What the hell. It's hot in here."

"You can drink outside if you don't like it in here."

"That wouldn't make scents, it's just as hot out there. You got an air conditioner in here?" Leo asked.

"Yeah, we got one." He pointed to the ceiling. "See them vents."

"Can you turn it on?"

"Yeah I can," the man said and parked himself upon a stool.

Leo stared at the man and gestured by laying his hands on the bar palms up and spreading his fingers. "Well, are you going to turn it on?"

The man looked at the vents and at Leo. "No reason to."

"There is a reason. To cool the place down."

"Wouldn't cool it. It's broken; all it blows is hot air."

"How long you been tending bat, fellow."

"All my life."

"You know those twelve years between six and eighteen. You were supposed to have gone to school."

"I went to school; I have you to know."

A man and a woman came in and took seats two stools from Leo.

"I didn't want come in here, Willard." the lady said.

"Nobody asked you, Mavis, did they. Now shut your mouth. Give me two bottles of Bud," the man told Red.

"I don't want a damn beer," Mavis said. "It's hot

in this place here."

"You are going to drink a beer and like it. Hey man do you have an air conditioner in here?"

"Yeah we got one," Red said.

Loe blurted out. "It's broken."

"Well, now, that is just dandy as hell. We come in here to get out of the heat and the air doesn't work."

"See there. It's so hot I can't drink in here," Mavis said.

Willard grabbed the woman by the hair and shook her head. "Shut the hell up, bitch. We are going to drink beer like it or not. Hurry up with those cold beers. I want one of those eggs."

Mavis got off the stool. "You sorry bastard. It's hot as hell in here, I'm leaving."

The man slapped Mavis knocking her down. "It is hot outside too, you dumb ass."

Leo stood, walked over, and hit the man, knocking him off the stool.

Leo had no idea Red was friends with the man and woman. Red swore Willard did nothing. The woman swore she fell of the barstool.

Leo was charged with assault and battery. After looking at his past record he got six months. That was two months before the virus hit.

CHAPTER 6

The Rangers

Three Hummers pulled into Sparta lead by Ball in his 1958 Chevrolet. He suddenly let off the gas causing the pipes to bellow. Next, he hit the brakes hard causing a chain reaction behind him.

Dawson was looking at the stores through the left door glass as they eased through the town.

"Stop," Mike yelled.

Dawson jerked his head to the front and applied the brakes when he was inches from the bumper of Balls car. "What the Hell, are you stopping for, Ball," he yelled.

"Mike tapped on his door glass. "Over here. Those things there are, what the Hell he stopped for. They are blocked behind that van, and we couldn't see them until we were right up on them." He held up a finger counting as he moved it from left to right. "Eight damn horses all saddled up and tied to a rail. Like they were ridden in here."

"No shit Sherlock. You don't think they toted them do you?" Dawson said.

The four Rangers walked up beside Dawson and tapped on the window. "Why did you stop suddenly in the middle of the street.

Ron Saint

Mike pointer and said, "Horses."

"I'll be damned. Who would ride horses to town?" Crier said.

"Men not strong enough tote them," Mike said."

Ball walked up beside the four men. "Look over there, guys."

They all looked at the sign attached to the building above the door. Their mouths opened.

"Wooee, son of a bitch. I don't believe it." "What in the world is that?"

"Just what it says I guess," Ball said.

West spoke up "Someone playing a joke maybe?"

"Let's check out the joke," Jes said and read the sign aloud. "Hell's Rejects Saloon."

"I don't know," Virgle said. Look at that other sign it says enter at your own risk."

"Check that sign, up there." Walker said and read it. "Our girls are the best in the territory. Bring your own gun, knife, axe, hammer, ball bat or whatever you have. Please drag the bodies outside."

Jes touched the handle of his knife hanging on his belt. "Sounds like our kind of place. Check your weapons. Who wants to stay with the Hummers?"

Carl stepped up. "I will."

"Someone will spell you in a while. Sit on one of the M60s."

"I'll meet you guys at the door. I need to get something from my car." Ball walked to his car and retrieved a 357, shoved it in his belt and walked to the door. "Shall we go in?"

Dawson pushed the two-swinging door open and stepped inside followed by his friends. They stopped five feet inside the room and looked around. Along one wall a wood burning stove sat furnishing heat. A smoke pipe sticking up four feet, turned and exited the room through a hole cut in the wall.

"Come on in fellows. No need to be bashful," said a man standing behind two twelve-inch-wide ten feet long boards resting three drums. He was surely six-six, a top hat resting on a bushy head of hair and eight inches of growth on his face. "Step over here to the bar and pick your poison." He scratched his belly through a hole in his dirty wool underwear shirt.

The men eased cautiously to the makeshift bar. Behind the bartender on shelves were several bottles of different alcoholic beverages. On the floor cases of beer were stacked five high from the front of the room to the back.

"Whiskey, scotch, gin, tequila. You name it, we got it. And of course, beer."

Ball counted the cases of beer to himself. Twenty stacks, five to a stack. One hundred cases of beer. Twenty-four hundred bottles of beer. He sang to himself. "One hundred bottles of beer on the wall. Take one down and pass it around." That's a lot of beer for now days, he thought.

"What are you taking in trade for your beverages?" Jes asked.

'Bullets work best. If you have ammunition to trade, you can drink. In the old west cowboys would trade a bullet for a drink. So, it was called a shot of whiskey. My name is Ram by the way."

Jes looked around, spotted a sign that said. To the toilet. Take your own paper.

"Yes, sire three bullets and you get one beer," Ram said. "It's the only beer for miles around. And the same for a shot of whiskey. Three bullets."

Jes thought, our M60 fires 600 rounds per minute. We have sixty-thousand rounds. A hundred minutes of firing. The M4 will dispense 950 rounds at the same time. For those we have forty-two-thousand rounds. He did more math. Forty-four minutes of firing.

"Ammo, are you kidding? Who would give up their ammo?"

"You would be surprised, soldier boy."

"You see a boy, kick his ass, old man," Dawson said.

"The bartender looked at the patches on Dawson's arm."

"I take that back, men. How about a beer on the house." The old man sat six open beers on the bar. "I had these outside. They are golden and cold."

The rangers picked the beers up, turned and leaned on the bar looking at the three women smiling at them from across the room. They were wearing dresses you would see saloon girls wear in western movies. Four men sat at a table playing cards and a man sat alone at the table next to them. It was easy to tell who was winning. He had a large pile of bullets in front of him. On the floor next to him were several cans of food. A fourth woman sat back from the table about a foot next to the lucky man with all the bullets.

One of the men slapped his cards on the table and yelled. "Damn this is just not my day. I Can't bet on this hand either."

"When Rock is around, it's nobody's day except his," one man said and dropped his cards on the table. "I fold too."

One man spread his cards on the table. "I call.

Three jacks." He reached to scoop the pot to him.

"Not so fast." The man they called Rock looked at the man with the jacks. He spread his cards on the table. "Three Kings. It must be my day."

"Deal the damn cards, maybe I can pull one out this time," The man who folded first said.

The hand played and Rock won again.

Dawson straightened up and rolled his shoulders. "I know those types playing cards. Excuse me." He walked over to the four men playing. "What's the game fellows?"

"Five card draw. You are welcome to set in if you got something worth losing?"

"How about some MREs?"

The man who asked him to play shuffled the cards and looked up. "Food is always good. My name is Rock."

"I'll be right back," Dawson said and headed out the door.

"Any of you other guys care to sit in on this game?" one of the men at the table asked.

Before either could respond, Dawson opened the door and walked in with two cases of MREs. He pulled an empty chair to the table, sat the cases of goods on the floor and took a seat.

"You do know that is from your stash. I just hope you know what you are doing," Jes said.

"He's a pro at cards, Sarge," West said. "He's played at a few of the tournaments in Vegas. And did exceptionally good.

One of the girls went and sat at the table with the lone fellow. The other two other girls made their way to the bar and struck up a conversation with the other

Rangers. "I am mighty thirsty how about one of you handsome men buying me a drink."

Jes stared at the girl. "You are barking up the wrong tree. We don't hand our bullets out."

She smiled at West. "That's a shame. Because we have other stuff for sale."

"Not interested, lady," West told her.

A woman came out of the back room and walked over to the Rangers. "Sit down, you two."

"You mean, a girl can't strike up a conversation around here."

"Not with these men you can't." She looked at the Rangers. "My name is Catherine. Folks call me Cat. I own the place."

"Pleased to meet you, Cat. My name is Jes." He introduced the other men to the lady.

"Let me buy you fellows a beer," Cat said.

"Never turn down an offer for a beer," Jes said.

"Set these gentlemen up on the house, Ram." Cat looked at the card table. "Is your friend a good card player?"

"I understand he is," Mike said.

Cat paused a moment. "I hope he has a sharp eye."

"Are you saying there is some cheating going on in here?" Jes said.

"I suspect that Rock will, but no one has ever caught him," Cat said. If your friend is good enough he might get rid of Rock for us."

"For Rock's sake if he is cheating, he had better not let our friend catch him," Mike said.

Cat eyed the patches on their sleeves. "I know what you guys are and I know you are right about your friend."

Dawson was on a winning streak. His winnings were 9MM bullets for his side arm and a few cans of food. They stopped placed bets and fed into the pot. Dawson put in part of a box meal and the other guys put in five shells. Winner takes all.

This went on until the girl sitting next to Rock developed a habit of leaning on the table when he was shuffling the cards. And Rock increased the pot when he dealt.

This went on for several hands until Dawson acted on his suspicion and used an arm to move the lady back in her chair just in time to see Rock pull a card from the middle of the deck.

"That wasn't very nice," she said.

Dawson pulled his arm back. "Just stay right where you are." Dawson looked at Rock. "I prefer my cards from the top of the deck."

"Are you saying you think I cheated?"

"I know you did. I saw that card come from the middle of the deck." Dawson stood. "I knew something was going on when the girl started to lean on the table when you were dealing."

Dawson's team walked over to the table.

Rock pulled a pistol and pointed it at Dawson. "I kill people for accusing me of cheating."

The soldier grabbed the edge of the table and quickly picked it up just a Rock fired causing the shot to go wild as Rock fell back on the floor.

Dawson pushed the table aside and kicked the pistol from Rock's hand. He stood and waited until Rock staggered to his feet. When the cheater was up Dawson landed a foot to his face knocking the man back to the floor. Rock made no attempt to get back up.

The lone man at the other table pulled a pistol and pointed at Dawson. "Time for you to check out soldier boy."

One of the other players produced a pistol and fired at the man hitting him in the head.

The swinging doors burst open and in rushed a man about six foot six inches. He was wearing a gun belt with a six-shooter crammed in the holster on his side. He had a badge pinned on his shirt almost hid by his vest. "Who fired that shot?"

The gambler raised a finger. "He drew first Marshall."

The Marshall looked around. Anybody else see it that way?"

Hands went up. "He did come from two men."

Rock rolled over, picked up his pistol, stood and began to raise the gun toward Dawson.

In a swift motion the sheriff filled his hand with his six shooter and pointed it at Rock. "Drop the gun."

Rock eased the gun to the floor and put his hands up. "I'm good Marshall."

"There isn't anything good about you Rock. Alright who started this ruckus here?" The Marshall scanned the men.

"Rock has a habit of dealing from the middle of the deck," Dawson said.

"Any proof of that?" the Marshall asked. "Who else saw it?"

That Ranger did is the reason Rock shot at him. He just happened to miss. And I saw it." One of the other gamblers said.

Dawson pointed at Rock. "The middle of the deck

dealer didn't like being called out."

"He's lying Marshall. Rock wasn't cheating." The girl who was leaning on the table said.

"You shut up, Hazel. Nobody asked for your two cents worth. I wouldn't believe you anyway. Was she leaning on the table?"

"She sure was every time Rock dealt." One of the men in the game said and pointed to the cheater. "We suspected he was, and she was blocking for him. But I saw it this time when the soldier pushed her back."

"Alright, Rock, this is a respectable and peaceful town. We aim for it to stay that way. I want you and Hazel out of Sparta right now. I catch you back her I'll put you on the farm for a month. That your friend on the floor?"

"Never saw him before," Rock said.

"I think you are lying but we'll take care of him."

Rock started gathering his winnings off the table.

"Leave it," the Marshall said. "You may want to stop by, and have Doc look at your nose on your way out of town. It looks broken."

Rock walked to the doors and turned around. "Nothing in this one-horse town for us anyway."

"I counted eight horses out front. Dawson said.

A man limped into the bar with two men following him. He limped over to the sheriff. "Pat what is going on in here?"

"Well, Lester, glad to see you show up after everything is over," Pat said.

"These two fellows finished their time in the camp. They worked hard and never did give us any trouble. I thought I would buy them a bee before they left town."

"Alright, Lester, set them up. They may want to stay and become citizens of Sparta."

West looked at the sheriff, the bar owner, Cat, and Lester the limping man and thought back to the reruns of the old westerns he watched on television when he was young. Damn, he thought.

Jes walked over to the sheriff. "You have a prison camp in this town?"

"We sure do. Beats having them sit in a cell all day. We need a few more detainees to get some repair work done on some of these buildings."

"Make them work for their food. Not a bad idea," Jes said.

"Yep, and after their time is up, we let them go about their way," Pat said.

"Good system you got here, Sheriff. And when their time in up you do cut them loose. You take care."

Out on the sidewalk West turned to Jes. "Did you ever watch western reruns on the television when we were kids?"

Jes grinned. "Any particular one you might be thinking about?"

West looked down the street. "Let's get the hell out of Dodge men."

CHAPTER 7

The mission

While crossing the Chattahoochee River on 285. Ruth slowed down and scanned the water below.

Bentley thought about all the times he spent with friends who lived in the apartments next to the river. He thought about one girl in the group that he liked a lot. She showed some interest in him too. Not easy to develop a relationship when you drive a truck over the road. He now thinks of her as the one that got away. His heart strings tugged at him. Just a short look. "Stop for a couple of minutes. I want to get out and look at the river."

Ruth stopped in the outside lane going East. Everyone exited the vehicle, walked to the edge of the bridge, and stared at the flowing water below.

Bentley focused on the grassy area they parked chairs on to watch the people coming down the river boats.

His concentration was broken when Ruth said, "The wind is cold, but it is peaceful and quiet here. I could stay here all-day."

Billy had a smile on his face. "I heard that one of the radio stations in Atlanta used to sponsor a raft race here."

"That's right one did. It was before I was spending time here," Bentley said. "This entire area was popular years ago. We missed it all."

"Ruth folded her arms in front of her and rubbed the top of them. "My friend told me she read about it. It was before she and I were born. She said hundreds of thousands of people would come to the river. It got too expensive to hire security and clean up, so they stopped it in 1980 after eleven years."

"Wow, it started over forty years ago," Billy said.

"It was everything you heard or read about," Jerry said.

"Really, did you ever come to it. Did you go down the river on a raft?" Ruth asked.

Jerry grinned. "Not on a raft but a boat. I only did it once. But I showed up four times, in my teen days."

"Wow you were a part of history," Ruth said.

Les gestured by raising an arm. "And now look at it. Not a single person in sight,"

Jerry held an open hand to one ear. "Listen, I hear something. It sounds like a boat motor. Can you tell where it is?"

Wherever it is, it's moving toward us. It's coming slowly down river toward the bridge." Billy said. "Maybe they hadn't seen us because we are six lanes from the other railing."

They followed the sound, as it neared them.

It's under the bridge now," Les said. He put a finger to his lips signaling silence.

Jerry walked to the opening between the East and West bridges and eased a look at the water but saw nothing. He looked at the others, shook his head and they all walked back to the other side.

They were looking at the river when the front of the boat came into view. Two men were standing in the front. When the men looked up and saw them, they fired shots at them without hitting anyone. Les motioned for everyone in the group to spread out on the bridge and return fire. They cut both men down. The boat began taking water from the bullet holes in the bottom. A tarp in the front of the boat began to move, and a woman crawled from under it. She stood and raised her arms showing her hands were tied together.

"She'll drown when the boat sinks," Ruth said.

"The woman screamed, "Help me, please. Help.""

The back of the boat dipped, and it began to sink. The water surrounded her feet, and she looked at the group on the bridge. "Help, please."

"You will have to make it to the bank," Les yelled.

The boat disappeared from under the woman, and she went down with it."

"Oh, my God, no. Please no," Ruth cried out.

"Look, over there." Bentley yelled. "It's her. She's swimming with just her legs."

The woman was kicking her legs as she moved at an angle down river and toward the bank. Her head went underwater for a couple of seconds and came back up.

"She is going to drown," Ruth cried out.

Les quickly pulled his boots off and shucked everything he had on but his pants.

"You can't go in that water it's too cold.

Before Ruth could say another word Les dove off the bridge. He came up beside the girl, as she went under. He reached and grabbed a hand full of dark hair and pulled her up.

He's got her," Billy yelled.

Les was too cold to say anything as he cut the ropes bounding her hands.

The crowd above watched as a big log brushed by and pushed them under. The group stood watching and waiting for them to come up. The only thing that happened was the log changed its path and angled toward the bank. For five minutes the log slowly floated closer to the bank and stopped.

"They never had a chance with the water so cold," Ruth said. "I'll bet their bodies ends up thirty miles from here."

"That damn log pushed them under," Billy said.

They stood watching the river flow around a bend.

"Damn, look, I believe it's a hand. See below the log beside that rock. It's her, she is on the ground behind the rock. I see Les."

Richard retrieved a sniper rifle from the suburban, came back, held it up and spotted the rock with the scope. "It's an arm alright. Look around, for anyone below the location in the trees around it. We don't know where those guys in that boat came from or where they were going." Richard scanned the area above the rock with the scope on the rifle. "I don't see anyone, how about you, Jerry?"

"Nothing below the rock."

Richard handed Jerry the rifle. "Ruth, drive me and Billy to the end of the bridge. The rest of you wait here and keep looking. Ruth will come back here. We have plastic garbage bags in the back. Let's get two each and grab a couple of blankets."

The others watched for unsuspected guests while

Bentley watched Richard's and Billy's back. The two men pulled the bags on and taped them around their legs and stepped onto the wet ground. They climbed over boulders and walked through mud on their way to their friend and the woman. At one time they came to a narrow branch, jutting off from the river. The water was icy cold and came to the top of the bags covering their legs.

"Look at that would you." Jerry pointed to a big buck that came out of the trees to drink. It was down river about a hundred yards from where the two lay."

When the men reached the rock, they found Les and the woman lying on the ground. The leather straps Les had cut loose were still on her wrists, but her hands were free from each other.

Billy untied the straps as she groaned and passed out. Give me those blankets, they're ice cold."

Les began to move his body around and shucked his clothes. Immediately he stripped the woman's clothes off, leaving her panties and bra intact and ran his hands up and down her body. "Friction will generate heat," he said wrapping the blanket around her body.

Billy put a blanket around Les. "Keep moving." He stood waved his arms and did a thumbs up.

Richard turned, raised his rifle, and took aim.

Billy turned expecting to see a person. He saw the deer as the rifle cracked off a shot. The round hit the buck's head the instant it tried to run causing it to do a flip and hit the ground.

"What was that shot for?" Les asked.

"Richard bagged a big buck. We need some wood for a fire." Billy said and began picking dead branches.

"Good she will need some protein to get her strength back." Les held up his wet clothes, so his friends on the bridge could see them and bring him some dry ones.

Bentley grabbed some clothes from the back of the vehicle, ran to the end of the bridge and climbed down to the water.

Five aluminum boats rested on the bank. Richard and Billy passed them by because they didn't want to be a target on the river for anyone hiding in the brush.

Bentley untied one of the boats, climbed in, picked up one of two oars and began to paddle.

After starting a fire Richard and Billy searched for tracks but didn't see signs of anyone. They both went along the bank and looked around. After determining that the guys in the boat were alone and must have entered the water North of them, they went back to the two warming by the fire.

Bentley stopped and gave Les his clothes. "I'll come back for the deer after we get you guys back on the bridge."

The girl was barely alive, and her breathing was shallow. They fed her some water.

She coughed a couple of times and said, "Don't put me in the water. Please don't throw me in the river."

"You're okay lady. Nobody is going to throw you in the water. We want to help you. Just lay here next to the fire and take in some heat."

"The lady's eyes opened, for a few seconds. "You were on the bridge," she said and passed out again, but she was breathing steadily.

Les motioned for Bentley. "Pull the boat over here

next to the rock. We need to get her on the bridge."

Can we put some smoldering wood in the bottom of the boat?" Billy said.

Bentley tapped the bottom with a foot. "Sure, it's metal."

The boat was wide enough so that some of the hot wood could be placed beside the girl. Billy and Richard piled some small branches in the boat to make it soft.

Les dressed now handed Billy his blanket. "Lay this in the bottom on the branches."

After laying the girl on the in the boat everyone except Richard climbed in.

When they reached the bridge Les and Billy carried the girl up the bank.

Bentley went back to pick Richard up and retrieve the deer.

Ruth jumped in the suburban and drove to where she let the two men out earlier.

The girl was placed in the middle seat of the vehicle with the heater on high and the air from the rear vents blasting on her from the top. Ruth drove them back to the others.

The deer was field dressed and quartered using a knife and a hatchet where the boat was parked, so it would be much easier to handle.

"Woo, hoo deer steaks tonight," Ruth said.

The woman opened her eyes and was startled to see the men standing around the vehicle.

Ruth, sitting in the front seat gave her a smile. "You're safe with us."

"Yeah, we're the good guys," Jerry said from the front seat. "No one will hurt you now. We have food and water when you are up to eating let us know."

Her nakedness under the blanket caused her to feel uneasy. She asked Ruth, "My clothes?"

"Modesty wasn't an option for you. They were worried that you would go into hypothermia," Ruth told her.

The woman nodded "Yeah, I was freezing and worried I would too. So, where are my clothes?"

"Yours are, uh, I think back where you came out of the water. They were in rough condition. You will have to go without until we can find you some."

"Find me some?" the girl blurted out.

"Just kidding." Ruth threw some clothes on the seat. "We are about the same size. You can wear those until we find something."

"Can I go with you guys?" she asked.

"You bet you can. We'll be on our way in a few minutes. What's your name?"

"Natalie Wilshire. Former Army officer, MP, GBI and my last job was a private investigator." She slid her fingers through her brown hair. "Where are you guys headed?"

Ruth paused. "Good question. First, we have some business in the town of Sandy Springs. Our destination is somewhere in middle Georgia. I'll explain later."

Les raised the rear glass, opened the tailgate, fumbled in a box, closed it back, walked to one of the side doors and opened it. He held out both hands. "Peanut butter with jelly or a fried chicken breast or both?" he said.

Natalie took both. "Thank you for the third option. Was that you who came in the water for me?"

"Yep, like to have got both of us killed. Glad you are okay." Les went back to the men who were discussing how to transport the deer.

"I believe it is 28 degrees, so we can put the deer on the trailer. Just keep it away from the gas." Jerry said. "Or we could tie it on top of the car."

Billy spoke up. "Hey, I saw on television, I think it was a news show. A man wrapped a steak in aluminum foil, raised the hood and tied the steak on his engine and after driving for I don't remember how long. But the meat was cooked, after a while and he ate it."

"After we find Ruth's friends, we can find some foil and try that," Bentley said.

"I like my idea better," Richard said.

"What is your idea," Billy asked.

Richard held up a lighter. "Build a fire and cook several steaks at once."

"You know I like that idea better myself," Billy said.

Thirty minutes later the group was on their way with their new addition.

A few miles later Ruth saw a sign letting them know they were approaching their exit.

"Yep, this is the road to where my friends live. It's to the left and up a couple of blocks."

Les looked around. "Stop at the bottom of the ramp. This was a highly populated area. Stop here."

Ruth pulled over and stopped. "I see them. The cars on the bridge."

"The question is how long have they been there," Les said.

"I don't see any movement. Did you remember seeing them when you left, Ruth?" Richard asked.

"No, they were not there." Ruth pointed to the West bound ramp across the wide Interstate. "I went down the ramp over there and didn't cross the bridge. But there were no roadblocks. That was four months ago."

"It was put there about three months back. I was hunkered down in a house close by until three days ago." Natalie said.

"Three months is a long time to maintain a roadblock nowadays," Les said.

"Let me check things out," Richard said, got out, went to the back, and opened the hatch. When he came back and got in he was carrying an M16. "Got a fully automatic mode on this baby."

Ruth took off and went under the Roswell Road bridge and drove five hundred yards. She crossed the median and headed back to the ramp.

"No one on this side either. Go to the top of the ramp and stop," Les said.

Richard and Billy got out when she stopped. They scanned the area and saw no sign of life or movement at the roadblock. They eased toward the roadblock. The men were hit with a foul stench when they got close to the cars.

"Wow, what is that smell?" Billy said.

"You're fixing to find out and it won't be pretty."

"Anything smells that bad can't look good."

They stepped between two cars and found the source of the foul odor. Two bodies half gone from animals feasting on them and decay.

"Oh, I can't take this." Billy threw up and ran back to the others.

Les stared at him for a moment. "What's the matter, Billy? You look like you seen a ghost?"

Billy wiped his mouth with a rag from his pocket.

"Worse, I'll let Richard tell you."

"How many," Les asked Richard when he got back.

"Two."

"How long would you say?"

"A few weeks at least," Richard said.

"Where from here," Les asked Ruth.

Ruth pointed. "Three blocks up." She made a right turn and eased the vehicle along, everyone's eyes searching left, right to the front and the rear. "They are on the bottom floor of that high rise."

"Not the best floor to be on," Richard said.

"A gang came to the building one day looking for food. They threw a male resident out of a window from one of the upper floors."

"I retract my statement. The first floor is the best to live on." Richard said.

The Town

The two women Ralph and Betty rescued from the three men were taken to the clinic in town. They had several bruises and scratches and were malnourished. They will need some time to heal mentally.

Millie and Maria had volunteered at the clinic that day. After their exam Millie put them in their car to drive them to the community building. The women had told them they hadn't eaten in three days.

"Oh, poor things, first things first." Millie stopped at her house and invited the women in. They bypassed the living room and went straight to the kitchen.

She looked around and said, "No, no. This way."

She led them into the formal dining room, stopped and patted the antique large mahogany table that was left in the house by the previous occupants. "Have a seat, ladies. We are going to have some lunch." Once they were seated Millie said, "Through all the excitement I did not ask you ladies your name's."

The older woman spoke up. "My name is Norma. And this is Louise, my daughter. She is sixteen."

"I hope you decide to stay. I would enjoy getting to know the two of you."

"It seems to be our only option, and it is a good one," Norma said.

"That will be great. I will be right back with our lunch." Millie went into the kitchen and checked the pot she had left on the stove with a small fire under it. She picked up a big spoon and stirred the vegetable stew she had prepared the night before her and John's supper last night. There was plenty left over.

She placed the bowl on a tray and carried them into the dining room. Millie placed bowls in front of the ladies and one for herself and took a seat. "I am so glad to serve guest in my home again. It's been a long time."

Several times people had shown up in the town needing help, so the people had prepared a building to handle their needs. A shower had been set up using PVC pipe with holes drilled in it. The pipe was attached to a has coming from a large tank on a platform ten feet off the ground. Water was added to the tank by plastic one-gallon buckets attached to a conveyor belt that was dragged through a vat of water on the ground and up to the tank. The bottom of the bucket would catch on to the lip of a board and tilt it enough to pour the water into the tank. The conveyor returned the buckets to the water vat to fill again. A mule walked in a circle to make it all work.

If they needed clothes some would be brought in while they were showering.

The people would be fed a healthy meal followed by a shower and clothes. This was the first time Millie had fed anyone at her house that had dropped by.

Sometimes a person will be passing through on their way to find their family and just ask for a meal. Most are looking for a safe place to call home. Usually if a person stopped at the town and was just passing through, they would decide to stay. If the people had not eaten for several days, they usually didn't have the energy to shower, so they would be fed first. Which was the case for the two women.

After being fed and showered the women were allowed to pick through the clothes from the community store. The merchandise was all donated and was free. No one ever abused the system and there were plenty of clothes and canned food. What the town was short on was coffee and sugar. It was not kept in the building or offered.

After choosing the cloths they wanted the ladies sat for a rest.

"Where are you two from, Norma," Millie asked.

"Tennessee," Norma said. "Our family died from the virus. We were living in a house on a farm and had canned food at first. We cut down on eating. Then the food got down to a couple of jars of corn and beans. A few days ago, three men showed up asking for something to eat. I informed the men there was only a jar of corn and a jar of beans in the house. They said they would take that and when I argued with them, they tied Louise to a chair and said to cook the food on the wood stove, or they would kill her."

My family found out how mean people can get," Millie said. "So, you did the only thing you could do."

"When they finished, our hands were tied, and they dragged to their truck and put us in the back. One man climbed in with us. One of the men knew about this town but he didn't know anyone was living here."

"A lot of people have stopped, by and we fed them." Millie told her.

They were going to put us and two of the men out and have one man drive it and see if he could get food. Their truck ran out of gas about two miles from where the town, so we had walked to the town."

"I don't know how you two walked that far."

"It was terrible, when we were close to the gate one walked around the curve to check it out. He came back and said there were armed guards. The men took us to the edge of the trees next to a field and said to stay put. Believing they were going to kill us we took off running across the field hoping the men wouldn't shoot and the guards would see us."

"You were fortunate the guards spotted you and radioed to our police chief," Millie said.

Norma said, "Hearing shots behind us, I thought they were shooting at us. I would rather be dead than go back to those men. So, told Louise not to stop."

Dean the police chief asked if I would bring the by the police station so he and Jerry could ask you some question."

Millie dropped the women off, so Dean could talk to them. Since John would be leaving on a mission in a few days he had dropped in to hear what the women had to say about what was going on outside the town. He was sitting in a chair across the table with his arms folded on his chest. "Did the men say anything about having friends or a group they were part of."

Norma nodded. "Yes, one of them did. He acted like the leader. Said something about meeting a large group of men who were headed this way. He called them an army and said they had a retired colonel leading them."

Dean sat next to John tapping his fingers on the table one at a time in a sequence. "An army sounds like a lot of people. But now days what would be considered an army?"

Ralph spoke up. "Just Regular Army, National Guard and Reserve had 1,005,725. Counting what the virus took, we would have about 201,145 thousand. That would have left 4,022.9 per state. Before countless others died for other reasons."

John thought for a moment. "Even if there were half of those."

Ralph said. "That would be—.

"I got that, 2,011," John said. "There is no way to feed that many people on the go for very long."

"We should send someone to check on them." He spoke to Norma. "Did he mention where he was to meet them?"

"Somewhere close to the Tennessee State Line is all he said."

"John that people finding mission you are going on will give you a chance to seek out this group those men told the women about. Are you taking Ralph?"

"Yeah, I feel safer with two of us going."

CHAPTER 8

The Rangers

It was mid-day when the Reverend Allen Ball stopped his chevy in the middle of the street in the town of the Eatonton. He got out and motioned for the men to do the same.

"What have you got on your mind, Allen?" Jes asked him when they were gathered.

"Since we are in no hurry, I would like to check in on someone. We can relax for a while. And we are going to need a place to sleep. The house is big enough to accommodate all of us."

"Are you sure there is no one there?" West asked.

"I checked it out after I got my shot. There was no one there." He paused. "I haven't been here since. It's on the edge of town up a long driveway. If you didn't know it was there you would never see it. So, it will be safe."

"Lead the way. Can we get the Hummers up the driveway?" Jes asked.

"Yeah, and we can park them around back out of sight if anybody happens up on the place." Ball said.

They followed Allen Ball to the house he told them about and stopped on the street across from the driveway.

"Look how the weeds and bushes have grown up on both sides of the driveway." Allen said. "You guys go first and pack those bushes down, so they don't scratch my car."

"By all means we will protect that road beast," Dawson said.

Ball got in his car.

"I believe he loves that car," Mike said.

"Of course he does. It will outrun the Devil," Jes said and looked at the Black Chevy. "Lead the way, Dawson. Drive close to the side of the driveway and pack the brush down. We'll do the other side. It wouldn't do to have the preacher scratch that classic he's driving."

The men made their way to the house driving over the bushes on both sides packing them down while Ball followed driving in the center of the driveway. They found the yard behind the house to be paved with asphalt and big enough to park the Hummers without being seen. They killed the engines, got out, stretched, and looked around.

Ball got out of his 1958 Chevy and walked around it inspecting the body. "Not a scratch on it. Thanks guys."

"Anything for a place to sleep," West said.

"Darn big place to be in town," Dawson said.

"Who lived here, Allen?" West asked.

Ball was silent as he looked around and parked his eyes on a fixture in the back yard. "Her name is Laura. We used to sit in the swing in that gazebo."

"You said no one was here the last time you had come by. She had gone out for a while. Look for anything that suggest she's living here," Mike said.

"Let's check the house. I'll know if anything has changed since the last time I was here. Follow me." Ball led the men up on the porch and pulled the screen door open. He put his face to the glass as he turned the doorknob. "The door is unlocked. I locked it when I left." He pushed it open, took two steps inside and stopped to listen. He looked around. "Laura, Laura, it's me Allen. They heard nothing.

"You guys search the place while West and I bring some food in," Crier said.

Ten minutes later everyone was back in the kitchen with a portable stove, fuel, three cans of beans, two cans of corn and seven cans of tuna, all from the marriage ceremony. They also brought in two MREs and seven bottles of water. And chocolate bars for each man.

Carl pointed out a window. "We should check inside that shed. There might be something in it we can use."

Let's go, Jes said. "We'll cook this stuff when we get back."

Dawson picked up two chocolate bars. He handed one to his codriver, Mike Hand. "Have to look out for my gunner."

They filed out the back door and into the yard.

"You'll not find anything useful in that shed unless you want to manicure the lawn," Ball said. "Oh, and a bicycle, retired years ago. And some tools."

Forget about the shed for now, let's check our map and pick a route around Atlanta." Jes said.

Ball walked to the gazebo, climbed the two steps, walked to the swing, and sat down. He began to swing and sing the hymn. Rock of Ages.

"Hey, listen to Ball would you. He has a surprisingly good voice," Carl Wilcox said.

"Well, I will just be damn—darn you are right, West said.

The reverend lowered his head and began to pray. He stopped, looked up, stood and walked down the steps and out into the yard.

"I'll warm up some of the grub," Dawson said, walked to the house and entered the kitchen. He stared at the table where they had placed the food. After scanning the contents, he stuck his head out the door and called the others. "You guys need to get in here."

"What's going on?" Jes asked as they walked through the door.

Dawson pointed at the food. "What do you see on the table?"

West turned his attention to the table and scanned the containers. "Two cans of tuna and the MREs are missing."

"Let's do another search of the house," Jes said.

The men spent twenty minutes searching the house for the second time.

On returning to the kitchen, Dawson went to the Hummers and returned with two cans of tuna and two MREs.

"Got any plates we can divvy this stuff up on?" Jes asked.

"Laura always had paper plates for the several guest her father would invite over for cookouts in the back yard," Ball said.

After eating the Jes said, 'Let's to go to the town and check for any survivors that might be hanging around. Leave that can of tuna and one MRE here. If it is gone when we get back, we'll know we have to go a better search."

When they were outside Ball told them. "You guys to go on without me, I wanted to hang around the house."

West patted the Reverand on the shoulder. "Sure Allen, is there anything you want us to try to find for you?"

"Nothing I can think of."

The Rangers piled into two of the Hummers. Allen watched them disappear down the driveway, packing the brush down more.

While the Rangers were cruising through the town, Ball used the time alone to think back to a happier time in his life. He was back in the gazebo swing following his thoughts back before the virus hit. He closed his eyes, and the picture of a girl came into focus. Her blonde hair was a foot past her shoulders, shining like gold, blue eyes the color of the sky on a clear day. A radiant smile warm as the sunshine on a summer day.

He didn't know how long he had slept but when he opened his eyes, he was looking at the house. Suddenly he thought he saw a curtain moving on one of the upstairs windows. He jumped up and ran to the back door and opened it. Glancing at the table he noticed the canned tuna were gone.

He hurried to the stairs and climbed them, taking two stairs at a time. Running from room to room he came up empty-handed just like the other times they searched. He had an idea and hurried back down the steps and out to his car opened the driver's door. In his back seat there was something surely to draw attention. What red blooded American could refuse a chocolate bar. Hershey at that. He pulled one of the bars from the bag, slid it in his shirt pocket, pitched the bag in the back seat and closed the door.

He made noise opening the door so whoever was in the house would hear him. "Nothing like a chocolate bar," he said in a loud voice. "Mmm, boy that tastes good. I'll just leave this other one on the table for later. I'll go back out now." Allen opened the door and pulled it to hard enough to be heard throughout the house and eased into the pantry to wait.

After twenty minutes he gave up, picked up the candy bar and went upstairs. Being quiet as a mouse he went to Laura's room. Standing quiet as could be he thought he heard whispering. There was a bookcase taking up three feet of the wall space. Ball eased over and put his ear to the wall. There was one person talking. Allen went into the room adjacent to Laura's room but saw no one. When he was about to give up, more whispering could be heard. Ball went over and leaned on the wall. It sounds like a child talking, he thought.

There was another noise. One that sounded like something sliding on the floor. Ball eased to the door and waited.

A young girl and boy walked out of Laura's room. After the kids were out of sight he eased to Laura's door and peeped inside. The bookcase was moved to the right exposing an opening in the wall. Ball walked to the opening and discovered the wall has a three feet wide room. He went down the stairs and sat waiting for the children to come back. When the kids got back to the stairs, Ball was sitting on the third step from the bottom. Seeing him the two kids froze with their mouths and eyes open.

"His hands went up. "I'm not here to hurt you. I'm looking for the girl who lived here."

The kids didn't say a word.

Allen pulled the candy bar from his shirt pocket and held it out. The kids backed up.

"It's chocolate." He tore the wrapper off and held it up.

"She's not here," the girl said and reached for the candy taking it out of Ball's hand. "Some men took her when we were walking in town."

Excited, Ball put his hands on the girl's shoulders. "You mean some men got Laura?"

"Oh, you are hurting me," the girl said, while the boy stood wide eyed and quiet.

Ball let the girl go. "I'm sorry, I didn't realize I was. Do you know how many men they were?"

"I counted six of them."

"I have some friends who will be coming back in a few minutes. There are six of them, but they are not the men who took Laura. My friends are Army men. Do you understand about Army men?"

"Yes, my daddy was in the Army. He wore a uniform."

"These men will be wearing uniforms too. And they are good men. Do you know where the men took Laura?"

The girl shook her head. "We don't know."

"I might have to get another candy bar for you two. What do you say to that.?

"I think so too," the girl said.

The boy answered. "Yes, me too."

"They are in the car, as soon as my friends get here, I'll get you another one. What is your name."

"Rebecca, my brother is name is Luke."

"How old are you, and your brother."

Judging by the way Rebessa talked she Ball though she was short for her age and expected her to say ten or eleven.

"I'm eight, Luke is five."

The boy held up five fingers. "I'm five."

He girl shook a finger at her brother. "Luke you are old that you don't need your fingers when someone ask you your age."

Ball heard food steps on the porch and stiffened. He heard the door open. "You two be quiet." He relaxed when he heard Jes and the other Rangers talking.

"In here, fellows on the stairs."

The men walked through the kitchen to where Ball called from.

"Well, what or should I say who do you have there, Ball?" Jes asked.

"The takers of our missing food. I'll explain later. I was sharing my candy with them. This is Rebecca and that little fellow is Luke."

"How did you find them?"

"I heard them. There is a secret room in the house. It's just not soundproofed."

"Do they know what happened to your friend?" West asked.

"Yes, Rebecca who is eight but comes across as older said some men took her when they were in town. She doesn't know where they took her."

Jes asked, "Rebecca, have the men brought Laura back here."

"Yes, they did not long after they got her. They got the food." Except what we had in our hiding place."

"Do you remember how long ago that was?" Ball asked.

"I made a calendar, and I have been checking the days off."

Dawson returned from the bathroom. "Have you kids been using the bathroom?"

Rebecca shook her head. It doesn't work."

Your girl might have left a message," Dawson said, "I believe the people who took her have more people and they are making them work on a farm."

"A farm?" Ball said.

"Yeah, come look on the bathroom mirror. She must have gone in there."

Ball followed Dawson to the bathroom. "See, hard labor," Dawson said.

"She wanted whoever seen this to know she was having to work hard," Mike said.

"No, no that's not what that means. That's the name of a state park about twenty-five miles from here."

"So, they have turned the park into a community," Jes said. "Let's check it out. If we can get in the park without them spotting us, we can set up a planned attack."

"Anybody there will hear the Hummers coming a long way off," West said.

"We can use my Chevy," Ball said.

"Are you kidding? We heard you coming two blocks before you got to us on the base," Dawson said.

"That is because of the glass pack mufflers I installed on it a couple of years ago. The original mufflers are in that shed out back. If I put them back on it will be quiet enough that we can get in the park without being heard."

"Get it done," Jes said.

"You must have been close to this family, for them to let you store your car parts here," West said as they walked to the shed.

"Laura and I were high school sweethearts. Her parents liked me." Ball stopped at the shed and pulled the double doors open. He stepped inside and pointed. "They are over there on that shelf." He walked over and shook one of the mufflers. "These things are heavy; I'll need some help."

"Coming your way," Virgle said.

Carl entered the building, walked to the shelf, and picked up one of the mufflers. When he came out carrying the steel cylinders he commented, "This thing is heave." He laid it on the lawn next to the Chevy.

Jes came out with the other muffler. "Do you have the tools to change these out," he asked.

"Ah, I'll be right out." Ball appeared from the shed with a toolbox. "One more thing." He went back into the building and came out with a jack in one hand and a two-foot steel rod to operate the jack in the other hand. Ball sat the jack on the ground next to the car, went to the trunk and opened it. He reached in and pulled out a pair of coveralls and began slipping into them. "I carry these just in case. The car is old, and I never know when I will need them." He buttoned the cover and walked to the shed, reached down, and lifted a foot square wooden block. He walked back and dropped it on the ground next to the car.

"Reminds me of when I drove my old klunker to school," Walker said.

Dawson gave his friend a confused look. "Both days you went?"

Walker flipped Dawson the bird. "I got your both days Einstein."

Ball went down on his knees and laid on the ground beside his Chevy. He slid the jack under the car and placed it below the frame. He began to move the steel pipe up and down and the Chevy began its journey upward by raising and stopping in slow increments as Ball pumped the jack handle. when it was high enough Ball shoved the block of wood under the machine and wedged it under the frame. "In case the jack doesn't hold," he said.

"Smart idea, I was worried about that jack being old and not used. The seals could give way," Jes said.

"I'll be finished in about thirty minutes fellows," Preacher said.

"Good that will give us time to finish our surveillance of the park before dark," Jes said.

In the time Ball gave himself to swap the mufflers he was finished. "Now, let's go get my girl," he said when he slid from under the car, moved the block, and let the jack down.

"That we will do," said Jes, but it not as simple as going there and getting her. We will have scope the place out and see how many men they have. And the type of weapons they are using.

Reverand Ball slipped out of the coveralls and put them back in the trunk. He walked to the driver's door, reached through the window, turned the switch key and starting the engine. The only sound they heard was the starter turning. He pulled his arm back. "Purrs like a kitten doesn't it."

"Is it running?" Mike asked.

Ball raised the hood and showed them the fan turning. "You wont get a car made today to run that quiet."

"That is the truth," Carl said.

"Enough the car. What can we do with the kids?" West asked.

"I have been studying about that. We can leave them here with some food," Jes said. "They've survived this long having to find food. A few more hours shouldn't madder."

"We can do it in a few hours?" Ball asked.

"Sure, Ball what do you take us for?" Carl said.

"Darn professional Randers, that's what. Right."

All heads nodded in agreement.

Walked slapped Dawson on the stomach with the back of his hand. "Give it to us, sarge. What is the move."

"We'll drive the hummers to the closest town to the park and hide them. Walker, you West, Mike and Carl will wait with your radios ready. I want to see how many hostages they have. We'll free them before we engage the gang," Jes told them.

"I can't believe just two hours ago I thought I would never see Laura again. And now in a few hours I'll have her back with me again. Thank you Lord."

CHAPTER 9

The mission

Three blocks up the street, Ruth stopped at an intersection and pointed to a building. "That's where they live."

Les inspected the surroundings. "Park underneath in the parking garage."

Ruth pulled under the building. I'll turn around, so we are facing out."

Park alongside in the middle. That way we are not blocked either way. It's wide enough that you can swing left or right for a fast exit."

After Ruth was parked and looked around. "I don't see my friend's car."

"I want to be in on this," Natlie said. "You guys saved my life. The least I can do is help save your friends."

"Sounds fair to me," Les said. "Richard, you, and Bentley stay with the car. The rest of us will check the building."

Richard stepped out with the M16. "I'll guard it with my life. We wouldn't want to walk to Middle Georgia. Bentley you take your rifle and go to the opening the and look outside. If you see anyone put up a finger for each person there is."

Les motioned to the door. "Let's go, People. Ruth, you walk behind me and tell me where to go." Billy, Jerry, and Natilie followed behind Ruth.

The team halted at the door to listen. Les eased inside and checked the hallway. He motioned for the others to follow. Ruth pointed down the hall to her right. They moved to the fourth door, stopped, and listened. Les turned to the others and held up a flat hand. They stood in place while he eased the door open and stepped inside. Les scanned the room before motioning for the others to follow. The apartment had a foul odor and almost gagged them as they searched. After going through each room, they were standing in the living room. The front door slowly opened. Les grabbed the knob and yanked hard, pulling a man in, so fast he fell face down on the dirty carpet. Les and the others had their weapons pointed at him.

"Please don't shoot me. You can have anything you want."

"What are you doing breaking in this apartment?"

"I didn't break in; I was pulled in when you yanked the door open. But I live here. I was living here before the virus hit." The man rolled over and stared in the faces of everyone.

Ruth surprised said, "Edwin, is that you?"

"Yes, I'm Edwin." The man looked at the female. He patted the floor moving his hands around. "My glasses fell off."

Billy found his glasses, held them up and looked at them. He handed him the glasses. "They look like coke bottle bottoms. You can't see shit without them, can you?"

"No, nothing at all." He put the specs on and

looked around. "Ruth, oh my God, I am so glad to see you. Where have you been all this time? I thought you were dead."

"I am very much alive. Never mind where I have been. Where is Angie?"

"They took her. The men did."

"Who are the men and where did they take her."

"I don't know who they were. They just came to the building and took all the women. Under and over a certain age that is."

"Do you know where they took them?"

"Yes, I was out looking for food one night. I was on my bike and saw their truck and followed them. They didn't see me in the dark. They were stopping and checking houses and apartments. That's how I was able to keep up with them."

"You can come with us and show us."

"Come with you? I don't really want to tangle with those guys. I'll give you the address. There's two of them upstairs right now."

Les spoke up. "You mean on a floor above us?"

"Yes, on the fourth floor right above this apartment. They threw the old couple off the patio that lived there. They landed outside my sliding door. I heard them scream and I saw them hit the ground."

Ruth put a hand on her friend's wrist. "Edwin, you do want to get out of this building and go to a safe place with nice people and live, right? If you do, go with us so we can take care of those guys and get Angie back. She needs to go too."

Edwin was silent for a moment, then he looked up. "I'll go, and I kill those bastards and get Angie back." He walked to the kitchen and got on one knee and reached into the cabinet under the sink. He stood and held up a snub nose pistol. "They are in a house. Let's go."

Les looked up. "First Billy and I have some business on the fourth floor."

"You mean you are going to their apartment?" What if their friends come while you are up there?"

"You have Jerry and Ruth here; they'll take care of them. And Natiley. Just keep an eye on that sliding glass door. Did I mention I teach flying lessons?"

"Flying lessons," Edwin said looking confused.

Les grinned. "You'll see. Where are the stairs?"

Edwin opened the door, stepped into the hall, and pointed. "Its next to the front door."

The two men quietly climbed the stairs to the fourth floor.

The door was no match for the size fifteen boot Les wore. When he kicked it the door opened so fast it broke loose from the hinges. Les and Billy were in and pointing their weapons at a tall skinny man and a short, skinny man before the men knew what was happening.

"Who the hell are you?" the tall man yelled.

"Glad you asked. Keep them covered, Billy." Les opened the sliding glass door to the patio. "We are here to give you two fellows your one and only flying lessons."

"Flying lessons? What in hell are you talking about?" short man asked.

"You are fixing to find out." Les stepped onto the patio and inspected the ground below. "Good ole solid concrete. Perfect for a landing pad." Les stepped back inside and grabbed the two men he outweighed by

109

seventy pounds and pulled them out the door.

Down below the others heard a commotion from above as they kept their eyes on the patio four flights up. They saw two objects pass by the patio doors from above. It was only a couple of seconds between the screams, and two dull thud sounds when the two men hit the ground.

"That would be the two tenants from the fourth floor," Ruth said.

Natalie grinned. "They didn't do so well. Sorry it's only a one lesson class, guys." She looked at Ruth. "I believe I am going to like your big friend."

Ruth gave her a sudden glance.

Natalie caught the look. "Professionally that is." She smiled.

"Oh, God, I must get away from here," Edwin said.

"We had better get out of this apartment before we pass out," Jerry said.

The house is across Interstate 285 a few streets and make a right.

Les asked Edwin, "Wow many men strong is this gang."

"The best I could tell, there were twelve. Well, now just ten."

Les asked Natalie if she wanted to join in the fun.

"Where is my gun?" she asked.

"Atta girl." Les said as he handed her a 1911. "It has a full magazine."

She checked that the gun was ready to fire. "Sweet, baby sweet. They might be the gang those men who took me belonged to. Payback time, assholes."

"If so, there are only eight men now," Les said.

"Edwin, did they wear a red sash around their waist?" Natalie asked,

"Everyone of them wore one. I wonder why they did that?"

"It dates to the eighteen hundreds. Outlaws wore them and called themselves, 'The Cowboys.' The leader could be a western movie fan. Wyatt Earp or his foes."

"Well, the wild west is back," Billy said.

Let's load up and hit the road," Jerry said.

They went back to the garage and told their two teammates what they had planned.

"Sweet music to my ears. Let's get them," Richard said and ran hard toward the wall, walked up it far enough to kick off himself into a back flip and land on his feet. With the M16 above his head. "Wahoo who, I'm ready to go."

"Are you psyched up now?" Jes said.

"Is that your psyche dance?" Natalie said.

Richard twirled the rifle in his hands. "One of them, I got plenty. Shall we go."

They loaded up and Ruth pulled out of the garage and turned right into Roswell Road. When she reached the bridge over 285, to get around the roadblock she had to take the ramp onto the Interstate, cross the medium and drive back up the ramp on the other end of the bridge.

Edwin pointed to a street. "Thats where that gang turned the night I followed them."

Les looked at the houses as Ruth drove. "A shame all these fancy homes going to waste. Let Ruth know when we are one block from their street. We'll park there and walk through the yard to the back of the house. Do they go out at night?"

"They go out anytime they take a notion. There's no one to stop them," Edwin said.

"Tonight, will be a better time to attack. But at least let's wait until some of them leave, it will better our odds if we break them up." Les said.

"Edwin what about the girls they took. What ages are they? And how about Angie, when did they get her," Ruth asked.

"The girls are twenty on up to forty-five. I guess they'll wait for the younger girls to get older and replace the girls who get too old. They got Angie one night when I was out on a food run. I was coming down the street on my bike as they were putting her in a truck. That's why I was able to followed them. I was going to try and get her from them. I was going to try to get her back, but they were to many of them. We should have listened to you about the food running out. It had always been there on the shelves in the stores. I guess we were what you would say spoiled stupid."

"I would say Rotten but stupid works," Ruth said.

"We both lived off a trust fund. We never had to work like our friends did. I just want my sister back." Edwin pointed. "This is the last street before the one they are on."

Ruth turned on the street and pulled to the curb in front of a two-story house and stopped and shut the engine off.

Edwin said, "They are living in two houses. the house behind this one and the one to the left of it."

"You will have her back today. And the question is what to do with all the women," Richard said.

"I guess that's something we need to think about," Ruth answered.

"I have already thought about it," Jerry Tilson said. "And it's simple. If either one of them can read a map."

"I can read a map well," Edwin said.

Jerry opened the glovebox and pulled out a folded paper. He picked it up, opened it and showed Edwin with his finger pointing to their town. "Can you get the girls here if you have transportation?"

"Yeah, I've been there. Angie and I drove up to North Georgia one weekend. A couple of our friends were with us. I was the map reader for that trip."

"What happened to your friends? Are they still around?" Billy asked.

"They're living in a house not far from me." Edwin looked as though he was trying to remember something. "Come to think of it I haven't seen them in five days."

"We had better check on them after we finish here," Jerry said.

Les opened his door. "Richard let's get a closer look at that house." He stepped out and eased the door shut.

Richard followed. "I'll go to the left. I can't wait to go psycho on those Basterds."

The men disappeared around the house. Les on one side, Richard on the other side. Bushes planted between the houses across the back yard formed a fence supplying them with plenty of cover. They eased across the back yard to the bushes and slipped through to back yard of the house the gang was held up in. They stood listening and looking for a few minutes.

When they were confident they would not be seen they moved to the rear corners of the house and eased to the front corners and nestled behind some bushes.

For fifteen minutes there was no activity. No noise, no movement of any sort. Then a man came out the front door and walked to a tarp, raised a corner, and threw it back. He changed positions and pulled the tarp off exposing several five-gallon cans.

"We'll take those with us," Les said to himself.

The man picked up two of the containers. Each had a hose on them about ten inches long.

Someone stuck their head out the door and yelled, "Hurry up will you shit head. I want to get out of this stinking house."

"Yeah, yeah, hold your ass will you. These things are heavy." He walked to one of the trucks, sat one can on the ground, opened the filler cap door and removed the gas cap. He was a short, skinny man with a bald head. He strained to get one of the gas cans high enough to get the hose in the filler hole. He finally made it and tilted the can up to pour the contents in the tank.

The same man yelled out the door, "Are you not finished yet, you damn half pint."

After a few minutes, the man lowered the can but held on to it and picked up the other can and moved to another truck. He put one container beside the truck and finished emptying the first one into the tank of the second truck. He swapped cans and struggled to get it up. When he did gas blew back on him; he cursed and lowered the can. After placing the empty cans back where he got them from, he went back into the house.

A few minutes later four men came out and got in two of the trucks.

Les and Richard waited five minutes before they moved.

No one in the SUV saw the trucks that left the house, stop and let two men out. They also didn't see the men walking up behind them. The men walked up beside the suburban and pointed guns at the six passengers.

The Rangers

The Rangers piled into the Hummers. "Where to," Ball asked.

"Let's find those guys. Jes said.

"Ball went and got in his Chevy.

They drove to the nearest town to the park and hid the Hummers behind a convenient store.

Dawson and Jes got in the car with Ball.

"Now let's go find those guys," Jes said.

Ball pulled the gear lever into drive. "I would say the front gate would be a good place to start."

I sure wish I had something they would trade for," Jes said.

"Hold on a minute," Ball said, got out, went to the back of the car, and opened the trunk. He reached in and brought out a brown paper bag. He closed the lid and walked back to the door. "I have just what they might want," he said after getting back in the car." He handed Jes the bag containing a quart bottle of Whiskey.

After a few minutes, Ball stopped the Chevy at the front entrance to the park.

"Well, here we are at the front gate, and no one is

home," Jes said.

"But the door is open." Dawson said.

Jes looked around. "Let's go in."

"Hold on a minute. Look up the road," Ball said.

Fifty yards into the park, two men stepped from the woods onto the road with rifles pointed at the Chevy. "That's far enough," one of the men said, walked to the driver's door and asked Ball, "What's your business?"

Jes spoke. "We want to talk."

Standing the man couldn't see Jes across the seat. He put a hand on top of the car, leaned down and said, "Got nothing to say except turn around and be gone."

Ball pulled the lever to reverse and let off the breaks. The Chevy eased back a few inches.

Jes held the bottle of whiskey up. "Whatever you say."

The man looked at the bottle and licked his lips.

"Just hold on fellow. Go ahead and talk, I'll listen." The man pulled a tin cup from his pocket and reached inside the car. "My name is Ted."

"How about your buddy, does he imbibe?" Jes said as he filled the cup half full.

"The man raised up. "Get your sorry ass over here, Nate. Fellows got something for us. Get your cup out."

"Mind if we get out and stretch our legs," Jes asked.

The man opened Ball's door. "Long as you bring that bottle you can." He turned his cup up.

The three men exited the vehicle and walked around to the driver's side.

Nate spotted the bottle and held his cup out. "Fill it up. This is the first we had in eight months."

Ted held his cup out. "Fill it up this time. That first one was just enough to wet my whistle."

After letting the men down three cups, Jes spoke up. "You know we were really looking to run across some women. I'd swap the rest of this bottle for a woman."

"You would huh. Well, what do you think, Nate should we tell them where they can get one?"

"How much is left," Ted asked.

"Jes held the bottle out. "A little over half."

Ted swayed side to side. "I don't know. The boss would be upset if we gave his women away."

Jes nudged Ted with his elbow. "Your boss wouldn't know. We wouldn't stay but an hour."

"What do you think?" Ted asked Nate. "One hour for the bottle?"

"Hell, yeah tell them where they are," Nate said.

Ted pointed. "First cabin on the right around the curve."

"Now, we don't won't to get turned around and end up in boss's cabin. So, which one is he in," Jes asked.

Ted took a drink from his cup. "Oh, yes that would be bad if you did. His is the third cabin on the right."

"The girls are two hundred yards down on the right," Ball said. Being familiar with the park, he knew how close they could get to the cabin the girls were in without being seen. "Let's go, I know where to park."

Ball drove into the park and stopped the Chevy twenty yards from the women's cabin. The three men exited the car.

The men walked through the trees to the cabin and stood next to a window.

Jes whispered. "Let Ball see if Laura is in there."

Ball looked through the window. He saw two women but not Laura. He scanned the room. A girl walked through a door from another room. It wasn't Laura. Ball looked at Jes. "I don't see her," he said, turned and faced the window again. Another woman entered the room. "There she is." He tapped on the window, startling the girls, causing them to go to the other side of the room. Laura looked out of the window. She recognized Ball and cried out. "Oh, my God, Allen." She rushed to the window and tried to raise it. "I can't get it open."

Ball motioned to the front door.

"Okay, but it won't open."

Jes went to the door, turned the knob, and found it locked. He backed up and rammed his shoulder into it. The door couldn't stand up to the large, framed man. When it opened Ball ran through the door passing Jes on his way to Laura. They hugged until Jes told them they had business to take care of. Dawson closed the door, so it looked like everything was normal.

Jes questioned the girls and found out they were the only ones there. The men who kidnapped them were going to deliver them to another gang that day.

Dawson eased the door open just enough to see a man coming their way.

A man stepped out of the cabin he came from and yelled, "Don't leave those women until we are ready to take them." The man went back in the cabin.

Jes looked at the busted door and noticed the only

damage is on the inside, unnoticeable to anyone coming in. "Dawson, you and Ball, take the girls into the other room." Jes backed up to the wall so the door would hide him when it opened.

The boards creaked as the man stepped upon the porch and walked to the door. Having no clue, it was not needed, the man put the key in the lock and turned it. The door opened slowly. Jes thought the man might suspect something. He was thinking about something more important than the door.

"Well, hello, girls' today's your last day with us. So, I think I will get a going away present. Come out wherever you are and let me choose one of you." He walked into the room, leaving the door open.

Jes pushed the door so it would slowly close. The man turned and saw, The Big Ranger and reached for a pistol hanging on his belt. Jes reached out and put one hand on the front of one shoulder and grabbed the back of the other shoulder, spun the man around and grabbed him around the neck. He twisted it one way and quickly jerked it back the other way causing it to make a snapping sound. He walked him into the other room and let him fall to the floor. "You girls go, out the window."

In the front room, Dawson pulled a multi-use tool from his pocket and opened the screwdriver blade, removed the screws holding the window shut and raised it. "This way everybody. It's a five-foot drop so, you first Ball. When you get them in the car, make some noise leaving. We want those men out of the cabin, so we can deal with them," Jes said."

The preacher jumped down and helped the women. After they all were on the ground, Ball rushed them over to the Chevy. When the women were loaded Ball jumped in and fired the engine up. He turned around and blew the horn as he headed toward the gate.

Six men ran out into the yard and watched the Chevy leaving.

When Ball passed the gate, he saw the two guards lying on the ground passed out.

"Are those men dead?" Laura asked.

"Only dead drunk. They'll wish they were dead when they wake up."

Jes and Dawson stepped on the porch with weapons pointed at the men.

The men looked wide eyed at the two men wearing Army uniforms. "Who the hell are you people," one man said.

Jes fired a round at the feet at the men. "You men have committed a federal crime. Drop your weapons and take a prone position on the ground."

"What do you mean, a federal crime? There is no government anymore."

"Do you see two men standing in front of you?" Jes said.

"Yes, we see you," one of the men said.

Dawson spoke up. "What are we wearing?"

One of the men said, "Army uniforms."

"That's right. So, drop the weapons and get down. I said get down," Dawson fired a round at their feet.

The men dropped their weapons and laid on the ground.

"Who's the head man of you fellows?" Jes asked.

All the heads on the ground looked around and at

the cabin door.

"He must have not come out," one of the men said.

Jes keyed the handheld two-way radio. "Head this way when Ball gets to you and leave him with the girls."

West keyed the mic. "We are on our way. Ball you wait here with the women. You got that gun of yours handy?"

Ball patted his waist. "Handy Dandy as can be."

Jes and Dawson stood guarding the men. "What does your boss look like?" Jes asked.

"Tall with a beard and slim."

"Everybody's slim now days. What is he wearing?" Dawson said.

"Jeans and a red shirt. Where is our friend that came to the cabin?" the man asked.

"He's still in the cabin," Jes said.

"What kind of shape is he in?"

"He's lying on the floor. Dead," Dawson said.

The man said, "Yeah, I kind of thought that."

Three Hummers stopped at the cabins.

Jes yelled, "We are going inside and see if we can bring your boss out. Just hope he is as smart as you guys."

"I believe there two other guys in there with him," a man said.

There was a noise at the rear of the cabin like a door slamming. Jes and Dawson ran to the rear of the cabin and saw three men run out the backdoor. Jes yelled for them to halt and put their hands up. They chose not to and turned and fired on the two soldiers. Jes and Dawson cut them down.

"That did not have to happen to you fellows," Jes yelled knowing his words fell on not only deaf ears but dead. "Neither of them was wearing a red shirt. The Boss is still missing. Give me the mic," Jes said.

Mike handed Jes the microphone to the Hummer's PA system.

Jes pushed the button. Men in the cabin. This is Master Seargent Jes Crier and platoon. If you toss your weapon out the door and exit, nothing will happen to you. If you choose not to comply, we will turn that structure into something that resembled Swiss Cheese. You have two minutes to make up your mind, which is not a lot of time, so I recommend you start thinking about your options.

Two minutes later passed and the boss made no appearance.

Jes tapped Dawson on the shoulder. "Come on let's take a look in that cabin."

They found food, ammo, some clothes, and shoes but no men.

They went back outside and Jes spoke to the man he determined was the second in charge. "Any other men."

A voice came from one of the men. "The boss got away while you were taking out the guys who ran out the back door. I saw him go out the window."

"Fellow," Jes said. "By not saying anything you have killed him. We need to get back to Ball and the girls. That guy might run up on them. You all get in your trucks and follow the lead, Hummer. We'll be behind you. Do you know what that is on top of those vehicles," Jes asked.

"They look like machine guns to me," one man

said.

"You are wright but not just any machine guns. Those are M60s, and they can take all of you down in just a few seconds. Stop at the gate and pick up your two friends."

"We'll stay right between you guys," The leader said.

Jes and West, being the last Hummer out of the park, stopped and retrieved the two passed out drunk guard's rifles and their buddies loaded the two drunks in their truck.

They reached Ball and the girls just in time to see a man wearing a red shirt with a rifle on his shoulder approach Ball.

"That's the boss man who got away from the cabin," Jes said.

The boss man peeled his weapon off his shoulder and was fixing to aim it at Ball. The preacher beat him to the draw, fired and put around in the man's stomach. He looked at Ball in disbelief before he fell face down.

The convoy stopped and Jes got out and walked toward Ball who was standing beside the man.

Jes could hear the man talking in a weak voice. "Turn me over. I want to see the blue sky one more time before I die."

Ball bent and took the man by an arm and rolled him over not noticing the hand on a pistol in his belt.

In a weak voice the man said, "You dumb ass. Thake this." And he squeezed the trigger. A split second after a size fifteen boot pushed his arm down causing the shot to go off wild.

"Damn," boss said, and his eyes closed.

Ball looked at Jes. "I could have died because of my stupidity."

"Maybe not the oldest trick but an old one." Jes said.

One of the girls yelled. "May is shot. That bullet caught her in the shoulder."

Everyone focused their attention on the blood coming out of the woman.

Walker hurried to one of the Hummers and grabbed a first aid kit. He ran back to May as he opened a package of gauze. He opened a bottle of alcohol and washed the bleeding wound and wrapped it with the white cloth.

"What are we going to do?" one of the women said. "She needs a doctor."

One of the other women spoke up, "Where can we find a doctor?"

"There were five in Eatonton, but I believe they all left.?" Laura said.

West snapped his finger. "Do you guys remember what Sheriff Pat said to that gambler before he left?"

"Yeah, Dawson said. He told him to go by and let doc look at his nose before he left town."

They were a couple of doctors there a few months ago," Laura said.

"Let's go fellows. She is bleeding. Which is the quickest route," Jes asked."

"We'll have to go back the way we came, so we can get the kids," Laura said.

"Put her in the back seat of my car. It's the fastest vehicle." Ball said.

"We'll follow you," Jes said. "Laura, will you ride with Walker and Carl to your house and pick up the two kids we found there?"

"Yes, I was so worried about them," Laura said.

"We need to figure out what to do with the guys we captured. After that we'll all meet in Sparta." Jes said.

West spoke up. "Why don't we take these guys to Sheriff Pat, back in Sparta, he has a jail, and he can put them to work. He said he needed more help."

Jes looked at the guys they had taken. "Good idea. He said he has a work camp with guards. We'll follow Walker and Carl, with those guys between us."

CHAPTER 10

The mission

When Les and Richard got back to the yard of the house Ruth parked in front of a men yelled, "Nice of you to join your friends. And don't try to be a hero because my friend has a rifle pointed at your passengers. It would be a shame to waste such pretty ladies. Stop right there and drop those nice weapons. I see that one is an M16. I'll have that for myself."

A slim man stepped in front of the two Rangers. He was about sis feet and his face and head was void of ant hair.

"All right you win, no need hurt anybody," Les told him.

Another man about five feet tall approached them. He looked at their SUV with the trailer attached and smiled. "Look at all that stuff he can use."

The taller man said, "Every day for the last three months I have crossed this street at the same intersection. I know every vehicle parked on it. Then I see one I have never seen before and pulling a trailer."

"My bad," Les said.

"Yep, you are right. Everybody out," the taller man said.

Everyone exited the vehicle and stood next to it.

"Look at them two babes," the short man said. "Our lucky day."

"The day's not over with yet, you short shit," Richard said. "The biggest part of you ran down your mama's leg didn't it."

"I'll short shit your ass."

"That'll be enough of that shit."

"Did you hear what he said about me," short man said.

"We have more pressing issues to take care of. And it is the truth."

"I'll take care of you later," short man told Richard.

The taller man said. "We are going to take a little walk to that house you have so much interest in. It doesn't smell good but it's pretty on the inside. So, move out."

When they entered the Livingroom, they were met by four other men with long stringy hair and beards. All shorter than the tall man who brought them there but all taller that shorty. The house smelled of sweat, human waste, dead animals, and deodorizers.

"This place smells like you folks look. Like shit," Natalie said.

"You don't look all that great yourself. Your hair looks like you took a swim," one of the men said. Besides, you'll get used to it."

"Let's go shorty, we have an errand to run," said the tall man who brought them there. He opened the door, and the short man followed him out.

"Where are the women that were taken from their homes?" Ruth asked.

"Who are you to be asking questions?"

"Just curious," Ruth said.

"You'll see them soon enough when you join them." He pointed to two men. "You and you, go see what's on their trailer."

"Not yet, I want to check out the fresh meat."

Les and Richard standing in the back of the group, bent a knee bringing a foot up. They reached in their boot and pulled knives out. Then something happened that must have been meant to be.

Les pointed. "Look your man can't walk. One of the men looked out a window at a man lying on the ground. Next to him was a limb that had fallen from a tree and knocked him down."

Richard gave out a loud yell. "Yeah ha." And several things happened at once. He rushed one of the men flipped him around, wrapped an arm around his neck, reached around and drove the nine-inch blade into his body under his rib cage and upward.

At the same time, Les did the same to one of the other men but without the yelling.

The third man turned, raising his rifles. Natalie quickly lifted a foot and gave him a kick in the groin causing him to drop his weapon. Billy hit another man in the jaw causing the bone to snap and Bentley ripped the gun from his hand, shot him and the man Natilie kicked. Another man appeared sleepy eyed from another room with a pistol. Jerry kicked the gun from his hand and landed a fist to the side of his head. Ruth Hurriedly reached down and retrieved the weapons and shot him.

Les looked around. "We need to find the women."

Ruth yelled a few times for Angie. "It's safe to

come out now. You girls are free." A moment later several women appeared on the landing at the top of the steps. They were all naked. Ruth spotted her friend and ran up the steps and hustled the girls into a room. She hugged Angie and told her she was safe now. She looked at the women and assured them everything was going to be fine.

Jerry said, "Les, you and Richard wait and see if those men outside searching the trailer heard the shots. If not, we'll go out and take care of them. There's another one unaccounted for."

Ruth yelled from upstairs. "This room is clear."

"I'll help Ruth with the girls," Natalie said.

"There's no one else here," Ruth told them after searching all the rooms.

Natalie came to the top of the stairs. "We are getting the girls dressed then we'll be down."

After a few moments Les said he and Richard were going out to check the fellow the tree limb fell on. And wait for the two men to come back.

By the time the ladies were dressed, Les and Richard came back and announced they were ready to travel. But they wanted to wait inside for the last two men to get back.

"They won't be long. I heard one of them say, they are going to a house close by to get a girl they saw yesterday," one of the girls said.

Fifteen minutes later a truck pulled into the driveway. The two men got out.

"They make up the eight," Richard said.

Edwin shrugged. "I guess I got it right."

Shorty pulled a woman out of the truck and headed up the walkway to the house.

"I got first dibs on her since I was the one who spotted her yesterday," shorty said.

Les told Edwin to stay inside. He and the other four went men outside and faced the men with their weapons pointed at them.

"I'll take her gentlemen. If you want to live you will let go of her and drop your weapons."

The men froze for a moment. Shorty let the girl go and both men dropped their weapons. The girl took off running across the yard.

The two men seized the opportunity and reached for their rifles.

Les and Richard fired dropping both men.

Billy and Jerry followed up and put rounds in them to make sure they were finished.

Bentley took off after the girl.

"You, guys, were not supposed to pick your weapons back up." Les said to the dead men.

Ruth and Natalie hurried the women out of the foul odor house. "We couldn't stay in there another minute," Ruth said.

Bentley ushered the girl back to the group. She knew two of the girls who had been at the house.

They were standing in the yard telling everyone about their town. All the girls and Edwin said they would be glad to go there. The new girl told them she was alone and wanted to go.

Jerry spoke. "All my years being a Georgia State Patrol I never shot a person. I could have never shot an unarmed man or someone who had given up. But things are different now. Those men would have kept on doing what they were doing. I feel justified."

"It's a new world we live in," Natalie said. "The

good people are very good folks you can count on and there are a lot of them. The bad are very bad. They must be dealt with accordingly."

Les asked the girls if there was any food in the house that they could take. The women said the men lived next door and would bring their food over. They would take the girls they wanted and bring them back when they were finished with them.

They searched the house next door and discovered a good supply of food.

The men they killed had collected twelve young girls and women and brought them to the house. All were between twenty-one and thirty-five years old. None were as old as Edwin thought.

There were two F150 Fords and one F250 all four doors and all full of gas at the house.

One of the women asked, "Do you have a need for a boat in that town."

The men looked at Jerry. He said, "Damn, we can always use a boat. What kind is it?"

The woman spoke up. "A twenty-eight-footer, with a cabin. It's at my house. My husband and I used it often, it is in excellent condition."

Billy walked over and checked the trucks. They all have a hitch. Two have one of those with three different size hitch balls."

After all the food was loaded, they drove to the woman's house and hitched the boat trailer to the F250 truck.

"Who can drive pulling this thing?" Jerry asked.

The owner said, "I can pull it. I have done it many times. My husband made sure I could. He trained me to do a lot of things. He wanted me to be able to take care of myself." She went to the back of the boat. "Would someone help me get in, please."

Jerry walked over, locked his fingers together and put his hands down. "Here you go. Step right up."

She put a foot in Jerry's hands and heaved herself up on the ladder and climbed in the boat. She ran her hand along the side and eased into the driver's seat, took hold of the steering wheel, and looked out over the windshield. "Marcus and I had so many fun days on the lake. Being on the water would magically take us to a trouble-free world." She put both hands on her head. "My hair would be a mess, and my face would be wind blistered from a few days. He loved boats." She looked up to the sky. "We are going to take our boat, darling."

When they were ready to load up, Les asked, "See if there is a map in one of the trucks."

The lady who supplied the boat said, "I have one in my garage."

"Of course, you do," Les said, and told them, "We are going South to look for a town that will be more suitable for our community. You guys follow Edwin, he knows where to go."

"Edwin, will you show me the town on the map?" asked the boat owner? "I just hate not knowing where I am going."

"Do you think we might meet any more bad guys like those we took out?" Natalie asked.

"From my experience there are plenty around and yes I am sure we will run across some of them," Jerry said.

"Then I would like to go along on your journey, if possible," Natalie said. "Not that I am a sadistic killer,

I believe I will be a big help to you guys."

"After seeing you in action in that house. You will be more than welcome," Jerry said. He added, "Why don't we all stay the night somewhere and get a fresh start in the morning."

"We all can stay here in my house. It's clean and I have plenty of room." The boat owner said.

"Good idea, those apartments were not livable. I was sleeping on the patio," Edwin said.

Ruth stayed by Angie's side consoling her. She would burst out crying as some of the other women would. Some sat silently with their heads down.

One of the ladies refused to give in and let what had happened spoil her life. It was the boat owner, and she got the ladies' attention. "Girls we have been through a terrible ordeal. I wasn't going to tell anyone my name because I didn't want anybody to know who I was if we were rescued, and we were. I thought if no one knew my name they couldn't say there is so and so, thugs raped her. My plan was to remain alone. That frightened me. So, my thought was, going to that town and staying away from everyone would help me forget it. But now I realize I need all of you as a support group. Let's help each other. I am the oldest of us girls and I had been married to my wonderful husband for thirty years."

One of the girls said, "You don't look old enough to have been married that long."

"Thank you. I have been blessed that way. I really think if those men had known how old I was they would have killed me."

"Maybe I shouldn't ask but you have my curiosity up. How old are you?" a girl asked.

"I am fifty-five and my name is Jenifer."

"No way you are past thirty-five," the girl who asked her age said. "Thanks to these God sent people we are alive with a chance for a life."

"There are fourteen women here who will live thanks to all of you," Jenifer said.

"They have saved the life of fourteen people today, Natalie said."

Jenifer looked around the room. "Who are the other two."

Ruth spoke up. "Natalie was our first. We pulled her out of the ice-cold river. After sinking the boat, she was in and killing two thugs who had her. Edwin, we got from his apartment. He and Angie are my friends," Ruth told them.

"Natalie, did you have a husband before the virus?" Jenifer asked.

Natalie stared at the women for a few seconds looking like she was searching for an answer. "Yes, I did have a husband. He didn't die from the virus. He's still alive. He is in Savannah with his two children. We were getting a divorce before the shit hit the fan. I miss those kids so much. We had been together since they were babies. I am their mommy. They are twins, a boy, and a girl. Eight years old."

"You guys just couldn't get along?" Ruth asked.

"Two's company, three's a crowd." Natalie turned and looked out a window at the moon.

"The rat fink," one of the girls said. "After you helped him raise his kids."

"Well, it's sleepy time for me. I am going to sack out right here on this thick carpet," Ruth said.

The women did the same. Some stretched out on a

sofa. Others found a bed. Les and Jerry said they would take the first guard shift. The others found the carpet to be comfortable.

Ruth spoke up. "Include me in the guard duty."

"Me too," Natalie said.

The next morning, before daylight, Richard and Bentley were pulling the last shift on guard when they spotted two men walking on the street. They were looking at the houses but not stopping to inspect any of them. They stopped in front of the house next door to Jenifer's. The men walked down the driveway to the back.

"Richard whispered to Bentley, "I'm going to see what these guys are up to. Richard knew that not all people who looked suspicious meant harm to anyone. He also knew you had to be cautious. The men were walking toward Richard. He stopped and waited for them to make it to the backyard. One of the men pointed to the boat connected to the truck. "You think she did that?" he said.

The men almost had a heart attack when Richard popped up in front of them and halted them with. "Who goes there? Speak up men," he said when they didn't say a word. "Do you know what kind of rifle I'm holding?" He realized they were too scared to speak. "It's an M16, very powerful. If I shoot you from here, you'll have two ass holes."

Richard spun around and caught a third man that was going to take his head off with a ball bat on the side of his head with a boot. He was back facing the two men before they knew what had happened.

One of the men spoke up hurriedly. "Lester what

was you thinking coming at this man with that bat?"

Lester lay on the ground rubbing his head. "I thought he belonged to that gang that attacked us."

The man that scolded the man on the ground said, "I live next door. Or I did before it got too dangerous to stay here. I left two days ago.

"Is that right? It looks like you overstepped your property line."

"We don't mean any harm. I promise. We're all worried about the gangs around here," the man said.

"Is that part of your promise to slip up behind me with a Louisville Slugger?"

"We have no idea who you are. Like I said we have been attacked by gang members."

"I'm not going to hurt you guys I just want to know what you are doing sneaking around in the dark," Richard said.

"Jenifer disappeared three days back didn't she Denton?" He nodded to the man next to him. "And I went looking for her. When we couldn't find her, I thought she had been taken by one of the gangs around here. We came back to see if she made it home. We were just wondering about the boat being hooked on that truck. It wasn't when I left."

"You know who lives in this house?" Richard asked.

"Yes, that's Jenifer's house. We lived next door to her and Marcus for twenty years. If you want the boat, take it. It's not doing anybody any good."

"We intend on that. You said his name is Denton. What is your name?"

"My name is Albert."

"Alright, let's go see if the lady of the house can

identify you. Walk ahead. If you try anything funny, you will have another hole in your back."

"You mean Jenifer is here."

"Yep, and some other ladies."

"Thank, God," albert said.

Jenifer was in the living room when Richard marched the three men in. She was up and greeting her neighbor before Richard had a chance to speak.

Albert, Lester, and Denton accepted an invitation to join everyone and drive to the town in North Georgia. Albert informed the group that he had an RV in his garage that was almost new. This was good news because it meant they could load a lot of stuff on the trucks. And it would ease the overcrowding in the pickups.

He opened his garage and had one of the trucks pull in front of his RV and connected jumper cables to the battery. The engine turned a few times, and it started. It held a lot of food and clothes and other items the ladies thought they would have to leave behind.

Edwin was driving the lead truck and Jenifer next to last in line pulling the boat. The three pickup trucks and motor home followed Jerry and his crew until they reached Interstate 75, then they took it North.

Some of the exits were blocked with cars but there were no people present.

Jerry, Les, and the others drove around Atlanta on the West side. Backtracking across the river where they rescued Natalie. That saved them from going through Dekalb County. East of Atlanta always had a lot of congestion, and they wanted to avoid what might still be there.

Crossing the Chattahoochee River, Jerry pointed up the hill to his right. "There used to be a building with glass windows overlooking 285. It was a nightclub called Baby Doe's. I went there a few times."

"I have an older friend who went there on the weekends," Bentley said. "He told me it was a good place to view the river."

"The river is pretty crossing this bridge," Ruth said.

Natalie spoke up. "The only thing I can say about the river, is it is hellishly cold this time of year."

"It appears a lot of the gangs have died off or given up holding onto territory," Jerry said. "We didn't encounter anyone in this area six months back when we came through here."

"I heard about John Carstairs and his family's journey to the town. It was scary," Ruth said.

"They are a brave bunch. John saved Dean and me from being shot," Jerry said.

"He knows how to take care of himself for not being a military man," Les said.

Jerry nodded. "The jungles of South America were his stomping ground for a while."

When they reached the exits for Interstate 20, they found them open but empty as the other exits were.

Approaching Cascade Road, they heard gunshots coming from below the interstate. Les rolled his window down and listened. There were multiple shots firing.

"It must be a gang war going on down there," Jerry said.

The shooting stopped as they were passing the exit ramp.

"One group must have killed all the opposing gang," Les said.

Suddenly a black SUV came up the ramp on their right and cut in front of them. It was followed by a second black SUV. The second vehicle almost sideswiped them. Ruth braked and avoided a collision. Shots were being traded between the two vehicles. The first vehicle's rear window exploded. Next a tire blew apart and the SUV careened off the road and flipped over the guardrail. The second SUV kept going.

"I don't believe for a minute they are going to ignore us," Les said.

The SUV moved into a lane to the right and sped up.

Ruth increased her speed. "They're in a big hurry to make that exit."

"They want to make that exit and come back down behind us before we get well ahead of them," Les said.

"It wasn't long before Les was proven right. The Black SUV exited and reentered the highway behind them.

"Let them catch up to us. Get in the far-left lane. That way the person in the front seat will have to shoot around the driver. Richard will have a straight shot. Everyone try to keep out of sight. The tented glass should make it difficult for them to see who is in here."

Ruth moved to the left lane and eased up on the accelerator, allowing the SUV to slowly catch up.

When the vehicle pulled beside them. The driver and passenger concentrated on the rear door windows trying to see in the back seat. The rear window lowered exposing two men in the back holding rifles. The driver yelled, "Me and my friends would like to know where you two folks are going?"

"Grandmas house to bake a pie," Les yelled.

"I don't believe you," the driver said.

"Not important you believe me,"

"Are you two alone," the driver shouted.

"I'm not telling you anything else because you didn't believe me."

"I believe you two are alone. So, how about you pull over and we'll lighten your load and you two can go about your business."

"What if we don't want to pull over?" Les yelled.

The man in the SUV smiled. "Then your ability to do any business will end."

Les yelled. "You are right, you shouldn't believe me."

"You mean you are not going to bake pies?"

"Not today, sucker."

"Don't make me tell you again. Pull over, now."

"Ask my buddy if I should pull over," Les yelled.

"Hey driver," the man yelled at Ruth. "Don't you think you should pull over?"

"Not that buddy," Les yelled and pointed with his thumb to the back. "That buddy."

Richard lowered his window. "No, they are not traveling alone," he said and stuck the barrel of the M16 out the window with it set to full auto. He yelled, "Ah ha. Take this you dumb bastards." He pulled the trigger and sprayed the SUV with bullets. They watched the vehicle swerve a few times before it careened to the right running off the road and crashing into a line of trees at Camp Creek Parkway.

"Call me a liar will you. Even if you are right." Les yelled out the window.

Ruth moved to the center lane and piloted them around 285 to Interstate 75 South.

CHAPTER 11

John and Ralph

John Carstairs stepped out of the front of his crew cab pickup, slid his arms into his coat, pulled it together to cover his thick chest and zipped it. He reached in and retrieved his M4 and slung it over his shoulder. There was a slight breeze, blowing across his face and the temperature stood at thirty degrees.

This being John's first time away from the town since arriving with his family last July he was excited. He has been itching to hit the road for the past few weeks. The uncertainty had kept him home. It was a different world now. And being separated from his family at the beginning of the virus and not knowing if he would ever see them again caused him for the first time to realize that he could lose everything and what it would be like if he did. All the other times he felt he was in control, and he knew they were home, and he would be back with them again.

At the last town meeting it was decided that someone would be sent out to scout for other survivors of the virus. And to see if any new communities had risen. John volunteered for the job. Or more like he demanded that he be the one to go.

People were in short supply, and they were needed.

especially good people. They would welcome every honest and trustworthy person they found. The community population had stopped increasing at a little over five hundred. It had been months since a new person had shown up.

Young women who could bear children and strong healthy men were very welcome. As people grow older, they won't be able to do the work it takes to keep the town going.

What the town needs are future laborers. In thirty years, ones losing the ability to work will outnumber the ones who age up. The community would die off. Like tribes that have disappeared.

This was a mission to search out young people, but John will take anyone he finds.

Being one who loved to travel, John never stayed home longer than a couple of months before he hit the road. He took a job as a long-haul truck driver for five years just to be able to travel. He finally grew tired of it and did something else. When he was at home, he spent time being a karate instructor.

He took a job with a company that supplied help with tracking drug cartels. John spent a few years wandering through the jungles of South America weeding out drug makers. Then the company that employed him decided to just supply security to companies that sent their employees down there. They also figured younger inexperienced help could do the job, maybe not as good but cheaper.

Now after six months of staying home he was on the road again and he loved it. He turned his nose to the sky, took in a deep breath and yelled, "Smell that fresh air."

Ralph Bishop popped up in the back seat and looked around. "Christ, John you sure know how to wake a man up."

John was standing beside the driver's door rolling his shoulders. "Step out and enjoy the cold weather."

Ralph eased the door open, stepped out and stretched. He reached in and pulled his coat out. "The last time we were on the road the weather was hot."

John rubbed his hands together. "And we were in South Georgia. This time the weather is cold, and we are in North Georgia. It was easier to find food too."

Ralph scanned the woods on both sides of the road. "The food is all gone now. We have almost depleted the deer population close to the town. I'll bet there are some around here. If they haven't been scared off or killed.

John reached into the bed of the truck just behind the cab and slid a cooler to the rear as he walked. "We'll have to be patient and wait for them." He made it to the back of the truck, let the tailgate down and pulled the cooler onto it. Inside the plastic container was fried chicken breast, thighs, legs, apples, boiled corn, baked potato cakes, cornbread fried fritters and one ten-inch square slab of cornbread. The bread was made from corn grown in a ten-acre field and crushed on a waterwheel run grinder. He also had four pounds of beef jerky and five pounds of smoke meat, fried sausage, and plenty of water. "If we can get a fire going, we can have a cup of coffee,"

The two men gathered wood and built a fire under a wireframe rack. John placed a percolator filled with coffee and water over the flame.

Ralph backed up to the tailgate and leaned on it.

"How bad do you miss the old world, John?"

"Really bad most of the time. Sometimes not at all. Millie and I had many years of it. But my daughters and my son-in-law didn't get as much as we did. What I hate the most is my grandchildren were cheated out of all of it. How about you?"

Ralph stared at the trees swaying with the wind, the sun trying to peek through a cloudy sky. "What's most difficult for me is not knowing things. Even though my wife divorced me she was my first love. And me loving betty now, it will always bother me not knowing what happened to her. And my house. Is it being lived in by strangers or is it rotting away."

John rubbed a hand through his hair. "When we get the people moved would you like to try to find the answer? I'll go with you."

Ralph scratched his forehead. "Something to think about."

The percolator began to play a tune, and the smell of coffee flowed through the air.

"Ahh, that is one smell I will never get enough of," Ralph said.

They sat on the tailgate, and each had a piece of chicken, a slice of cornbread and a cup of coffee.

After a second cup of coffee John walked to the driver's door, opened it, reached in, and pulled a map off the dash. He walked to the back of the truck, opened the map, and spread it on the floor of the truck bed. To keep it from blowing away he moved the cooler onto one side and held the other side down with his forearm. He traced a line on the map. "Ten miles to the next town. How close has our mail carrier got to those towns?" He asked Ralph.

"It's a long haul from our town, so they don't go that far. Not likely many folks there," Ralph said. "Statistics wise there wouldn't be fifty or sixty people left in some of these places. Less in others. Unless they had a good stash to start, it would have been difficult for them to survive. Country stores were not heavily stocked."

"I'm sure they were cleaned out in a few minutes."

John secured the cooler, folded the map, opened the driver's door, and tossed it in the front seat.

Ralph studied the road to the top of the hill. He put a hand to one of his ears. "Do you hear something? It sounds like an automobile?"

The two men stood listening; their eyes fixed on the rise in the road.

"It is a car or truck. Sounds like it has a hole in the muffler," John said, and picked up a pair of binoculars and put them to his eyes.

The top of a red car came into view. The front end began to come into view. As it topped the hill, and the entire vehicle appeared the noise grew louder.

"It looks like a Ford," Ralph said.

"You are correct. It's a Ford Explorer."

The Ford bellowed when the driver let off the gas and coasted off the rise. The two men kept their eyes on the Ford as it rolled next to them and stopped.

The passenger window came down and a man leaned across the seat and spoke out the window at John and Ralph. "Howdy, fellows. My name is Jubal Mack. My family and I are looking for a farm that should be around here somewhere." He smiled as his eyes went from one man to the other.

John started to say that they are from a

community, but he realized the man was not talking about their home because it was too far off.

The man introduced the woman next to him as his wife, Mary. In the back seat were a girl and a boy. Both looked like they were in their late teens. Jubal pointed to the back seat with his thumb. "Back there is my daughter, Kimberly and my son, Hollis. They are twins, eighteen years old."

We are pleased to meet you, Jubal, Mary, kids My name is John."

Ralph peered into the window. "My name is Ralph."

"You fellows mind if we get out and stretch our legs?" Jubal shoved the gear lever in park and opened the door. "Get out Mary. Come on kids lets talk to these gentlemen." When Jubal unfolded, he stood six feet five inches. The top of Mary's head came to his jawline. She was a pretty woman, slim with blonde hair and top heavy. Kimberly was blonde, tall as her mother and had the same built. Hollis was as tall as his daddy. They all looked refreshed in clean clothes. The girl's hair fixed and in place.

"Lord do have mercy," Jubal said. "I would swear I smell coffee. Am I right gentlemen?"

"That is what you smell. Would you care for a cup?" John asked.

Jubal smiled. "If you have a cup to spare, I would love some coffee. That smell will make you kiss your momma."

John asked. "Are you a preacher by any chance?"

"Not hardly," Jubal said.

Ralph asked, "Were you ever one of those pitch men on television."

"No, he was not. Jubal, settle down these men don't want to hear your clowning around," Mary said.

"Let him talk. Times have been hard on all of us. A little humor is what we need," John said.

Mary said, "If you can stand him, but it is so out of character for Jubal."

"Have you folks had breakfast?" Ralph asked.

"No, and I do hate to drink coffee on an empty stomach, but it does smell wonderful."

John walked to the cooler and pulled out four corn bread fritters stuffed with sausage patties. He walked over and handed each of the family members one of the fritters.

"Look at this, Mary, Kids. We have stumbled upon the door to heaven itself."

"Coffee is over here folks."

"I am the only coffee drinker in our family," Jubal said. "I'll tell you something. I was going straight before I made that last turn. When I got to the middle of the intersection something told me to turn left, and I did at the last second. Ain't that what I told you, Hon?"

Mary took her husband's hand. "Yes you did. Somebody has been taking care of us on this trip. Jubal just can't follow directions at all. Neither one of us is any good at it either."

John nodded. "The lord will do for us the things we can't do for ourselves sometimes."

John lifted the pot, filled a cup, and handed it to the man. "I have some powder creamer and sugar."

"Straight up is fine with me," Jubal said. "And what you said about the Lord doing for us is true. I have been asking him for a good bit here lately. And he has delivered on the things that counted."

John nodded his head. "Good for you Jubal." He put the pot back on the fire. "Do you have directions to that place you are trying to get to?"

"I have them written down and a drawing, Sheb Hanks gave me. That's my friend's name I worked with before the virus ruined the world. He wrote it down for me. The place is a farm that belongs to him. He was at my house when things started. He is who got me to asking the man upstairs for favors.

After a few months he told us he was going to try to get home, and he left out on a bicycle I gave him. I sure hope he made it. He told me to bring my family up here if things got bad. And things got ruff. So, I'm taking him up on his offer." Jubal pulled the paper from his pocket and unfolded it. "Do, you have a map?"

"Yes, we were just studying it," Ralph said.

"Good, I followed the directions best I could, but I may have gotten turned around. Like Mary said. I'm just no good at following directions."

"I am sure we can find it for you, Jubal," Ralph said. I'll look at the map and the directions you have while you and your family enjoy your breakfast. And soon as we get packed up, we'll head that way."

John thought he was stressed and worried about his family. He doesn't know if he can trust us. That's causing him to overreact to our kindness. "Jubal, you, and your family have been through some tough times. I have a wife, two daughters and two grandchildren. Ralph is going to be married soon to a wonderful lady. Both of us have been in dangerous situations with our loved ones. We will help you any way we can."

Jubal covered his heart with a hand. "Lord, Lord. We are so thankful for any help we can get. It is scary being out here. And worse not knowing where we are going," Mary said.

"Ralph and I are going to figure some things out first."

"You go right ahead." Mary turned to go to her family. She looked up. "Thank you, Lord."

John told the family which way he and Ralph thought it would be best to get to Sheb's house.

****

All the women who came to the town with the Carstairs family were gathered in the park in the center of town. They were sitting around a firepit with their coats on. The temperature was twenty-eight degrees. The women had been couped up in their houses for two weeks.

John's wife Millie was with their two daughters Julie and Peggy. Julie's husband Donald had their son Ben, who is two and a half years old in his lap. Their daughter Anna, who is seven, sat in a chair next to Julie. Betty Larkin who is the women's USA champion sharpshooter with a rifle was cuddled on a bench with her seven-year-old son, Jammie. She was thinking about Ralph Bishop, the man who along with John rescued her and Jammie from a house while on their mission to find John's family. She and Ralph had developed a relationship. Maria is telling them about her experience of being the manager for her husband The Great Juan, a professional wrestler. William and Debra Dunbar were neighbors and friends with Millie and John before the virus hit.

William and Debra were the only people to escaped the neighborhood alive thanks to John and his family.

William has a brother who is a recovering drug addict that credits the virus for saving his life that the drugs was surely to take. The only way he could stop using was for the drugs to disappear.

"I wish we had some way to communicate with John and Ralph," Betty said.

"None of us ever thought we would lose our ability to communication," Millie said.

CHAPTER 12

The Dreads Gang

Ringo sat on a bench holding a forty-five automatic in his right hand. He wore a red blazer, a white dress shirt and a pair of blue dress pants. He could have stood in front of a camera telling you to buy a used car from me and pay weekly. Or he looked like the type anyway.

A man stood in front of him talking about a community in North Georgia.

Ringo patted his leg with the pistol. "What is your name?"

"Walter, Sir. Walter Hite.

"Tell me all about this town, Walter Hite."

Walter told Ringo several hundred people were living there. They grow food and raise chickens, pigs, cattle, and a few horses. He told him the name of the town and that it was well protected.

Ringo held the pistol up, pointing at nothing and rolled it back and forth. "Why did you leave that nice town that had all the food you could eat?"

Hite replied. "I got caught stealing food. They ran me off."

Ringo waved his gun up and down. "How many

times did they catch you stealing?"

"Three times."

How do we get the town to just hand over their food?"

"You will have to figure that out. There are some hills around you can shoot from."

"I could plant one of my good shooters on one of the hills and plug a couple of their citizens. That would get their attention."

"What do you want for this information?"

"I'd like to throw in with you guys."

"Go introduce yourself around."

The snitch turned and walked off. After walking ten feet, he may have heard the shot that pierced his back. He may have felt it for an instant but no longer.

Ringo got out of his chair and holstered his pistol. "You would just end up stealing from me. I hate a thief."

The man next to Ringo had a deep voice. "You two men come over here and take out the garbage." He turned to Ringo. "Do we want the food or the town?"

The clean-shaven Ringo looked North. "Both." He laughed, "Ha, ha, ha. We'll take it all, Jefferson. What do you think?"

"Why settle for less than all."

Ringo patted his friend on the back. "Jefferson. How did you get that name?"

"It was my parent's name. What the Hell did you think?"

"Oh, pardon me, I thought that was your first name. You know, Jefferson Davis."

The man gave Ringo a hard look. "No, it did not

come from the president of the Southern States."

"Oh, excuse me. Of course not, man," Ringo said.

"It came from the television show," Jefferson said.

"For real. You were named after that television show?"

"Jefferson laughed, "Ha, Ha, Ha. Just kidding.

"You are a jack ass. Time to grab a bite. Why don't you join me, Sir Jefferson?"

"Excuse me, do you have any Grey Poupon?"

Ringo smiled. "I remember that one. It was a good one. Too bad we don't have any."

Jefferson stopped before going through the door. "What is that noise. You hear it?"

Both men turned their heads and saw a man pushing a homemade cart followed by a woman and a young girl. The women followed him in a manner as if they were being dragged along by a rope. The squeaking was caused by the wheels turning on a dry axle.

Jefferson lifted a foot and placed it on a bench beside the door. He rested a bent arm on his knee and leaned on it. "Well, look at that, would you."

He watched the three looking straight ahead oblivious to them standing in front of the building. They were thin from lack of food, dirty faces, and ragged clothes. The young girl looked to be around sixteen. Both women had blonde, stringy hair.

Jefferson and Ringo went inside the building. Half a minute later Jefferson came back with a paper bag in his hand. He walked out in the street and told the man to stop.

The man did and looked up at the face of the tall strong looking Black man. "We have nothing, Sir."

Jefferson had been mistaken about the man's age. He had thought he was old, but up close he looked like he was about forty. The same for the woman. Jefferson pulled three cans from the bag and handed one to the man, woman, and young girl. Next, he handed each of them a fork and motioned for them to sit on the bench he had rested his foot on.

The fellow thanked him and tried to open the can, but he didn't have the strength to lift the ring on the top.

Jefferson took the can from him and opened it. When he handed it back, the man passed it to his wife.

Jefferson said. "That's right, fellow. Let your wife eat first. You must be a good soul." He opened a can for the girl and one for the man.

Holding the can up the man said, "Thank you." And jabbed a piece of meat. He put it in his mouth and swallowed it without chewing.

Jefferson placed three bottles of water on the bench. "Careful fellow you don't want to choke." He disappeared inside the building again.

He reappeared and held up a can. "Grease, I'll put this on the axles." He greased the wheels and placed the can in the cart. "You take care fellow," he said and went inside the building to join his friends.

The gang known as the Dreads was a group of thirty men. They had developed a month ago under the leadership of Ringo. He stands six feet tall, weighs one-eighty, muscular, short blond hair. Before the virus hit Ringo had been a trainer at a gym. That was after he had gotten released from prison. He did six years for a molestation charge.

They had made their way from Lithonia to Tucker

and were held up in a lumber yard on Main Street by the railroad tracks.

The gang stole, robbed, killed, and raped along the way. They had no destination in mind. They seemed to go where the wind blew. Until ten minutes ago. Now they are going North.

Thirty minutes after going into the store, Jefferson stepped out onto the sidewalk and stopped by the bench the family had sat on and the meat. There was no trace of the man and the two women.

His thoughts went back to a woman. Tall with long dark hair, brown skin and dark eyes, a soft touch, the body of an athlete, a smile warm enough to melt a man's heart. A young girl, fifteen years old and a carbon copy of her mother. The three of them were running on the beach a little over a year ago. He closed his tear-filled eyes and winced as he thought about digging two graves and slipping their bodies into the dark holes and shoveling dirt on them. He had no control over his thoughts when they would come.

Ringo interrupted him by slapping him on his back. "I am going to sit here and think about that town that thief told us about." Ringo took a seat, leaned back, and crossed his arms. "Do you think he was telling the truth and there is a town like that up North?"

"If you lie, you will steal, if you steal you would kill. He admitted he was a thief."

"As the saying goes, huh. Look at it this way. If I had allowed him into our gang and I was sent on a wild goose chase. He knew I would have killed him. I believe he was telling the truth. I'll send a couple of men to check it out first." Ringo stretched his legs out and rested the heel of one boot on the toe of the other.

Jefferson rubbed his bald head. "We have eaten good the past week. It would be a shame to run out. How far is that town?"

The Dreads had sent out scouts to search for anything usable and edible. What the scouts found was a group of men, women and children living in houses and apartments close to what had been a water treatment plant. They discovered some plowed fields that had been planted and picked.

They also discovered that the community was well guarded because they lost three men just scoping the place out.

"First, I want to raid that community, Irvin told us about," Ringo said to Jefferson.

Jefferson gave some thought to the idea. "We lost three men just looking it over. I hate to imagine the outcome if we try to storm the place."

"That is the reason we are not going to try to fight our way in, Jefferson my man."

"What are we going to do, just roll up to the gate and ask them to hand over their food?"

"That is precisely the way we will do it. Of course, we will have something they want," Ringo said.

John and Ralph

John pulled his pickup off on a dirt road a quarter mile from the farm and stopped. The Mack family car pulled in behind him.

Ralph got out holding a Remington M40A5 and took off through the woods toward the house.

John walked to Jubal's car. "We'll give Ralph twenty minutes to get in position before we go in."

"That's a clever idea checking the place out first. I would have barreled on in there not thinking about it being taken over," Jubal said. "I have got a lot to learn."

"If I had just left my place for the first time, I wouldn't know any better myself," John said."

"Desperate times cause people to do desperate things," Mary said. "I am worried for my family."

After giving Ralph twenty minutes to get set up, Jubal followed John up the driveway to the farmhouse.

Six men walked out of the house onto the porch as they pulled to a stop. One by one five of the men walked down the steps to the yard and spread out.

Jubal, smiling, asked. "Is this the Hanks home?"

"Sure, who wants to know?" one of the men asked.

"Tell him Jubal Mack is here with his family."

The man that asked the question stepped next to the Ford and peered inside, checking the front and back seat pausing to get a good look at the women. He backed up. "Get out folks."

Jubal and his family got out and stood beside the car.

John exited his truck and walked over to Jubal. "Do you see your friend?"

Jubal scanned the men. "Is Sheb around."

"Somewhere. What do you folks want with him?"

"He was with us for a few months in the beginning. He told me I could bring my family and stay with him if I took a notion."

The man stood looking at John. "Are you part of

the family?"

"A distant cousin," John said."

"So, you not being a member of Jubal's immediate family you were not invited here."

"I might like it. Any objections if I decide to stay?"

"Yeah, I object, so you can go." The man eyed the women. "Welcome ladies."

The youngest man of the group looked to be in his early twenties Stood gawking at Kinberly. He looked at one of the other men.

The man nodded his head. "Sure, boy go ahead."

The young man walked over and stood in front of Jubal's daughter. "Baby those are the prettiest things I have ever seen." He raised his open hands ready to touch the young girl's breast.

"Daddy," Kimberly yelled."

Jubal who was talking to the other man rushed over and shoved the man away from his daughter. "You keep your hands to yourself, boy."

The boy came toward Jubal with his arm raised, fist closed. Jubal slapped the boy across his face hard, causing him to stumble backwards.

A man yelled out. "What do you think you are doing hitting my son." He stepped in front of Jubal and drew back a fist and thrust it forward. Jubal put a hand up and caught the man's fist.

"That's enough of that," the man yelled from the porch. He looked at the crowd and walked down into the yard. "Who are you folks?"

Jubal told the man who they were and asked where his friend was.

The man told him he was in the house.

"That fool slapped Junior, Boss." the man who

was going to hit Jubal said.

"That boy was fixing to put his hands on my daughter."

Boss looked both women up and down. He looked at Junior. "He's a young man. There are no young women here. Been a year since he has seen a female. I heard you say you brought your family here to live. You and your family are welcome to stay."

"I think I'll pass on Sheb's invite. Where is Sheb anyway?"

"Don't you worry about your friend. Me and the boys want you to stay with us." The man pulled his coat back showing a pistol in a holster on his belt. He looked at one of the men holding a rifle. "We want them to stay, don't we. The women anyway. You men should take off."

The man with the rifle nodded and smiled.

In an instant John was behind the Boss. He wrapped his big arm around Boss's neck, drew a pistol and shoved the barrel to his neck.

The man with the rifle pointed it at John. "Mister, I would advise you to let my daddy go."

A shot rang out and the top of the man's head who was holding the rifle went flying into the air.

"That came from my friend in that tree line over there. Another shot rang out and the window in a truck shattered.

One of the men yelled. "You're the cause of this by bringing those women here." He raised his pistol at Jubal.

A shot cracked from the trees and the man's chest began to spew blood.

"Son of a bitch, I'll kill all of you." Came from a

man raising a rifle.

John, still holding Boss turned his pistol on the man and put a round in his chest dropping him.

The boss pulled free and pulled his pistol but before he could get off a shot, a round from John's pistol pierced his forehead.

The last two men standing fired, but they lacked the accuracy to get the job done and were put down.

Jubal went into the house looking for his friend. He came out a few minutes later and walked down the steps to the others. "I didn't see Sheb or his wife."

They loaded into their vehicles and left the house of Jubal's friend.

John spotted Ralph standing on the side of the road and stopped. The Ford pulled in behind him.

Jubal pointed. "Look, somebody is walking toward us through the woods. It's a man and a woman."

Ralph, standing beside John's truck, raised his rifle and pointed it at the two people coming toward them. It was a man who looked to be in his late sixties and a woman.

The man quickly raised his arms and yelled. "Don't shoot."

Jubal bent and looked at the couple through the trees fifty yards away. "Sheb is that you?" he yelled.

"It sure is. I have been wondering if I would ever see you again."

Jubal said. "Come on down here. Things finally got bad, and we had to leave home. What the heck is going on at your house?"

"I'm sorry for what happened at my house. Those men came by a month ago and took over. This is my wife, Elly. They let us stay but I had no control over them."

After, Jubal introduced his friend to John and Ralph. He asked him how he had gotten away from the house.

"I saw you and your family through the screen door, so Elly and I slipped out the back." Sheb said. "I was hoping we would make it to the road before you left."

John told Sheb the name of their town and asked if he knew where it was.

"I know the town and how to get there. I have a friend who lives there with his wife. His name is Elbert Lewis. Do you know him?"

"I've heard his name several times. Look him up when you get there," John told him.

CHAPTER 13

The North Atlanta Community

Early in the morning three women from the water treatment community had gotten on bicycles and left what they now call the farm. They wanted to scout some of the businesses for anything that could be of use to them.

The first couple of stores had been completely ransacked. The third store produced a few pairs of shoes that were hidden under a door that had been torn from the frame and fallen on the floor covering the boxes. The person who broke in must have been to lazy to lift it. The girls swapped their old shoes for a pair of new ones and went in search of something else.

After a few more searches the girls were getting hungry. A table and chairs in front of sandwich shop provided a place to eat. Each lady had packed the same lunch. A baked potato, ear of boiled corn and a cup of pinto beans.

They were sitting on the curb in front of a service station eating and discussing their new shoes. Four pick-ups pulled up and stopped next to the ladies. Two members of the dreads unloaded with rifles in their hands. They approached the women and ask them where they were from. When they told them the men loaded two women in the bed and one in the cab of one of the trucks with the driver and another man.

"Alright lady, tell me where to go," the driver said.

She pointed. "That way. I'll have to show you."

When they reached the entrance to the buildings the driver spotted two men with rifles standing next to a pickup.

"They'll not let you in," the lady said.

"For your sake they had better."

The lady stared out the windshield. "What do you mean?"

"If he lets us in you get to live. If not you will die along with those two-standing guard and your friends in the back."

"You mean you would just kill us."

"I believe that is what I said. So, you had better hope they like you."

They were met by the guards and were asked what their business was.

A man in the back with the women pointed his rifle at the oldest woman's head. "My business is getting in here. Your business is letting us. Or the population of your community will drop by three."

The man looked at the women laying on the floor of the truck bed. "I'll need to escort you in."

"Mighty thoughtful of you. Take us to the food storage building," The man with the gun said.

"Let them through," the guard said, got in his car and drove ahead of the four trucks trucks.

They stopped at the door of the building where the food was stored. The driver of the car blew the horn. The doors began to roll up. When they stopped the driver of the car led the trucks in. The men in the back stood next to the three women pointing guns at their heads.

Several women were milling around, gathering vegetables, and putting them in baskets. Everyone stopped and stared. The sight of the men was frightening.

"Five men coming across the field with guns, Ringo," one of his men said.

Ringo fired off a shot at the approaching men. "Listen up you, guys. If you do as you are told no one will get hurt. If anyone tries to be a hero, you will all die. You men stop where you are and put your weapons down."

The men stopped and dropped their rifles.

Ringo pulled one of the women off the floor of the truck. "You see what I have. Now get on the ground, face down."

The men got down.

Jennie spoke up. "What do you want?"

"Well, let's see. What are you willing to give up, so you can stay alive?"

The girl stood silent. No one else spoke.

"I take that as everything in here is what you will give up," Ringo said.

"Just take what you need and leave us with the rest. We worked hard for it," Jennie said.

Ringo walked over and stood in front of the little lady. "I already see what I need as you put it. Load half of everything on our trucks."

"You rotten piece of crap," Jennie said.

"We don't have room for half of everything," Jefferson said. "Unless you want the men to walk to North Georgia."

"Load what you can. We'll double the men up in the trucks." Ringo took Jennie by the arm. "Leave room for this one in my cab."

Jennie pulled away. "I'll not go anywhere with you. You filthy pig."

"We'll see about that. Load it up."

The men pulled the trucks inside the building and went to work stacking as much in the beds as their trucks would hold and still have room for them.

After they had loaded all the trucks could hold, Jefferson told Ringo. "We're ready to roll."

Ringo opened the passenger door and looked at Jennie. "Get in, now."

"You go to, Hell."

Ringo leveled his rifle and fired. A red dot appeared on the chest of an older woman, and she fell. Her heart was blown apart, so there was no bleeding.

Everyone stood with harrowing looks on their faces.

"You son-of-a-bitch," Jennie said.

"Are you going to get in or do I." Ringo looked around and pointed the gun at a ten-year-old girl.

Jennie ran to the truck. "I'll get in."

"Nothing like a little persuasion."

Jefferson stood like a statue with his mouth open.

"Are you coming with us, my friend. I did get that right, didn't I? friend?" Ringo said.

"That was uncalled for." Jefferson started to get in the driver's seat of one of the trucks.

Ringo yelled, "Come drive me and my date." He opened the back door, shoved Jennie in the seat and got in beside her.

Jefferson slid in behind the steering wheel. "I

would have never thought you would stoop that low."

"Just drive. I 'am going to relieve some of my tension."

As soon as Jefferson pulled out of the building, Ringo pushed Jennie down onto the seat. But she wasn't one to give up easily. She fought, scratched, bit, and jammed a knee between Ringo's legs. He drew back and hit her on the side of her face, knocking her out cold.

He sat up. "Damn little bitch has spunk. I can't wait 'til she comes around."

"I wouldn't count on that. I believe you will have a fight on your hands all the way," Jefferson said. He checked Ringo out in the rear-view mirror. I hope she kills you. I'll give her a gun.

As the trucks exited Interstate 285 to enter Georgia Highway 400 they saw the entrance blocked by two Military trucks.

"What the Hell is this," Jefferson said, and stopped fifty feet from a man with his arms raised. "Look at this fool."

Ringo looked at the man, then he searched the area seeing no one else. Pull up and see what he wants."

Jefferson eased forward, stopped beside the man, and rolled his window down.

"What can we do for you?" Came from Ringo in the back seat.

"Gentlemen let me introduce myself. My name is Olie Berdash, Bird Colonel. I am not your enemy. Call me, friend. I have had a couple of my men keeping an eye on you. What do you call yourselves?"

"We call ourselves the Dreads." Ringo said.

"And what is your name and position in the

Dreads."

"I'm Ringo and I run the gang."

Berdash looked at the girl asleep in the seat. Her jaw was swelling. "Something tells me she said no. I hope you can command your men better than you can your women."

"What do you want from us?" Ringo asked.

"Pool our men and take a town, so we can live happy ever after."

Ringo studied the man's proposal. "Do you have one in mind."

"No, but I have heard about a couple up north. And with our combined forces we stand a good chance of taking one. If you are interested, follow me up the road and let's find a place to let our men get acquainted."

Berdash exited at Abernathy Road, turned right, and stopped at the first intersection. It was a five-lane road both ways, giving them room to park. He got out and ordered his men to do the same.

The Colonel began by telling Ringo that he had seventy men. That was more than twice Ringo's thirty. It they combine it will put them at one hundred. By today's standards that was a good size army. He laid out his plan which put him in charge of the operation, and he will have control over the men. Ringo would be his second in command. That is the way it will be when they take control of a town. Ringo agreed part out of joy and part out of fear of the seventy well-armed men they would have to face.

The Colonel displayed that he had the experience of leading an army.

Ringo's men lacked the discipline of a soldier. He

could keep them in line, most of the time. They were members from various gangs that had dissolved because most of the members had been killed or starved to death. Times were different, so people acted differently, gang members included. Their loyalty followed the food and water not the person. Some panicked and turned on each other when the food ran out and they had no means of getting more.

Anybody who came along and proved he had the authority and experience to bring them in line had themselves a gang. Especially if that person had food and water or a promise of.

Ringo rubbed his chin and told the Colonel he had a town in mind to take over. First, we are going to see about getting some of their food. Whether or not we can take it depends on how easy it will be getting those supplies. Ringo would tell him the name of the town after they finished raiding it.

The Colonel agreed to the terms and told Ringo to meet him at the end of Interstate 575 in a few days. The one who gets there first should wait on the other.

"What if I get there ahead of you and I just go ahead and take it," Ringo said.

"Have you ever heard of General Armstrong Custer?"

"Yeah, He got his ass kicked by the Indians, didn't he?"

"Yes, because he went it alone. You don't go it alone," the colonel said.

"You, bet I won't."

Berdash stared at Ringo. "And one last thing, uh, don't hit the girl again. Cowards hit women."

The Dreads pulled out of the intersection and

went North. Ringo wanted to see what was left of Roswell. He wanted another piece of transportation, a pickup preferable and more food, but he would take anything he found.

What he found was a town with plenty of vehicles that would not start and was empty of people and anything usable.

Jefferson stared out the window. "We can cut across to Marietta and go North on 75 to 575 from there."

"We are but first let's search a couple of the subdivisions here. There is one with a large lake and the lots are wooded."

"I know the one you are talking about. It's by the river. There's a school."

"Yep. You and Lonnie take the area close to the river. I'll search from the school to the lake. We don't want to spend a lot of time here just scout it out."

Jefferson had driven on a few of the streets working his way to the lake without seeing anyone. He made a right turned. "I believe this place in deserted." He drove to the end of the street, turned left and suddenly stopped at the first yard he came to. All he could do was stare. He could not believe his eyes. He shook Lonnie who had fallen asleep. "Look at that house on that hill, man."

Lonnie looked at the house that was fifty yards off the street. "Oh, my Heaven to Betsy. I must be seeing things."

Jefferson not taking his eyes off of the yard. "You are seeing things, and they are real because I see them too. I never thought I would see a yard with this many flowers again and plants."

"Did you see that?" Lonnie asked. "A woman standing behind a tree out of sight. She poked her head around."

"Let's check it out." Jefferson drove up the driveway and stopped.

The two men got out and walked to the tree the woman was hiding behind. She didn't see them until they spoke.

"Hello, your yard looks gorgeous," Jefferson said.

The startled woman jumped. Her mouth came open, but she didn't say a word she just stood wide eyed and trembling. She was an older woman seventyish or so. She glanced to her left at the 3006-rifle leaning against a tree.

Jefferson followed her gaze. "You don't need that we mean you no harm. That is the God's truth." He looked around and saw several raised garden beds hidden behind a wall of bushes that looked like they had been in production last summer.

"Did you have a productive season?" Lonnie asked.

The woman nodded. "It fed my husband and I."

"You got enough to carry you until the next season?" Jefferson asked and looked at the truck in the driveway next to the house.

"It will if we keep our portions low."

"My name is Jefferson. This fellow is Lonnie."

"My name in Mavis."

After a conversation about the situation and swapping names. They talked about how they were getting along and her yard with all the plants. And how she should be very careful.

"How long since you two had any food that didn't

come out of a can?" She reached in a basket next to her and brought out two big potatoes and held them out. I keep them dark and cold so they will last."

"You don't have to give us your food," Jefferson said.

"They'll go bad if I don't get rid of them. We can eat only so many. We were blessed with these. My beans just didn't do so good." I miss not having them."

Jefferson took the two big spuds. How did you grow these so big?"

She managed to smile. "I don't know but they are good."

Jefferson was looking across the yard. "What I miss the most, is desserts. I loved something sweet after a meal."

Hold on a minute, I will be right back." Mavis went into the house and returned in a couple of minutes later with two pieces of cake. "You and Lonnie sit down and enjoy some dessert." She motioned to two lawn chairs.

After they finished the cake Jefferson said, "Lonnie and I thank you. That was good and sweet."

"You are welcome. I have sugar, I just don't have any salt or any seasoning."

"Well, let me see what I can do for you." Jefferson walked to his truck, opened the door, reached in, put a few items in a paper bag and walked back to the woman. He handed the her a round box of salt and a box of pepper. "We ran across a store two weeks ago and found this. And these." He handed her the bag.

The woman looked in the bag and saw two clear plastic packages of dried beans and smiled. "Thank you. Pinto are my favorite."

After an education on the types of plants in her yard and finding Mavis was a doctor of alternative medicine Jefferson told her. "You take care. For the next hour stay out of sight. And hide that truck until then. Our boss is not so nice."

After they were in the truck and on the street Jefferson told Lonnie. "That woman is intelligent and friendly. And that is not all. I'll bet there some folks around here and she takes care of them. She seemed like that kind of person."

They pulled beside Ringo sitting in his truck in the school parking lot. "I was concentrating on the devastation thinking what is going to become of us."

"We are going to survive and repopulate the world," Jefferson said.

"Get over here and let's go You're driving me."

Jefferson switched trucks and got behind the steering wheel." Where to Boss?"

"Go where you want to."

Jefferson took off. "Marietta it will be. We might find a truck there. It's a good size town." He looked in the rear-view mirror. That colonel Berdash will make mints meat out of your ass, Ringo. And mine too if I stick around. I believe I will make my exit before he gets enough of you.

They drove around the town until Ringo spotted a truck, he wanted sitting in a parking lot."

"Yo, Bro, over there." Ringo pointed at the truck.

There was a man and a woman standing beside it. The woman was around twenty-five, slim with blonde hair, wearing tight jeans and a snug fitting sweater. She was heavy up top.

Jefferson pulled beside the truck and stopped.

"Nice wheels, my man," Ringo said. "What would it take to get it from you?"

"I don't want to part with it."

"In that case I'll just have to take it." Ringo stepped out and pulled out a knife. He walked toward the man moving the blade side to side. "You step aside. Your girl can get in the truck."

"Your ass," The man kicked the knife out of Ringo's hand, then he delivered a high kick and caught Ringo on the side of his head.

Ringo staggered. "You bastard. You're dead." He swung at the man hitting nothing.

That gave the man time to land a blow to Ringo's jaw knocking his head sideways. The man pulled a gun from his pocket, spun Ringo around, grabbed him around the neck and shoved the barrel into the side of his neck. "Today you die."

Jefferson said, "Hey, man let's say we just go about our business, and we leave you and your lady alone. Nobody has to die today. Think about it. As nasty a person is Ringo is there is no need to kill him. There aren't a lot of people left. And killing him would make one less person. Think of something else. Like Ringo is conceited and he will have to live knowing you kicked his ass. And he knows I saw it."

The man thought for a moment. "You and your men take off. I'll drive up the road a piece and let him out. I agree with you about not killing anyone."

Jefferson yelled. "Okay, guys take it up the road, so our boss doesn't get his brains splattered all over his truck."

The trucks drove off, everyone looking at Ringo

with the gun barrel buried in his neck.

"Okay, now you. When I clear the top of that hill, I'll let your friend go and you can come back and get him."

"How do I know you're not going to put a round in him?" Jefferson said.

"That's a chance you are going to have to take. Because if you don't take off. I am going to turn him into a corpse and baby doll is going to put one in you."

"How is she going to do that?" Jefferson looked and saw baby doll pointing a pistol at him. "Oh, okay."

"I am a very good shot," she said.

"You folks have a good day." Jefferson drove off.

The man watched the other trucks follow. Ringo was led to the man's truck and put in the back seat. The girl got behind the steering wheel. The man got in the backseat and pushed Ringo to the left door behind the driver and told him to sit up straight. This would shield his girlfriend from anyone wanting to take a shot at them. He told the girl, "Drive over the next hill while I keep this piece of crap in check."

Halfway down the hill the man had the girl stop. He got Ringo out and kicked him in the back causing him to spread eagle on the ground.

The man unloaded his pistol and walked over, put the gun to Ringo's head. "Say bye asshole." He pulled the trigger, and the gun snapped.

Ringo yelled out like a man fixing to die.

The man laughed. "Ha, ha ha." He kicked Ringo in the side with a pointed toe cowboy boot.

The girl slid over into the passenger seat.

"You had better hope you never run across me again," the man said and eased into the truck and drove away.

Jefferson waited longer than he had to before he went back to get his boss. When he found him sitting on the ground, he said to himself. "I thought that man was going to take care of you for me, Ringo. You lucky son of a bitch."

CHAPTER 14

The Rangers

After stopping to pick up the kids from Laura's house it was an hour before dark when Jes and the men pulled into Sparta.

Jes told the others to keep watch on the prisoners while he and West talked to the sheriff. They strolled to the saloon, pushed the doors open and stepped inside. They spotted Sheriff Pat sitting at a table with Cat and Lester, each having a beer.

Jes and West walked over and got the tall man's attention.

"You gentlemen have a seat," Pat said.

Jes pulled an empty chair out from under the table. West reached and dragged one across the floor and they sat down.

"Lester I believe it is your turn to buy," Cat said.

The deputy put on a big grin. "I tell you, I would but I am flat busted."

Pat starred at Lester. "You mean you sat there and let me, and Cat buy a round each and you drank yours. Now you tell us you are broke."

"I tell you Pat I got to shooting pool with Troy and he wiped me out."

"Lester you have seen Troy shoot pool, you knew better than go up against him."

"I know I have Pat, but I thought it might be my night to win." Lester picked his glass up and held it. "But I wasn't."

Cat smiled, shaking her head. "Sam, bring us all a beer."

Pat patted his knee. "What brings you Rangers back to Sparta.?"

"We have you some prisoners for you?"

"Prisoners, what did they do?"

"Stealing women and reselling them before we apprehended them."

"Been a good bit of that going on around here," Pat said. "I welcome them because I only have two working. The others done their time and were set free.

West asked, "How much time do you think they will get."

Pat thought for a minute, "I don't know yet. That will be up to the judge. He'll hold trial in the morning. They have committed a serious crime, so I'm sure they'll be here for good bit of time. Have they killed anybody?"

"That we don't know," Jes said then asked, "Do we need to be here to testify?"

"No, you have told me what they did. That's good enough. I know those boys. This is not their time visiting me."

"Swift justice keeps everything simple," Jes said.

Pat told them, "You stay the night and get an early start the next morning. We have a hotel in town. Where are those guys? I'll lock them up in our jail."

"Out front being watched."

Jes picked his beer up. "It makes no difference what time we leave in the morning. We are in no hurry."

The sheriff told them, "Well in that case I'll see that you men have a good breakfast before you head out. Cat will fix you up. Just tell her what time you guys will be here."

"Will nine be okay."

"I'll have it waiting on you and your friends?"

The next morning when the Rangers woke, they had been served eggs, bacon, grits, toast, and coffee.

Pat showed up wearing a black coat. After he was seated Cat sat a cup of coffee in front of him. He picked the cup up, took a sip and held it in front of him.

"What did the judge give those guys," Carl asked.

"Two years each," Pat said.

"On what we told you. I would like to meet that judge," Dawson said.

Pat reached in his coat and pulled out a gavel and tapped the table. "Order in the court."

"You are the judge. I'll be dammed," Dawson said.

Clyde Walker spoke up. "Where did all this food come from?"

"The people who lived here had small farms. The ones who survived continued as they were doing and some folks who ended up there took over for the people who died or left."

"The coffee," Dawson asked.

"Pulled it out of an eighteen-wheeler out on the Interstate."

Do the people pool what they grow like one big community? Carl asked.

Pat shook his head. That's not a good way to live. Everyone has their own land, and they work it. That way everyone works and takes care of their families. Just like it had always been.

We have some families that are bigger than other families, so they require more food. When everything is pooled together people began to resent that. They feel that they worked just as hard, and they use less food. Some feel others are not working as hard as they are. They get to thinking that someone got more than they deserved. Others took more than their share.

"I see what you mean," Mike said. "You get what you work for. Your family needs more, you must put more time in. Your family is smaller so, you don't have to grow as much but you don't have a lot of help.."

"Darn best way to have it," Dawson said.

"I guess we will be going now, Pat," Jes said. "Which is the shortest way to Atlanta? The Interstate or Highway 278.?"

"It is about six of one and a half dozen of the other," Pat said. "Just ever which way you want to go. I would stay out of the towns."

"Thanks a lot," Jes said. "We are out of here."

The Reverend Allen Ball was second in line between Dawson and Carl when they left Sparta.

Laura sat next to Ball in the front seat and the two children were in the back seat. The injured girl and the two other girls were from a town close to Sparta, so they stayed behind.

Reverend Ball and Laura were going to look for a preacher to tie them in the bonds of holy matrimony and they would raise the two children as their own.

Their intentions were to find a place in South

Georgia they could call home.

The Rangers pulled into a town next to Interstate 20 early in the afternoon a day after rescuing the women and getting the injured girl to the doctor.

The convoy stopped in the middle of the street in the downtown area, thirty feet from an intersection.

Jes and West exited their Hummer. "Just stay where you are guys. We want to check things out." He and West walked to the sidewalk and stopped.

Jes looked at each driver and ran his finger across his throat. Each driver shut their engine off.

After a scan of the area, they stepped upon the sidewalk in front of a drugstore, and listened, hearing nothing. He motioned for the others to get out.

Dawson planted himself behind the M60. I'll take first shift. For a while then I want to walk around."

"Allen and I want to take the kids in the drugstore and see if we can find something to occupy their time," Laura said.

Jes nodded. "Excellent idea. The rest of us will mosey down the street." The men took off listening and scanning the town as they walked.

Twenty minutes later everyone was standing beside the vehicles not saying much or making any noise.

Luke was sitting on a sidewalk bench rolling a truck he had found in the store. Rebecca had picked out a coloring book with pictures of animals in it. She was sitting next to Luke flipping through the pages. Next to her was a box of crayons.

Jes's fist went up and everybody went silent. He pointed to a store with the front door set back off the sidewalk between two glass display spaces. They all eased into the space and waited. They heard muffled talking.

Jes eased his head out just enough to see the corner of the building and didn't see anyone. He motioned for Dawson and West to follow him. At the end of the building the talking was louder, and they could understand what was being said.

"Let's stop here, I'm tired and hungry. Grace is hungry too." A woman said.

"I don't know about stopping here, we are out in the open. Somebody from that gang might see us," came from a man.

"Let's be quick about it then," came from the woman. "We did the right thing leaving that place and going back to our home. I bet more people will do the same thing."

"I know. And you are right, and it is a good thing we hid some food in the basement of our house. This is to open, let's go in one of the buildings." the man said.

"Hold on there you two," another man blurted out. "You folks are from that group at the college. Where do you think you are going?"

From his voice Jes could tell he was walking up the street toward the couple.

Another man spoke. "You get up and I'll take your head off, fellow. Young lady you sure are a pretty thing. I got plans for you."

"Open two of those cans and put them on the table. Me and Leo is hungry."

"Those are for me and my husband and daughter."

"That was before we saw you."

"We need to eat too," the woman said.

"You and your family can have what we leave."

Jes motioned for Dawson to make his way to the back of the buildings. "Your call on this one," he told him.

Dawson took off through the building to the back door.

"Hold on just a minute, Rip," Leo said. "I'm going to get me something first, even if I have to beat you for it." one of the men said.

Jes and West heard a slapping noise like a folded leather belt being stretched quickly.

"He's going to beat the woman." West whispered.

"Get your hands off my wife you bastard," the husband said.

"You are in no position to be giving orders, hot shot," Leo said.

"You had better keep your mouth shut before Leo gets good and mad," Rip said.

"I'll kill you when I get a chance."

"You think you going to have that chance," Leo said. "Come here pretty thing and let me see—."

"Stop Leo, you damn maniac. There's plenty of time for that. Right now, I want to eat. You know the sergeant will nail your ass to the wall." The other man said.

The sergeant, Jes thought, I want to meet that guy.

"I can eat anytime," Leo said. "Now I want her."

"Mommy, I'm scared," a little girl said.

"It's okay, honey. Go to daddy."

The woman yelled. "Please stop. Not in front of my daughter."

"Let's me and you go around the corner," Leo said.

"Over my dead body. You'll have to kill me first."

"Well damn you, if I can't have you, I will shoot you right in front of your old man and little girl."

Dawson stepped from behind the building, took aim and fired. Leo swayed a couple of times before his legs gave out and he sprawled on the concrete.

Jes made his presents and the other man froze. He looked from Dawson to Jes trying to decide which man to shoot. He raised his rifle toward Jes, but he was slow. A shot hit the culprit between his eyes, and he fell on one of the many tables set up next to the building. The table tilted and he rolled onto the sidewalk next to his buddy.

The woman turned and saw the stripes on the soldiers' uniforms. "Oh, there are more of them."

West put his hands up. "No, we are not part of those guys group. We are real soldiers."

"How do I know that?"

Her husband put his hands on his wife's shoulders. "Because they shot the other guys."

The woman looked at each of the men. "And your uniform looks more like what an army person would wear too. Our leader's is solid green and faded."

"The guy who convinced everybody to leave their home wears a uniform," The woman's husband said and told them, "He said he had been in the special forces. But he doesn't have those patches and stripes on his sleeve you guys have. I believe he is more special needs."

"Who is the sergeant Lee mentioned?"

The wife spoke up. "He's that guy I just told you about. The head of the group we are from. Those guys you shot are from another group."

"I have got to meet this guy," Jes said, getting agreements came from Dawson and West. "Where can we find this soldier want to be?" he asked.

"They're at the college across the Interstate," the husband said.

"Shall we enroll in class, gentlemen," West said.

"I want to meet some coeds," Dawson said.

West looked at the husband. "Where were you guys going? Do you live around here?"

"Yes, with two hundred and fifty people. Our home is south of the town. One day the sarge and a few other men rolled through and began telling everyone we would be better off if we moved to the college, so we could look out for each other. It sounded like a good idea, at first, so we all packed up and moved here. It turned out it wasn't so good. The food didn't last. And the arguing about who should have this and that started. We left out last night."

"Were you mistreated?" West asked.

"No, but those two laying there are mean. Their group all live off our food and threaten us if we refuse to give it to them." the woman said.

Jes slung his rifle on his shoulder. "Go with us and let's see what we can do to rid you people of those guys. First collect those guys' guns and ammo. You and your husband might need them."

Jes and the Rangers loaded the man woman and the girl in Ball's Chevy and headed to the college.

The group stopped in front of the library. "This is where the boss should be," the man said.

Jes opened his door. "Let's go in and confront him, West."

When the Jes and West entered the building, they saw a of six men standing across the room. There was one man talking to the group. He sounded like he was trying to convince the people not to leave the college.

The man looked across the room at the two Rangers. He stared open mouthed and silent for a moment. "Who are you guys?"

The two Rangers walked toward the group saying not a word. They stopped ten feet from the man who was doing the talking.

He was about forty years old, six feet and about a hundred and seventy pounds. He had dark shoulder length hair and a four-inch beard.

"I'm Jes Crier the gentleman with me is Thurston West. We are Sergeants in the U S Army."

"I can see that by your stripes on your arms. What are you doing here?"

Jes stepped closer to the man. "Can you read the patches under those stripes."

"Yeah, I can read them I'm not a dummy."

"We'll leave that thought open for now. Tell me what the patches tell you about us."

The man looked at the arms of the men. He hesitated for a moment before looking at the men's faces. "It tells me that you men are in the Special Forces. Airborne Rangers."

"Where are your stripes and patches? Where is your name patch?" West asked.

After a moment nervously he said. "Riley, and I don't have any patches. I lost them."

"You got any tattoos to tell us you are what you say you are?" West asked.

"I don't like them."

Jes looked at the group. Everyone was staring at the two Rangers. "I am not crazy about them, but I have one tattoo. Just to show that I am proud to be a Ranger. We'll put that subject aside for now. We just need to have a conversation about survival first." Jes said.

Riley turned his hands up and moved them up and down. "That is what I am trying to get across to these folks. That they need to pull together and work with each other to get things done and not argue about who does and who don't work."

"That's what we want to talk to you about. How to get everybody working." West said. "Tell these people to round up everyone and let's have a meeting. Where is a good place to meet?"

"The gym will hold everybody. Wait a minute. How did you all happen to find us?" Riley asked.

"We ran across some of your people in town. A mother and dad and a child are outside. Two of your friends will not be coming back. Their names were Lee and Rip," Jes said.

"Oh, those two huh. Those two were not part of our group. How is the family you found?"

"The family is fine. But they're hungry. Where is all your food?" Jes asked.

"We have food. Some of Lee's friends took it. They are not nice guys, and they are not bad guys. They will steal some of the food, but they have a source for most of theirs. They are more a nuisance trying to act mean than anything. You folks killed the two that were problems."

Jes looked around, at the books in the room.

"Did they go from house to house and get the

food.?"

"No, we kept all the food in one location and doled it out. Now some are complaining about having done more work than others and they think some got more than their share because they didn't work harder. Or they have a larger family, and they turn out more work. It's a mess," Riley said.

"I know, it is not easy feeding a community," West said. "Let's walk over to the gym. I'll give you a rundown on the way. Dawson have the men move the Hummers to the back out of sight."

"So, you guys have a solution for that?" Riley asked.

Jes nodded. "Yes, we do. Just stop right here and I will explain something to you. The first thing is. You are going to have to send everyone back to their homes and let them fent for themselves. Each family will have to plant and attend their own garden."

"You think so. Some of these people would go hungry."

"Not if they know they have to work to eat."

After everyone piled into the gym Riley gave them the news that they would be going back to their homes.

"Why is that?" one person yelled out.

"The sergeant here can explain it better than I can."

Someone from the crowd yelled, "Oh, that's all we need. Another army guy telling us what to do."

"This guy is not a phony. He is a real sergeant from the real army," Riley said.

Jes started out. "I'll get to the point. You people will be better off if you go back to your homes and live as individuals, working for your own families. You will grow your own gardens and live as you did before the virus."

"Are you saying it will be better than us living together and taking care of each other?"

West told them. "Yes, we have spoken with people in another community who went through what you folks have gone through. You can still look out for each other, just look out for your family. How many of you feel that you worked harder than some of the others?" That statement caused several hands to go up.

Jes asked, "And how many of you cut back on your work because of that?" After a few minutes, hands went up. "See what I'm talking about. It wouldn't be long before most of you would cut back, and the crops would fail." The mumbling in the crowd grew loud.

Jes whistled loud and did pushing motions with his hands in the air to get their attention. "If someone has a bad year with their crop people will help that person because they want to not because they have to."

"I agree with everything you men are saying," said a young dark-haired girl on the front row.

"You only have one mouth to feed. Your job will be easy." Someone from the back of the crowd yelled.

"She does have only herself, but she worked twice as hard as some of you." Came from a woman up front.

"That's right, she worked her pretty little self from light to dark every day," Someone yelled.

"And that is the way all of you will do when you go back home," West said.

"We will still have that gang coming around and

taking what they want. And that damn Rip trying to put his hands all over us women." a woman said.

Riley spoke up. "That is true but, Rip and his friend are both dead now thanks to these guys here." Cheers filled the large room.

"Let's do it today," Came from someone.

"Riley yelled, "Let's get at it. We'll start as soon as we leave here."

The dark-haired girl who everyone said worked hard walked toward the Rangers. She was about five seven and one hundred and twenty pounds. Her jeans and shirt showed off her figure that had curves in the right places. There was a slight twist in her walk. She smiled. "I really do appreciate you guys doing this for us. Especially taking out Rip and that scumbag friend of his. But that gang is still around, and they will come for what they want."

"How many men are we talking about?" Jes asked.

"I counted them one day and it was thirty. I don't know if they were all here," she said.

Jes couldn't take his eyes off the girl. Dammed if she isn't the prettiest woman I have ever seen. "What is your name?"

"Lindsay Vest. And you are?"

"Jes Crier." He put his hand out. "Pleased to meet you, Lindsay." They shook hands while he stared into her green eyes.

A man came running in from outside. "They're here. The gang is up the street looking for us. It looks like about fifteen of them."

Lindsay tensed up. We don't have time to deal with them right now. What are we going to do?"

Jes smiled at the girl. "Just leave those guys to my

friends and I. Seargent West, tell the men to bring two of the Hummers around front in five minutes. You and I should go out and introduce ourselves." He announced. "Everyone, plant yourselves inside here."

Jes and West went to the door, opened it, and waited for the gang to reach the lot in front of building. When it was time the two Rangers walked outside with their weapons pointing not at the men but at the ready. They stopped at the street and stared at the men in the trucks.

The four pickups eased next to Jes and West.

CHAPTER 15

With the engine running a man stepped out of the passenger side of the lead truck. He was around six four and muscular. He had his long greasy hair in a ponytail that touched his shoulders. His beard was about two inches long. "My name is Samson."

A girl got out and stood beside him. She was tall, slim and had blonde hair halfway down her back. Her lips were thick and painted bright red.

"Well, it looks like the Army has come to life." She looked at Jes's arm. "I guess you are the boss, you have the most stripes. Oh, my, you are a Ranger. And one who jumps out of airplanes." She looked at West. "And your friend does the same." What are you two doing here sugar?" she asked Jes.

"Trying to sweeten things up for these people here."

"How are you going to do that?" the girl asked.

"That depends on what you and your friends are doing here."

She puckered her lips. "Sampson saw something that upset him."

Jes fixed his eyes on Samson. "Several things could upset a person. Can you be specific?"

Ponytail spoke up. "I'll tell you exactly what we are

doing here. We found two of our friends in town with bullet holes in their heads. Would you know anything about that?

Jes thought about the two men they left on the sidewalk in town. "Let me think about it."

"You had better think fast because we have the Army out manned."

Jes looked at his watch and started counting down from ten. When he got to one two Hummers rolled into view with two men sitting behind the M60s. Jes raised an arm.

Dawson cut loose with his machine guns blowing the windows out of one of the buildings and chunks of concrete off the walls.

Jes looked at Ponytail. "Out maned yes, but we have you out gunned."

The man turned and motioned with his hands to his men, and they lower their weapons. He turned back to the Rangers. "Did you kill those men?"

"Yes, they were in the process of molesting a woman in front of her husband and daughter. They deserved to die."

The woman looked at Jes. "You are so right, sugar. You did the world a favor taking out those two."

"We'll, we can forget about those men and you guys leave," Jes said and pointed to the hummers. "Or we can get down to business."

"You are outnumbered three to one," Ponytail said.

"Not for long. Each of those guns will spit out six hundred rounds a minute. We have one more around back. In less than thirty seconds, we will outnumber you."

Ponytail looked at his men and back to Jes. "Six hundred rounds?"

"Yep. Look you will lose men here today or we can walk away. But not one of my soldiers will die. Your call."

The man opened the truck door. "Delilah, let's go, get in." They got in the truck and closed the doors.

Are you shitting me? Jes thought.

West turned away and grinned. "We met folks from a western movie. Now we have met a judge from a book of the Old Testament. He had better watch out s all I have to say, she will betray him."

Jes saw Lindsay walked out the door and toward them. He couldn't take his eyes off her. The twist in her walk was one hell of a calling card. He couldn't get over how snug her jeans fit when everyone else's clothes were loose on them.

"That was some demonstration with that M60. I think you made believers out of them," Lindsay said when she reached the men. Her remark was delivered with a smile.

"Do you know what that man and woman call themselves?"

Lindsay laughed. "Yes, I do. I wonder if she has ever thought about cutting his hair."

"I'll bet he is a light sleeper." Jes paused then asked, "How did you know that gun was an M60?"

"I just know some things. And I know something else. They will be back. So, I hope you have no intentions of leaving anytime soon," she said.

Jes found himself drawn to her. "Then we should prepare ourselves. Do these people here have any weapons? Preferable guns?"

'You bet we do and ammo. We are just short on guts."

"We'll," Jes said. "Things haven't gotten bad for them yet. When it gets to a live or die situation, those men will kill everyone here for the food and water. It will come to either fight or die. We will give them some guts."

"How do you do that?" The pretty girl asked.

"Train them and let everyone know that when those guys get desperate, they will be to kill them. Then they will do what they must do," Jes said.

"Then they can either sink or swim," West said.

"You might have better luck teaching them how to swim," Lindsay said.

"We'll see," Jes said. First, let's have a look at those guns."

"I hope you are right. Follow me." Lindsay turned and began walking toward the gym.

Jes stood and watched her. Anywhere you want me to, he thought. "Lead the way."

Halfway to the door she stopped and turned around. "I don't bite."

"Invite. Get your big self-up there," West said.

Jes caught up with her. "So, where are these weapons you mentioned?"

"We keep them hidden in the gym."

"Let me guess why they are tucked away instead of being used."

"How many guesses do you get."

"I only need one. The people are afraid to face the gang, and rather than fight they hide their weapons. Which is okay because up to now there has been no threat. That is fine but they all could be killed before they got to their weapons."

The pretty girl pointed "Here." And replied. "I know that, and you know it. But these people don't see it. I believe they are in shock from what has happened."

Jes opened the door, and they all walked into a large room with steel rows of shelves filled with rifles, shotguns, and pistols. The walls were lined with boxes of ammunition.

Jes picked up a 30-06. "Wow, this is enough to fight a war. With a gang. Where did all this stuff come from?"

"There was a big gun store in town. I told the people we should gather the weapons and bring them here so they wouldn't fall into the wrong hands. We raided it and here they are."

"These folks should learn how to shoot and fight."

"Riley and I told them that, but they don't seem to get the idea. We need someone with a stronger voice. That's why Riley told them he had been in the special forces. He was hoping they would listen if they thought he had been. But it didn't work."

"Why did it not?" Jes asked.

"I don't think they believed him. Would you? They are fine living the way they are. We have food and the gang hasn't hurt anyone. They just steal food."

"It won't stay like that. It is not going to be long before they come for the women and when they do it will get ugly. Your group had better be preparing for that day."

"I tried talking to them, but they are scared. If we had someone who had Ranger on their shirt and who looked like a Ranger. And that person stood up to that gang and got them to leave without taking our stuff. That person just might be able to convince the people here to stand up for themselves."

"Oh, you think so?"

"Yes, I do. But like I said. If we had somebody like that. And even more so if there were six of them. By the way, why is Preacher Ball tagging along with you guys?"

"You know the preacher?"

"I have seen him at my church a few times. He did short sermons at some of the churches. This is the first I've seen of him since the virus. I have seen the girl with him a few times but who are kids?"

"He hung around the Base for the past year." Jes said. "He is going to marry Laura and the kid's parents died. They are going to raise them."

"Good for them giving those kids a home and a family."

Jes picked up a revolver and bounced it in his hand. "You have ammo for this."

"Sure, we have 357 bullets," Lindsay said.

"I want this."

The girl smiled and nodded, "Good choice. I have one tucked way." She walked to a row of shelves loaded with boxes of bullets, took two boxes off a shelf, walked back to the men, and handed Jes the boxes.

Jes tucked the pistol in his belt and slid the ammo in his pockets. "West, you think you can talk these people into standing up for themselves?"

"Nothing like trying. If not, I'll teach them how to swim." He picked up a 1911 and asked where the bullets were.

Lindsay pointed. "There on the top shelf."

West grabbed two boxes and tucked them in his pockets. "So, you were elected to be in charge of the arms room."

Lindsay grinned. "Let's say I volunteered. No one comes down here except Riley. Shall we go?"

The three of them headed back to the gym to explain to the people what is coming and what is needed of them if they are going to survive.

After giving the people, the news Jes suggested they hit the gun store in town again. He told them they will need supplies to keep the weapons in good shape.

They piled into the Hummers and drove the few miles to town.

"This is a big store for a small town," Dawson said when they entered the building in search of paper targets and anything else they would need.

"Why such a big store in a town no bigger than this?" West asked.

"The store served people from all around. People from a hundred miles away came here. And some folks from Atlanta would come here," Lindsay said.

The gun store was the size of one you would expect to find in a large town rather than here. It was the size of a grocery store. There were all sorts of equipment they could use. What was missing was the guns and ammunition the people they were going to train had taken.

Jes stopped a cart he had grabbed upon entering next to the cleaning kits. "We should take all of these," he said and began filling the cart.

West called out to the men. "Each team grab a tent and some camouflage clothes."

"There is some bow and arrows and cross bows on this isle," Mike called out.

"Can you hit anything with one?" West called out.

"Is a pig's ass pork?" Mike called back," as he loaded two carts with the bows and arrows. "Got a very good, expensive cross bow."

"It looks like a lot of stuff has been taken but there is plenty left," Virgle said.

"They had some packaged food that we took. It was not bad eating." Lindsay said.

Walker spoke up. "I'll bet it's no match for our MREs."

"You are right about that," Carl said.

Attention, guys," West said. "Since we are going to be here for a while, I say we find a furniture store and grab six small mattresses."

Lindsay clapped her hands together. "There is a mattress store in the shopping center."

After leaving the store with six mattresses on one of their trailers Jes spoke up. "I noticed a gym on the other end on this place. We all need a good workout."

CHAPTER 16

The Town

Dean sat in his office tossing at tennis ball against the wall and catching it. "I find this life after the virus to be very boring," he told Jerry.

Jerry picked up a cup. "I tend to agree with you. I sure do miss all the traffic we used to have in town." He poured coffee into the cup. "Want a cup of coffee?"

Dean threw the ball at the wall and caught it when it bounced back. "Na, I've had two cups already."

The door opened and in walked the ex-Governor Roy Barnes. "Dean, I have something I need to talk to you about. I'll just get right to it. Are you aware there is a Black man living next to my wife and I?"

"Sure, I am he is one of the finest fellows I know," Dean said. Do you have a problem living next to a Black man?"

Roy noticed the tone in Deans remark showing he was surprised rather than sympathetic. "No, it's not that. He's a mechanic. I would prefer to be in a more upper-class area. If you know what I mean."

"You are living in an area with fine neighbors. There is no class separation anymore. Now, let's just forget that you said what you did."

"Oh, one more thing. I will be running for mayor of the town. I just want to let you know," Roy said. "And I will have a gathering of the minorities in the town to assure them that they will be represented."

Dean looked at Jerry and back at Barnes. "You go right ahead, Roy. It is your right if you want to."

"You mean you have no objection?"

"No, why would I. It's a free country."

"Well, I will be doing a lot of campaigning and speaking to the people. I will be holding a meeting in a few days. Thank you for your understanding, Bye now." Roy opened the door and looked out. It is a nice town," he said as he closed the door.

Roy had just closed the door when a message came over the walkie-talkie from the main gate. "There is a man in a Cadillac and a woman with him who looks like a walking jewelry store."

"What do you mean?" Dean Martin asked.

"I mean she is wearing more jewelry than you see in a pawn shop a week before well-fare checks come in."

"Did you search them and the car?" Dean asked.

"Yes, we did. They had two weapons. And the trunk of the car looks like Fort Knox. You know when they used to keep the country's gold there?"

"The woman said she is friends with the John Carstairs family. Her name is Lucy Jenkins."

"Take their guns and send them down to the second gate. John isn't here; I'll talk to Millie after I talk to them."

Dean talked with the couple and sent them to the park to sit and wait until he spoke with someone in John's family.

It was a good thing Millie was sitting on the couch when Dean mentioned the lady's name. She went limp and her jaw dropped. Finally, she said, "Lucy Jenkins? Are you sure that's her name?"

"That's the name she gave the guard at the gate and to me. She is wearing enough jewelry to fill a store. The trunk is full of gold. And silver."

"Oh, my. That's Bill Jenkin's wife all right."

"I've heard John mention that name." She's the nymphomaniac wife of that killer, Dean thought. "Wasn't he one of the head guys of the gang that came here in the truck last summer and tried to take us over? John said he was killed before you folks came here."

"I am afraid so. We never knew what happened to Lucy. We assumed she took up with someone. She certainly couldn't take care of herself. To tell you the truth I worried that she starved to death."

"What are your thoughts about her. Would she be trouble for us?"

Millie sat back. "I'm not sure what kind of person she is away from Bill and the drugs."

"We could send them over the valley," Dean said.

"You mean to Con Town? She would feel at home there. Or maybe not. Doing that to someone you have known for years is difficult. I would always wonder about her."

Dean rubbed his jaw like he was checking if he had shaved. "That fellow she's with sounds solid. I don't believe he is like her former husband."

Millie thought for a moment, then raised a finger to signal she had an idea. "Let me talk with her and get a feel of how she is now. People change when they get clean of drugs."

"That's not a bad idea. My sister's boy got clean, and he has been a different person ever since."

"And look at Freddie, he is fine now. His brother, William and sister n law Debra put up with him for years. We wouldn't want to send her somewhere she shouldn't be."

"I think I will walk down there right now."

"I'll walk with you and we both can speak with them."

"That's a good idea. I don't know that man."

Millie and Dean didn't see the couple when they got back to where Dean left them. They did spot them walking around the town square. They were holding hands like school kids would do or two people in love.

Millie could tell by looking at them, Lucy was a different person. She looks more alive and pretty. Before she had always seemed to be in a hurry, never having time for anyone. Now she seems settled as she walks. At least she is still taking care of herself. All dolled up like a walking fashion show as she had always done. And that is good.

Millie and Dean waited until Lucy and the man reached them.

Millie smiled. "How are you doing, Lucy?"

"Oh, Millie, I am, so glad to see you. I really didn't know you were here. I just guessed and ask the man at the gate if your family lived here. Oh, this is Carter Logan. We met not long after Bill left."

Millie put out a hand. "Pleased to meet you, Mister Logan."

"I guess it looks odd me showing up with another man."

Millie shook her head. "A lot has happened in the

past year."

"You know I have no idea where that husband of mine got off to."

"You mean you don't know what happen to Bill?"

"I haven't the foggiest idea. He just went out of the house one morning and never came back. I would never have thought he would have left me in the fix he did. Luckily, I had enough food to last a while. Millie, do you know what happened to Bill?"

"Why don't we go to my house, and we'll talk."

Lucy was in good spirits walking with Millie. She acted as though they had always been good friends. There was something Millie didn't understand. One is what was Lucy like before she indulged in the drugs. The other was Lucy working with a brain damaged by drug to the point she never would be her original self.

When they were inside Millie's house and seated, Lucy and Carter were offered coffee. Which they both accepted. "Dean I know you will have a cup too."

Carter smiled. "That aroma. I was sure it was gone forever. It is going to be a pleasure to indulge in your coffee. I can't thank you enough Mrs. Carstairs."

"You two get comfortable, it will be right out," Millie told them.

Millie went into the kitchen, removed the lid from the percolator and filled it with coffee and water. It was good she had a fire going when Dean showed up. She slipped another stick of wood in the stove and got it going again.

She went back into the sitting room and took a seat. "It will be ready shortly. We do miss our utilities."

"Oh yes we do," Lucy said. "I will never get used to heating water for a bath."

"Well, you showing up unexpected is a little shocking to say the least. The guard at the gate said you asked for John and me. How did you know we were here?"

"It was the day after all of you got back home. Bill told me that John was taking his family to a town in North Georgia. I just drove through a few before I came upon this one."

"You finding us was just a shot in the dark then I would say."

Lucy smiled. "I guess you could say that."

Millie put her hands together and smiled. "Oh, I am glad we have some of my biscuits left. I baked six more than I usually do for some reason. They are good with honey.

"Oh, you cooked biscuits. How great," Lucy said.

"It isn't like we can run to the store and buy some sweet rolls. Let me get you all one. John found some flour on a salvage run. The coffee should be ready."

"Dean and I brought an extra biscuit for you, and Carter. I hope you men want one?"

Dean took a biscuit. "Yes, I sure do. No one turns down food now days."

"I have to agree with you, Dean," Carter said. "I will say one other thing. I wasn't expecting to be treated with such hospitality. Thank you, Millie."

While they were eating and drinking coffee Millie talked with Dean to give them time to finish their bread and half of the coffee before, she engaged in conversation. "Lucy where have you been since we left?"

"That is something else strange. I woke up one day, and everybody was gone. I went outside and there was no sign of anyone. I got in my car and drove around looking for Bill and I never found him."

I stayed in my house for two weeks before my food started to run out."

Millie said, "There is something I want to tell you. But in private."

Dean stood. "Why don't I show Carter around outside."

"I think that is a good idea. Why don't we let the ladies talk?" Carter said. "I'd really 4853to see this pretty little town. Lucy, can enjoy her talk with Mrs. Carstairs."

Millie listened and heard the door close. "Lucy, I have some news about Bill."

"Oh, Millie please don't tell me he is in this town."

"Well, no he is not here."

"Oh, thank goodness, I am, so glad to be away from him."

Millie repositioned in her chair. "I knew you two argued a lot, but I had no idea you wanted to get away from him. How long have you felt that way?"

"Ever since he went to prison, but I wanted to wait until he got out. I confronted him about a divorce, and he said he would kill me. He said he learned how to do a lot of things in prison."

"Lucy, I had no idea things were that bad between you two."

"My parents were killed in a car accident, and I had no family."

"I wasn't aware of that."

"I did step out on him while he was in prison but that is the first time in years, I did things for myself. I couldn't help it. I was free and I went overboard. Then after he got out, he started me on those drugs. I hated them but he threatened to hurt me if I wouldn't take them."

"He should have been ashamed doing that to his wife," Millie said.

"The drugs caused me to do some things I am not proud of."

"They do cause people to do terrible things."

"Oh, my God. Millie, I am so ashamed of some things that I did. John may or may not have told you this. He came up to my room and got some guns and I was in bed with a man."

"No, he didn't mention it to me, but John is not one to gossip."

"It was all a blur to me, and it was a few weeks before I remembered it happened."

"Well, you made it easier for me to tell you this." Millie paused. "Bill is dead. He was shot shortly before we left."

Mouth opened Lucy stared at Millie. "He is dead?"

Millie nodded. "Those two brothers that were his friends are too. You said those days are gone and it was the drugs causing you to do the things you did. Put it behind you, Lucy. Carter seems like a nice man, and when I saw you two walking around both of you seemed happy."

"He is a great person, and I love him, and he loves me."

"When and where did you meet him?"

"It had been four weeks since I had seen Bill. My car ran out of gas, and I was walking on Holcomb Bridge Road, going home. A car slowed beside me, and the window went down. I was scared at first and didn't say anything."

"That must have been scary for you."

He held a candy bar out the window and asked if I wanted a candy bar. Then he laughed and commented on how dumb that was of him. "You remember the old joke; you want some candy little girl."

"Yes, I do. That was funny," Millie said.

"Then he asked me if I needed some help. I didn't look at him and just kept on walking. He said, ma'am, I am not going to hurt you."

"But you didn't know," Millie said.

"No, I didn't but I had a gun in my purse. So, I stopped and told him why I was walking. Anyway, that's how I met Carter. He put some gas in my car, and I drove home leaving him standing on the street. I saw him the next day and we talked. After that, we hit it off."

Millie touched Lucy's hand. "I am glad it worked out for you two."

"Thank you for telling me about Bill. I am relieved that he is gone. Now I can move on. Is it terrible for me being glad he is dead?"

"Well, no I don't think so." Millie said. "I am pleased he is gone too. Make sure you move on. I will tell you more about him someday."

Lucy paused to take a breath and let it out. "Just, so you won't think I am a heartless person for being glad Bill is dead I want to show you something." Lucy stood and turned around. She undid her blouse and let it fall off her back.

"Oh my, Lucy, I can't believe a man would do that to his wife. Some don't look that old."

"Those two newest ones were from the last night I

saw him. He put ten there, two at a time. Over two years. After he joined up with those two men with the drugs, he didn't pay any attention to me. He told me he didn't care what I did, just don't leave him. He said if I did, he would make my front look like the back. He slid the knife down my back. I thought he might have turned gay in there."

"You were afraid of him," Millie said.

Tears began to trickle down Lucy's face. "I don't want anyone to know my husband treated me that way. I don't know how any man could treat his wife the way, but he did that to me."

"I can't start to imagine how you felt."

"I had better wash my face. I have my makeup in my purse."

"Down the hall on the right."

CHAPTER 17

John and Ralph

After driving a few miles, John and Ralph spotted a car on the right side of the road.

John eased off the gas. "Get ready. All I can see are two heads."

"I'm getting in the back." Ralph crawled over the seat, rolled the window down and positioned his rifle to fire out of the window.

John stopped beside the two-year-old Buick. The driver's window was down a few inches. The heads belonged to a young boy in the driver's seat and a young girl beside him. Both were asleep. He hoped. "Hey, can we help you?" he said his voice elevated.

The couple jolted awake, turned their heads, and looked shocked to see the man with salt and pepper hair in a pickup next to them.

"We are not going to harm you. Do you need help," John asked?

Neither said anything. They just stared until the girl punched the boy in the side.

He moved suddenly and said, "We, we sure do. Our gas tank is empty. So, a ride if you can't spare any gas."

The girl strained across the car to get a good look

at John. "Mister Carstairs is that you?"

"Yes, I'm John Carstairs. Who are you?"

"Take a good look at me, Mister Carstairs. I'm Regina Tomlin. I went off to college four years ago. I was only eighteen then. I'm twenty-two now, so you might not recognize me."

"Regina, of course, I remember you." He looked hard. "Now I recognize you. What brings you here?"

"I've been in Tennessee the last four years. I was going to come home last year but the virus hit. I am having a fit to see my mom and dad. Have you talked to them?"

"Let me pull in front of your car. You folks get out." John pulled in front of the car and stopped. He looked at Ralph. "This is not going to be easy. Her parents were in the group killed by Bill Jenkins because they wanted to leave. I don't know a good way to tell her. But she has to know."

"Oh, Lord." Ralph shook his head. "She should be told. You can't let her leave thinking she will see them."

The girl met them between the vehicles. "Are my mom and dad, okay?"

John lowered the tailgate and told the girl to sit down. She backed up, put her hands on the tailgate and lifted herself up and sat. The boy joined her.

John looked into her eyes. "Regina, I have bad news about your parents."

The hint of excitement of seeing an acquaintance drained from the girl's face. All she could do was stare at John. At first, her mouth moved without words, then she managed, "Are they? Are they? Oh, no." She fainted and fell over on her companion.

Ralph opened the back door of the truck. "Put her in here the heat is on."

"Just let me sit here. I'll be fine. I need the cold to keep me awake. I had worried that they would catch the virus."

John shook his head and looked back at Regina. "It wasn't the virus that killed your parents."

"It wasn't? Then what did.?"

"Do you remember, Bill Jenkins?"

"That creep who went to prison?"

"Yes, that's him. Our entire family was in Florda when everything started. It took us four months to get home. By the time we got home the neighborhood had started a watch committee. They elected Bill to head it up. Though I believe it was Bill who set the whole thing in motion. He also fell in with a bunch of the wrong people and had an idea he could take over a town in North Georgia. All our neighbors who were left walked away from him and he had his drug friends kill them."

She put her hand to her mouth. "Oh, my, God. They lived through the virus, and he killed all of them." Her tears came and she couldn't stop. When she had control, she said. "Most of them had children. What happened to them?"

"John handed the boy a water bottle. "He killed the children too."

"Oh, no, oh no."

John and Ralph walked to the front of the truck and stared at the bare limbs waving on the trees.

After several minutes Regina got off the tailgate, took her husband's hand and led him to where John and Ralph were standing. "I didn't introduce you two to my husband. This is Kenneth Waits. We married three months ago. My mom and dad never met him."

"I'm sorry, for that Regina. Pleased to meet you, Kenneth." John put a handout.

Ralph introduced himself. "Pleased to meet the two of you."

Regina asked, "What happened to Bill Jenkins?"

"He'll never bother anybody else," John said.

With her eyes filled with tears, Regina looked out across a field. "He's dead then?"

John took her hand and patted it. "And his two partners from prison are too."

"This virus hasn't hardened me, but it has taught me to accept things," the grief-stricken girl said.

John nodded. "That's the best I have heard it put."

Regina wiped tears from her eyes. "We had the shot but there was no gas to get us home. There was food in the cafeteria at the school. We went to some stores and gathered all we could. When the cell service went out, I didn't know what to do. With our food running low, we knew there wouldn't be any more, so we went out and found what we thought was enough gas to get us home. But everybody said to stay off the Interstate and not go through the big towns. We looked at the map and saw we could come home on the back roads. That took more gas. Then we realized our calculations was wrong about how much gas we needed. The car wasn't getting the milage we expected it would. I put five gallons in and set the odometer to zero. We drove one hundred thirty-three and six tents of a mile. After it ran out, we knew how far we could go on our gas. We didn't factor in the mountains and all the stops and starting up again on the back roads.

After we put our last five gallons in the tank and drove one hundred twenty- and one-half miles we knew it wouldn't get us there.

"You were getting twenty-six points seventy-two miles per gallon on the first five gallons," Ralph said. "You got twenty-four and one tenth on the last five gallons."

They both stared at Ralph with confused looks.

Ralph said, "It's eighty-six point two miles to your home. three and a quarter gallon would get you there on good level ground."

"For real. Where were you when I was sitting in math class?" Regina said.

"Teaching math classes."

John laughed. "I felt the same way when he did it to me the first time.

Look, guys, there is nothing to go home to in Roswell. It was a mess when we left six months ago. Things are only worse. We have our families in a town with a few hundred people who are open to newcomers. The younger the better. How would you two like to live in our town?"

The couple talked for a moment, each nodding their heads a couple of times.

Regina turned to the men. "That would be great, mister Carstairs. I don't know anything else to do."

"We'll give you gas and directions on how to get there. Millie, Peggy, Julie, Donald, Anna, and you don't know Ben, he is Julie's and Donald's youngest one. Are all there? They will be thrilled to see you and meet your husband. It's only fifty miles. Do you have a map?"

"Yes, Kenneth does and he's good at reading it."

"Good, most young people can't."

"That is true. We knew how to ask our phones." She spoke.

Ralph dragged a five-gallon container filled with gas to the rear of the bed. "Open your filler spout."

Kenneth went to the small door on the rear panel, opened it and twisted the cap off.

Ralph heaved the can off the truck and walked to the back of the car. He placed the spout in the hole and tilted the can and held it there until the liquid stopped flowing. "This will more than get you there, so you want have to worry about running out." He walked back to the truck and secured the now empty five-gallon can next to the cab.

"We sure do thank you and Ralph Mister Carstairs," Regina told them.

"We were scared as all get out about what we were going to do," Kenneth said.

"Tell the guards at the gate we sent you," John said as the two got in the car.

With Regina and her husband's car gassed up and ready to go Ralph and John took off to finish their journey.

Ten miles later they passed what they thought was an unpaved road on their right. John and Ralph turned their heads and saw it was a long driveway that went for a hundred yards off the road and up a hill. At the end sat a big white house. But that wasn't the reason John stopped. What had gotten their attention was a man sitting on a white horse at the top of the hill. The man on the horse was wearing a long black slicker with a western hat on his head. The coat was pulled back on each side exposing a pair of pearl handle revolvers sticking out of twin holsters.

John pulled the truck off the road and stopped beside the driveway, and they got out.

The horse began trotting down the hill, the man yelling. "I'll kill every one of you sons-of-bitches. Yee ha, get ready to meet your maker."

John and Ralph moved behind the truck with their rifles and waited on the man.

The man pulled his horse up next to their truck and spoke. "Hello, my name is Harlan James. Who are you two." Attached to his saddle was a scabbard with a rifle in it.

"Just passer byers," Ralph said.

He dismounted and checked up the road. His long white hair blew in the wind, whiskers short and a stern look on his face. He looked like he was sixty years old. "I'm going to wound or maybe kill some people in a few minutes."

John studied the horse and saddle. "Help yourself, Harlan. You sound like a man with a reason."

The white-haired man glanced up the road. "You bet your ass I have a reason. They should be here at any minute. How are you guys getting along?"

"Not bad," Ralph said. "Hope you don't mind us stopping. Running across folks is not common nowadays. We saw you at the top of the driveway and wanted to meet you. My name is Ralph Bishop. This fellow here is John Carstairs."

Harlan looked at John for a few seconds. "Pleased to meet you fellows. Always like to pow-wow with folks but you might have stopped at a bad time."

"A bad time?" John said.

"They came by five minutes ago going west. They'll be back any minute."

"Who will be back."

"The rats who are trying to run my wife and I out of our house. They came up two days ago telling us we had to go because they wanted it. "I told them over my dead body. That might be what they are coming for."

"Do you need some help, Mister James?"

"Just stand by. I fight my own battles."

"What kind of battle you got coming up?" John asked.

"You boys stand right there. I'm going to show you how a man protects his home."

Suddenly a roar could be heard coming toward them from over the hill."

"That sounds like motorcycles," Ralph said.

"You aren't wrong, that's them. You two just enjoy the show. You may want to move out of the line of fire."

Three two-wheel motorcycles and a three-wheeler topped the hill.

"They look like they mean business," John said.

Harlan yelled out. "Yahoo, come to poppa you no goods bastards." Harlan pulled the twin chrome-plated revolvers and stood beside the road.

The guys on the bikes steered with one hand and held guns in the other. When they were seventy-five feet from Harlan they started firing. Harlan fired back and hit a front tire causing the rider to lose control and run into a ditch and fly over the handlebars landing thirty feet away. They passed and Harlan fired again. This time he blew a rear tire, and the bike zig zagged a few times and ran through a fence, the top strand catching the rider's neck stopping him while the bike kept going. The two remaining bikers turned around and headed back for another pass. The hammers on Harlan's guns clicked on suspended shells. He put them away and pulled the rifle and emptied it on the three-wheeler's engine and tires. The bike turned over sending the rider skidding on the asphalt on his back. The last rider must have realized Harlan was out of shells and turned to make another run at the man. He stopped and let the engine idle making the sound only a Harley can make. He revved the engine and let it come back to an idle a few times. The third time he revved it he popped the clutch and came straight at Harlan now standing in the middle of the road.

What is he going to do now, John thought?

Harlan took the rifle by the barrel and when the rider came by, he stepped to the side and swung it into the guy's face.

The second biker to go down got up and pulled a three feet chain from a saddlebag on his bike and started running toward Harlan who now resembled a gladiator.

If you are the last man standing facing a lion, do you go toward him or get in the cage and lock yourself in. The biker ran toward him swinging the chain in circles above his head. When he was close to Harlan, the rifle butt went up and caught the chain. The white-haired man pulled the biker to him and planted a hard fist on his face. He pushed him back and pulled him toward him and hit him again. This time he let the man fall on the road, his face red with blood. Harlan could have called a victory then, but he wasn't finished. He walked over to the guy who rode the three-wheeler.

"Those things you said you were going to do to my wife." He drew back what looked like a size fifteen boot and kicked the rider in his manly parts. "You won't ever do to anybody." He kicked him again in the same place.

Strike one up for the white-haired man, John thought.

Three minutes later a pickup truck topped the hill, rolled up and stopped. Ralph and John pointed their weapons at the two occupants.

Harlan looked hard at the men inside. "You want to finish this?"

The driver looked around at his friends on the ground. "Mister, I had rather sandpaper a wildcat's ass. We just want to get our friends and be gone. The bikes we'll get later."

Harlan not even breathing hard said, "They are all yours."

After the truck left with their friends, the battle-worn Harlan told them the two in the truck were the last of them.

Ralph looked at the rifle in James's hand. "That's a reproduction Winchester 1873. I know you hated having to hit him with it."

"Yeah, I did. I got another one just like it up at the house."

"That's good you do," John said.

Harlan told them he and his wife have been living in their home for twenty years. The bikers said they would give him two days to clear their stuff out. They also insulted his wife. He had no idea why they thought he would just turn it over to them.

John told him he noticed he didn't seem to aim at

the riders, only their bikes.

Harlan told him he didn't need bodies littering up his land. And the killing had to stop somewhere. He had had enough of it. He thought maybe they didn't realize the world was down eighty percent of the people it had before the virus. Not enough people left to be killing them off.

They heard hoofs touching the ground and looked up to see a woman coming down the driveway on a horse that was identical to the one Harlan rode.

Harlan waved his hat to the woman. "Yessir, that's my wife coming there. She's just as comfortable on a horse as she is walking."

The woman who got down and hugged Harlan around his waist looked twenty years younger than him.

"My wife, Roxy." Harlan took off his hat and looked at John. "You don't remember me, do you?"

"I can't say that I do."

Back up several years and imagine me with dark hair."

"Harlan," John said. "Harlan James," he said again using the man's last name. "Yeah, we worked for the same outfit, in South America. And you came to the karate studio a few times when I taught there."

Harlan smiled. "We were the only ones who could give the other a good workout. Fifteen years and white hair will change a person. Come on up to the house and enjoy a cup of coffee."

"If you got some to spare." John said.

"I got enough for a cup or two."

Once inside Harlan sat a cup on the table in front of each man. "How you boys set with this stuff?"

"Got a little. We have one cup a day."

With the aroma coming from the percolator filling the kitchen, the men and Roxy sat around a breakfast table discussing their situations in the new world.

Ralph told Harlan he admired him for not killing the guys and his way of thinking about saving the population.

"Yeah, that was good thinking," John said. "My wife commented on not wanting to become someone we are not. And since then, I feel the same as you do.

"It was one thing hunting the drug guys who would kill us and anyone that got in their way. But it's another thing shooting Americans even if they are up to no good," Harlan said. "This situation has turned good people bad."

"And some bad people good. There's a community inhabited by prisoners from the jails and their families across the mountain from our town. We had some trouble with some of them several months back. The leaders turned the guys over to us. They come to our town on the first Saturday of every month with people from other communities to trade their goods. You and Roxy are welcome any time you want to come. I'll give you directions how to get there."

"That sounds like a good idea," Harlan said. "I'll tell you what. If you two spend the night here in my guest house, tomorrow I'll show you guys around."

CHAPTER 18

The Mission

Les scanned the area as the group neared the exit. He was impressed with the way Ruth handled the Suburban pulling the trailer. Her stops and starts were smooth and she maneuvered it expertly. "Pull off at the Morrow exit," he said. "I want to check the straps holding our gas reserves down."

Ruth picked a shopping center parking lot, to park the Suburban in. After she stopped everyone got out and scanned the area.

Ruth stretched and twisted her body. "I sure am glad we made it around Atlanta safe and sound."

Natalie did three trunk twists. "Why did some people stay around town. And what is their source of food?"

Jerry rolled his shoulders. "Like those guys we encountered coming here. They go from house to house gathering up what is still edible. Some canned foods will last a while. The smart ones planted gardens I guess."

Richard did a handstand, his body straight as a board. "Look I don't know which end is up anymore." He walked a short distance on his hands and thrust himself up flipped up right while in the air and landed on his feet. "Now I know."

"Not bad for a tired ole soldier," Les said.

Billy started to say something but was cut off by a scream that came from around the building.

"A woman in distress," Richard said.

"Les you and Richard go with me to check it out," Jerry told. The men grabbed their rifles and took off to where the scream came from.

When they got to the edge of the building, they saw two young men, a young girl, an older woman, and an older man standing next to a car. One of the young guys was pointing a rifle at the older guy yelling, "Get in the car and leave. We want the women."

Les and Richard raised their rifles and aimed.

When the man got in the car, the armed men grabbed the women by an arm and walked them toward a pickup. The women jerked free, shoved the men into each other and grabbed the young girl by a hand and took off running toward the building Jerry and his friends were watching from.

"You go girls," Ruth said.

One of the men shouted, "Stop or we will shoot."

The women kept running.

"Damn you I said stop." The man raised his gun. I told you to stop."

The other man raised his rifle. "Stop or you both will die."

Not today bastards," Les yelled. He and Richard fired.

Hearing the shots the women cried out. She checked Body for bullet holes. Finding none she slowly turned and saw the men on the ground with red spots on their heads. The women looked at the direction the shots came from and saw the three men step out from behind the building.

"You ladies are safe now. We're the good guys," Jerry said.

The older women put her arms around the younger girl, and both stood staring at the men.

"Is that your husband back there in the car?" Jerry asked.

Both acted as though they were in shock.

"You ladies are okay," Les said.

Finally, the younger girl opened her mouth and closed it a couple of times. "Help us."

The man got out of the car and hurried over to the women. "They are my wife and daughter. Thank you, men, so much." he yelled out.

The three men walked to the man and women. "Luckie for you people that we decided to exit when we did," Jerry said and asked, "What are you folks doing here?"

The man told Jerry, "We pulled behind the building last night to take a nap. Those two men snuck up on us about fifteen minutes ago. It was by the grace of God that you guys came along."

Les looked at their new Ford Explorer. "Yes, it was. We just wanted to check our load and stretch our legs. Where did you get the new car?"

"Ford dealership close by. We swapped our compact for it. There was only a small amount of gas in each of them. We siphoned the gas from several and got a full tank."

Les looked at what the men were driving. "I believe those men would want us to have their truck."

Jerry looked at the new Crew Cab Ford F150. "It

has gotten crowded in the Suburban. Red is my favorite color. Where are you taking your family?" he asked the man.

"Opelika, Alabama, my family should be there. We were in Virginia visiting relatives, but they all died. We have had a hell of time getting this far. It is less than a hundred miles to our home, and we almost got killed. I just hope we can make it."

"You are kind of off your trail, aren't you?"

"Yeah, we were forced off 285 onto 75. I kept driving to get away from Atlanta. I got off and that is how I found the Ford Dealership. I am going up to Jonesboro and take 54 over to Interstate 85."

"Watch yourself on those back roads. It will be lonely." Les said.

"You have a gun?" Richard asked the man.

"An AR15, but I used up all my bullets in South Carolina getting away from some guys."

Jerry pulled a magazine from his vest and handed it to the man. "This holds thirty rounds. Give me your empty mag. Pull around to our SUV."

"I'll get that truck," Richard said.

They brewed coffee and fed the man and the women. Jerry pointed out their town on their map in case he did not find his family. He told him to remember which one it was. If he marked it and someone else got the map, they would know the town was a significant place. The man agreed.

Before they loaded up to go, Jerry looked down the parking lot and spotted the front end of a large truck sticking out from behind a building. "That looks like the nose of an eighteen-wheeler. The type that pulls freight trailers." He told everyone to load up and pull to the side of the building.

The name on the door of the truck was a company that distributes wholesale food. There was a fifty-three-foot trailer attached to it.

"I bet that trailer has food in it," Richard said. And ran to the back. "The doors have a hefty padlock, on them," he yelled.

"Hold on a minute." Jerry walked to the truck and climbed up in the cab. A minute later he walked back and held up a key. He slid it in the lock, twisted it and pulled the lock open. The driver carries a key to each store and a key to the lock on the doors. It was the odd one."

Les pulled one of the doors open and stared at boxes of canned food. "We uh we. Look what we have stumbled on." He pulled the other door open and climbed inside.

What they found were cases and cases of cereal, vegetables, flour, corn meal, dried beans and more. Most were out of date.

"You guys should swap that car for a truck and load as much of this stuff as it will hold," Les told the man and his family. "We'll go to the car dealership with you and come back and help you load it."

Jerry locked the trailer door, and the team piled in the SUV and followed the family to the car lot.

Halfway down the second row Les pointed to a new F250 pick up. "That will haul one heck of a load. Let's siphon the gas from your car and some from a few more vehicles and fill gas tank."

Richard opened the driver's door, reached in, and turned the ignition key. "The battery is dead. I need those jumper cables."

Billy opened the rear door of the SUV and pulled out a set of cables and walked over to the F250. He clamped one end of each cable to the SUV's battery. "Here you go" He handed Richard the ends of each cable. "Black to the ground, red to the hot."

"No shit Sherlock, like I never done this before," Richard said, and connected the cables to the truck's battery. "Let it run for a couple of minutes."

After letting the battery charge a few minutes Les reached in and turned the ignition key. The engine truck fired right up. "We should get inside the parts department, get a new battery, and swap them out after they charge. That way you will always have a hot battery."

When they got back to the tractor trailer, they filled the bed of the truck with as many boxes of food as it would hold. Jerry and his crew loaded twenty cases in the pickup that had belonged to the two men.

Les climbed up into the trailer. He began moving boxes. "Where is it? I know it has to be here." He climbed on the boxes and went all the way to the front shining a flashlight and moving boxes. He turned and came halfway back slinging packages. "Ah, here it is," he yelled and slid several boxes to the back as he made his way to the door. I found it. I knew it had to be here."

"What are you talking about," Ruth said.

Les held up a box. "Coffee, what else."

"Oh, for the sake of all, yes of course," Richard said.

"Now we can get down to business," Les said.

Jerry showed the man where he was going to hide the keys. If he found his family, they could come back and get more.

"Thank you. And we will not take more than we need," the man said as they all got in their vehicles.

Jerry sat staring out the window. "The interstate is grown up in weeds compared to the last time Dean and I came through here," Jerry told them.

"I wonder who moved all the cars?" Ruth asked.

Jerry held a cup he filled with coffee before they left the family. He took a sip and lowered the cup. "When word got out about the virus, people stayed home."

As the crew approached Macon Jerry pointed. "Take 475 off to the right. Going through the town might put us head-to-head with a gang or two. And it is shorter going around."

"Not a bad idea," Les said. "Richard and I came through there after leaving Fort Stewart. My ETS date came up at the first of the virus. My paperwork went through the day before we got the news that no one was to leave the base. I was ready to kiss the Army goodbye. When the food ran out, we left. By the time the shipments stopped we had the shot, so we hit the road. A bunch of us grabbed the best weapons we could find. Twenty of us ended up with a MK 16 SCAR. One member of my group grabbed M249."

"That was a lucky grab for you guys," Jerry said.

"It proved to be a good choice not long after we left," Les said. "We went in different directions wanting to get home. I was going to Louisiana, but we got sidetracked and headed to Atlanta. Richard was going to Mississippi. That is where we were going to pick up his parents and head on to my hometown of

Monroe Louisiana."

"Do either of you have siblings?" Ruth asked.

"I have a brother named Leon and two sisters, named Karen and Lettie." Richard said. I hope they are still home.

Les, what about you? Any sibling."

After a silent moment Les spoke up. "I have a brother who is three years older than me."

"Do you know where he is?" Ruth asked.

"No, I do not the last I heard he was going to fort Liberty which used to be Bragg in North Carolina. That was a year ago."

"What is his name?"

"His name is Jes. He is a master sergeant in the army. Special forces."

"Wow a couple of bad asses. Jes and Les," Ruth said.

"His parents can't spell anything above three letters,"

"Alright smart ass." Les used his knuckles and tapped Richard on the head.

Richard gripped the back of Les's seat and pulled himself up. He was excited when he spoke. "Oh, hell, man when we came through Macon I counted fifteen burned buildings, and five were still in flames. We fought through a roadblock coming in and going out. I'd say we put down twenty guys between the two blockades. Their weapons were no match for what we had plus our experience."

"What stopped you two from going home?" Ruth asked.

"It was too dangerous, and we didn't have enough ammo left," Richard said.

CHAPTER 19

The Rangers

Dawson stood looking down the row of ten men and women lined up waiting for his orders. "You people on the first team line up with your weapons. The target is only twenty-five meters from you. They should be easy to hit."

"Weapons up, aim fire at will," he yelled after everyone was on the firing line.

Nine rifles fired. "June what are you waiting for. It is not going to fire itself." Dawson told the woman.

"It is so darn loud, and it is so destructive."

"Have you ever fired a rifle before?"

"Yes, a time or to with my husband. And it hurt my shoulder and made it blue."

Dawson smiled. "That is why I said to pull it snug to you. Now try it that way so we can move on."

June pulled the weapon tight to her shoulder. Closed her eyes and pulled the trigger. "Oh, that didn't hurt. Thanks."

Jes stood and watched Lindsay who was at the end of the line. I thought she knew how to shoot. He walked down the line and stopped behind the girl who he had his eyes on ever since meeting her. "You are a little off in your stance."

Lindsay turned her head and smiled. "Maybe you should show me how to stand."

Jes unslung his rifle, brought it up and pointed it toward the target. "Like this."

Lindsay raised her rifle and aimed at the target.

"Bring it a little closer to you," Jes said.

"I am more of a hands-on learner. Maybe you should stand behind me and set me up."

Not knowing he was being set up, Jes moved in position, reached around, and put his hand on her arms and moved then to the correct position. "Now lower your head and aim."

"I'm sorry I didn't hear you. Could you move closer."

Jes moved in closer and caught the smell of her hair and perfume. He paused before giving her the same instructions as before. "Are you comfortable?"

Jes delivered Lindsay the first smell of aftershave she had experienced on a man in over a year. Complements of a bottle he had grabbed from one of the stores, at the shopping center.

"That is much better, just stand there while I shoot." She closed her eyes for a moment. "Let me get comfortable," she said.

"The target is waiting. Are you going to fire?"

"Do I have to," she said before opening her eyes and pulling the trigger three times.

"Let's see how you did." Jes stood holding her for a moment before pulling a scope from his pocket and looked down range. She had put three rounds in the circle no larger than a silver dollar. Jes knew she had played him, and he loved it. "You listen well."

"I try my best. There is a lot more to learn."

"We will get to that, later." Maby some hand-to-hand stuff went through Jes's mind.

Dawson walked the line checking that all the weapons were empty. "This the only time those rifles will have no ammo in them. After your training is over when you leave the line load them and keep them loaded." When he got to Lindsay and Jes he turned and yelled, "Next, we will be doing some hand-to-hand combat training. Each member of our team will be your instructors. Let's go to the gym, so we can use the mats. Fall in behind us two abreast," Dawson said as five of the Rangers led off. Everyone followed four feet from the person in front of them.

Jes and Lindsay waited for the end of the line to reach them and fell in into place. They kept twice the distance between them and the others. Occasionally Lindsay would brush against Jes's shoulder.

"You did exceptionally good on the range. Do I take credit because of my instructions?"

"Sure, you can. You know just how to position a girl. Are you good at the hand to hand?"

"There is a lot of hands-on and close order drills."

Lindsay smiled. "Oh really. I can hardly wait."

Jes and Lindsay watched the door close behind the last group as they entered the building leaving them outside. When they reached the door Jes stopped.

He stood for a few seconds and turned to the girl standing beside him. "Let's not keep them waiting," she said, and reached for the handle.

Lindsay reached for the handle.

"No, you don't." Jes put a big hand on the handle and pulled the door open. "In you go."

"You Southern Gentlemen are something else."

"Have to take care of our women. Where are you from?" Oh, Jesus let her be a Southern Girl.

"I am from Atlanta, but I have lived in other places."

Jes looked up. Thank you, Lord.

Dawson was standing in front of the bleachers. "If some of you guys would pull some of those mats over here, we will get started."

After the mats were in place Dawson had everyone take a seat. "Our fearless leaded and instructor who has many years of martial arts training will give us a few demonstrations. Take it away Jes."

Jes joined Dawson on the mat. He looked at his audience. "I need a volunteer."

Before anyone else could speak up, Lindsay was on her feet and walking on the floor. She stopped five feet from Jes and stared at him. She took three steps toward him, jumped and aimed a foot at his chest.

Jes grabbed her foot and tossed her for a flip in the air.

In a split second it seemed as though he was going to let her fall and break her neck?

Two strong arms reached out and caught her before she landed headfirst and flipped her over planting her feet on the mat. Her hair was a mess, covering her red face.

"You got any more tricks up your sleeve?" he said.

"Yes, this one." She punched him in his rock-hard gut and turned to go back to her seat.

She was stopped by a big hand grabbed her arm. "We need five more people down here."

One person matched themselves with a Ranger.

Jes started off by telling his group that the best

place to kick a man in between his legs.

Let me try that came from some of the ladies in the room.

Jes was quick to speak. "I prefer we bring one of the mannequins from a store in town for that drill."

After two hours of training, it was time for lunch. Some of the older women in the group had cook enough vegetables to feed everyone.

On their way to the cafeteria Jes and Lindsay paired up for the walk. West was walking up ahead of them. He had paired with a blonde who was busy moving her hands while she and he talked.

"Who is the blonde my friend has latched onto?" Les asked.

Lindsay focused on the couple. "That is my good friend Joy Ingles. You don't pay attention do you. He has been eyeing her. She is a very good person. Maybe they'll hit it off."

"Hit it off? Hit what off?" Les asked.

Lindsay slapped him on his chest. "You know what I mean." She put her hand in his hand and locked their fingers together. They bumped shoulders as they walked.

His thoughts turned to Reverand Ball and the girl he was going to marry. How he had thought what a burden it would be having someone to tie you down. Having to worry about them constantly. Now he felt his life would be empty without Lindsay in it. Already he was worried about losing her and he doesn't have her. He knew he was not leaving this place without the woman walking next to him. Even if she did try to take his head off with her foot two hours ago.

He wondered how Lindsay feels about marriage. He thought how can I ask her. How do you feel about marriage? No, she would think I was going to ask her to marry me, and she would say, you are fast I don't even know you. She would think I ask every girl I have a conversation with to marry me. I know, I'll just ask her. But not how do you feel about marriage. Wait a minute, why am I thinking about it? Finally, he blurted out, "Have you been married?"

She tightened her grip on his hand and hesitated.

Oh, shit, I should not have asked, he thought.

She said, "No, I was engaged for a while. The relationship lasted a couple of years before he decided he didn't want to be tied down. He just up and left."

"You mean he just left and that was it?"

"Yes he did. He told me goodbye and hit the road, Jack and he didn't come back no more. A year before the virus. I don't know if he is alive or dead."

The Town

The gate guard pinged Dean Martin's radio. The Carstairs are popular this week. There is another car at the gate. This time it is a young couple. The driver said they met John and Ralph on the road, and they sent them here. The girl's name is Regina Tomlin. She grew up in the Carstairs's neighborhood."

Send them in," Dean said. I'll have a talk with Mrs. Carstairs.

"I'll sent them to their house," the guard said.

Dean made another trip to the Carstairs's house and spoke with Millie. "There is a young couple out front who said they know you and John. Her name is

Regina Tomlin."

Millie put her hand over her mouth when she got the news of the couple in the car at the gate. "Oh, my God, Dean this is going to be terrible. I wonder if John told her.

Dean stared at Millie who looked like she had just been told the virus was back. "I spoke to the couple before I came to see you. The girl said John told her that her parents were killed. If that is what you are worried about being, so terrible?"

"That is one of the things but there is something else. The girl, Regina Tomlin, and her family lived in our neighborhood. Her parents were two of the people Lucy's husband killed."

Dean slowly turned and looked out the window at the Buick parking out front. "And his widowed wife is here. This is a small town. They are bound to cross paths. Since you know the girl, it will be best if you tell her. Is there anything I can do to help with this?"

"I don't know of anything," Millie said.

"I'll leave you three alone. The girl has a husband."

"She is, so young. But that is good. She was mature for her age. I will have to tell her Lucy is here."

Dean walked to the door. "I'll leave it with you." He opened the door, walked out, and closed it behind him.

Millie got up and walked to the door and waited. She opened it when the couple knocked. It was hugs and greetings through tears for a minute. The introduction of the new husband. The sad faces of old friends brought smiles with more tears.

Regina found comfort in seeing her family friend. She didn't see Millie, as her mother's age. Now they seemed like friends from the past having a conversation on equal ground.

Neither did Millie see Regina as a child. Millie was amazed at how the girl carried herself. She was surprised she was talking on the girl's level. Had she regressed socially because of the lack of people she has conversations with? While in the town, her conversations were fewer now. There were times when she would shop and go back home without speaking to anyone. I must talk to more people.

Regina told Millie. "John told me what happened to my parents and who was responsible. It was horrible they lived through the virus and have bill do that. He was a mean man even before he went to prison."

"It was the worst thing we experienced since the virus started," Millie said.

Regina startled by the noise coming from the front door said, "What was that I heard?"

"That was the doorbell. There is a knob you twist to get that sound. It is a kind of harsh compared to what we had."

Millie's two daughters, Julie, Peggy, and their friend Debra entered the room. Regina and the other girls yelled with excitement when they saw each other.

Regina stood and hugged the two sisters and Debra and introduced Kenneth. "How is William? You two were always fun to be around. He treated you like a princess."

"Getting along, same as everybody else."

"He still treats her like that," Julie said.

"You girls are making me blush," Debra said.

Millie clapped her hands. "Girls let's everyone take

a seat. I have something to discuss with all of you."

"Oh, Mom, just when we were getting to know regina again," Julie said.

"I feel I should tell all of you about someone who just showed up. This will especially impact you, Regina."

"Oh, wow I just arrived too."

"As did the person I am going to tell you about. They arrived a day ahead of you. Which made you my second guest. I was not as pleased to see my first visitor as I was to see you. But I did learn some things. Anyway, Lucy Jenkins is here. She showed up before Regina."

An. "Oh no came from the girls."

Millie assured them. "I was as shocked as you girls are. And I was not pleased about her showing up, at first. I am going to clarify the at first statement in just a moment."

"It will sure need some clarification, Peggy said."

Millie took a deep breath and let it out. "Lucy tried to divorce Bill. And he had threatened to kill her."

"You know, mom, it could have been just talk to gain favor with us," Julie said.

Millie nodded. "That thought did enter my mind. Until she showed me the scars he put on her back with a knife."

"Bill had scarred her back with a knife?" Peggy said.

Millie nodded her head. "They were slice marks. I have no idea how she survived without going to the hospital."

The conversation went on about the drugs and why she did the things that she did.

Regina sat on the edge of her seat. "Should we believe her. I mean if she is telling the truth that would mean she was a victim of Bill's. Her husband was that mean, wasn't he?"

Peggy leaned forward in her chair. "Oh, yes he sure was."

Millie nodded in agreement with Peggy and regina. "I could not hide her being here from either of you. I still have reservations about her. She did seem different and the man with her seems nice, and they are crazy about one another."

Regina told them. I have come to accept things, the way they are. Lucy will need time to do some soul searching."

The conversation shifted when Julie mentioned a house next to her and her husband being up for grabs, if she and Kenneth were interested or if they wanted an apartment, there were plenty available.

Regina looked at Kenneth. "Do we prefer the house over an apartment?"

Kinneth responded. "I have never lived in an apartment, so the house will suit us better."

"The house it will be," Regina said. "I will keep my distance from Lucy until I have more time to think about what you just told us."

They all agreed they would not pursue a friendship with her.

"The situation is like a wound without medicine. It will fester and become inflamed before it heals. And we just might be that medicine," Millie said.

CHAPTER 20

John and Ralph

Ralph and John were walking around the farm with Harlan and his wife.

John looked at the hills around the farm. "This sure is a wonderful place you have here."

"I was living in Atlanta when I met Roxy. We both were tired of the city. This place had been on our radar for seven months. It never came on the market, but I knew the man who lived here wanted to sell it. We agreed that everything we did we would do when we were together. So, we waited until the day after we were married, and we bought it. Two hundred and seventeen acres."

"Were you a farmer before you lived in Atlanta?" John asked.

Harlan shook his head. "I didn't grow up being one. We lived in a small town in Alabama. I visited my uncle and aunt who owned a farm. I would stay with them in the summer. He taught me a lot. I loved the open space of the country, the smell of the fresh air in the morning. There is a certain feeling one gets standing in the warm sun in the morning. No noise except for the sound of the animals. I think back and tell myself that was as close to heaven as I may ever get."

"You think about that a lot, Heaven," John asked.

"I would guess we all had better," Harlan said.

Ralph spoke. "Is that's the reason you didn't kill those thugs yesterday."

Harlan's expression went from serious to a grin. "I didn't want them to get there ahead of me."

Ralph smiled. "Oh, well, I love the open space, too. When I was teaching at that college every weekend I was in the country and the woods hiking. I just never thought about it the way you do."

John breathed in the country air. "It seems like we all like the freedom of the outdoors. I could never stay home long before I had to take a trip somewhere. My desire had always been to be like a cowboy, but those days are long gone. So, I did the closest thing to it. I drove a truck across the country for a couple of years. I loved the freedom of traveling. That was what I liked about our job roaming the jungle. I would work a couple of months then go home for a month. I knew that I would always be leaving home for a while."

"Harlan spoke up. "I enjoyed working in the jungle until I married. After that it stopped being all about me. I had to think about what Roxy wanted, and she worried about me. That's one reason I quit after ten years."

Roxy spoke up. "He was right about me worrying. It really got to me when he left. I thought I was going to have a nervous breakdown the last time he was out. I told him about it, and he never went back. I was, so relieved." She reached up and kissed Harlan on the cheek.

Ralph thought for a moment, I guess this virus is not as hard on us as it is most folks. Maybe because we liked being outdoors more than having a big social group.

John stiffened his arms and bent them at the elbows. "About time we hit the road."

Roxy put her hands together. "Not before we feed you two."

"Eggs, bacon, grits, toast and of course coffee," Harlan said.

"What was that you said about being as close to heaven as you will ever get? That is just about the way I feel now," John said.

"Well, let's go rustle up some breakfast, so we can talk some more before you two leave," Roxy said.

The Mission

The group made it past Macon without any trouble. They stopped to spent the night at the Perry exit. Not wanting to chance getting trapped in a building they chose a motel that the doors opened to the parking lot. Worried that there might be a gang or two around because of the previous population they scouted the area.

The women were in one room and the men chose a room each all on the bottom floor. Two guards were on duty at a time, rotating every two hours.

Les and Ruth were up before daylight and intended on cooking breakfast for the others.

Ruth walked off leaving Les standing beside the SUV. She scanned the area before settling on watching for the sun creep up in the East. Les had his eyes fixed on her. He and his friends used to see who could come the closest to guessing a woman's size and he had gotten pretty good at it. He guessed that before the virus she filled out the jeans that now hung loose on her hips to be a size seven. So, she must be a size five. As small as she was, she still retained the shape that would turn any man's head.

Ruth turned and caught Les gazing at her. "I loved watching the sun rise back home," she said.

"You'll see it here in about thirty minutes. A few hours before the people in Utah can," Les said as he opened the back door of the vehicle and searched the contents. He reached inside, slid a box to the rear and pulled two items from it. "Look we have a can of bacon and a bag of grits. Complements of the trailer of food we found yesterday."

Ruth turned to Les. "Too bad we don't have eggs."

Les pulled a can from the SUV and held it up. "Oh, but we do. In the form of powder."

Ruth frowned. "Powdered eggs? I don't know about that. Are they good?"

"Yes, they are good. Very good if you haven't had eggs in a long time. And they are excellent if they are all you have."

"Well in that case," Ruth said. "I'll get the table." She walked to the trailer, lifted the three-foot square table over the rail and rested it on its edge, unfolded the legs and sat it upright.

Les pulled two chairs and two blankets from the trailer. "Come here," Les walked to the edge of the parking lot, unfolded the chairs, and placed them facing East. The sky was just beginning to show a trace of light. "Sit, we are going to watch the sun come up."

"Wow what about breakfast." Ruth said as she took a seat.

Les unfolded a blanket and draped it over her shoulders. He eased in the chair next to her and wrapped the other blanket over his shoulders. "They can wait."

Five minutes later the sky in the East was getting brighter. It really doesn't last long enough does it," Ruth said. She put her hand in Les's hand and squeezed.

It wasn't long before the sun showed itself.

The pair got up and walked back to the truck.

Les lined boxes and a can of eggs up on the table. Next, he retrieved a portable propane stove and lighter and placed it next to the boxes. After connecting the small bottle of fuel, he fired it up.

Ruth said, "Grits or coffee first?"

"Coffee, please," Richard said followed by the same answer from Bentley.

Ruth placed a pan on one of the eyes and poured water into it for the coffee. She placed a skillet on the other eye for the bacon. What do we need to cook the eggs."

Les spoke up. "Just mix with water. We'll cook them in bacon grease. That'll give them a good taste."

When the food was ready to be eaten one by one the others began to gather in the parking lot.

Billy was the first to dig into the hot breakfast by grabbing a paper plate and dipped some grits on it. "It's a good thing we all are from the South. Well except for Ruth."

Ruth piped up. "I have you to know, we do eat grits in Utah. A lot of restaurants serve grits and shrimp for dinner. Some serve them for breakfast. So, I'll have a bowl, thank you."

"I sure hope that family made it to Alabama." Billy said.

Jerry rolled his shoulders. "We'll never know unless they show up in our town," he said.

"If they do, I hope they bring their entire family," Natalie added.

"Yeah, at least we would know they were okay. Not to mention adding to our town's population," Bentley said.

"It's almost like we are back in the eighteen hundreds old west. Except we do have better weapons and automobiles." Ruth said.

Richard pointed to his rifle and to the pickups. "There will come a time when we do not have either of those."

"All I can say is, we had better start a horse farm," Les said. He also noticed Richard had grown silent and was fixed on something across the parking lot.

Ruth looked toward the sky; the sun was fully visible. "Oh, I do, so much miss riding the trails back home."

In a deep voice Les said, "Quiet, everyone." He pointed off to one side at five figures walking toward them.

Richard pointed his weapon at them. "That's close enough. We mean you no harm, but we will shoot you if you come any closer."

The people stopped. "Help us please." Came from a man. The five sat on the ground. One of them lifted a young girl off the asphalt and put her on his lap.

There was a man, two women and two children, both girls. The young girls looked to be about six and eight years old.

"What can we do for you?" Les asked.

"The man's voice was low. "We need food and water. Please. If not for me. Can my family have some?"

Les reached in the back of the SUV and pulled out several bottles of water. After a moment he told his group. "You guys keep a look out. You people come on over here. Are there any more people out with you? If so, you need to tell us now because we will protect ourselves."

"There is no one other than us. I promise," the man said.

"Come over here," Les said.

They got to their feet and walked toward Les and the others.

"We have food and water for you," Ruth said.

CHAPTER 21

John and Ralph

Ralph spotted something lying in the road as they approached an intersection. "What do you think?"

John stared at the object. "Looks like a body in a dress."

"What is she doing in the middle of the road?"

John looked around. "Over there is another one on the ground. Looks like a man. I don't like this at all."

"I'll ease up. You keep an eye on the woman. I'll do the same to the man."

Ralph eased the truck toward the body until he was ten feet from it. "It is a woman." He stepped out holding his weapon.

John eased out the other side with his rifle. Ralph walked toward the body. When he was five feet from it, she came up and pointed a rifle. Ralph put a round in her head twisting her around.

"On your left," John yelled and fired as the man raised up. The round knocked him backwards and he spread out on the road.

A round was fired from a hill off to their left and a man yelled. "Run, run."

They took off in the direction of a building as another round was fired from the hill. They stopped behind the building and looked at the road. There was a body that neither of them had seen before.

"Behind you. He's behind you," came from the hill.

They both turned and fired at a man aiming a shotgun at them. One round hit him in the head and the other got him in the chest.

"That's the last one. I'm coming down. Don't shoot."

They watched as a man made his way down the hill by jumping from rock to rock like he had springs on his feet. In no time his feet rested on the last rock. He turned around, held his rifle in both hands in front of him and did a back flip sending his long blond hair flying and falling to his shoulders when he landing on his feet. John and Ralph stared at the man as he walked up to them and put out a hand. "Derrek Trill. "Pleased to be of help to you. Truth is, I been after those guys for a week."

John's hand went out. "Well, we got them. John Carstairs. My friend is, Ralph Bishop. We are delighted you were on that hill."

Ralph's hand went out. "Thank you for your help."

"I been up there all morning watching those rats. I was beginning to think nobody was going to come by and take their bait. That was the only way I could get them. Waiting until someone came along with weapons and bullets. I am out of bullets."

"Glad we could help," Ralph said. "It's not every day we get to help take out the garbage."

Derrek looked down. "Garbage is right. They didn't factor in somebody shooting back."

"Who were those people?" Ralph asked.

Derrek told them. "I don't know who they were. We ran across some of their handy work last week. A few days ago, we were hiding on a rise. They drove up and stopped on the side of the road at the intersection and got out. We watched them for a good while until we heard a car coming and they got down on the road. When the car stopped the passengers got out to help them. That's when they pulled their stunt. I got two of them that time.

"You been stalking them?" John asked.

"Three young kids stopped a car and got out that day. They killed them all."

"You live up here in these mountains, Derrek?

"Have been for a few months."

"You got a house?" Ralph asked.

"Na, we go from house to house. Came up about seven months back. Whoever, lived in these houses around here must have up and left."

"Or worse. Have you seen any bodies?"

The blond guy shook his head. "Not the first one. That's why I say the must have left."

Ralph looked at the hill the man bounced down. "I never seen anybody come down a hill the way you did. You're light on your feet."

"Ah, nothing to it. For me anyway."

"You had anything to eat today," John asked him.

"No, ate the last of my food yesterday afternoon."

"It's late now, I bet that rock hopping made you a little hungry," Ralph said.

"A little don't quite describe it."

"Come on over to our truck. We got some extra. You can tell us about yourself," John said.

"Before you offer, I had better show you

something." Derrek turned, put a finger in his mouth and whistled.

They watched as a girl stepped from behind a tree and came down the hill the same way Derrek had. And like the blond man she looked like she had springs on her feet. She did the back flip off the rock sending her long blond hair flying. When she landed her hair came halfway to the waist. She walked over to the men, stopped smiled. She looked like she was just over five feet tall. Her right hand came out. "Hello. Sure, is good to see some people who are not shooting at us."

John and Ralph had surprised grins on their faces.

Derrek put an arm around the girl who was a foot shorter than him. "My wife. Her name is Jasmine."

"I was wondering why you kept saying we," Ralph said, then asked them. "How old are you two?"

"We are both twenty-five."

"Fantastic," John said. "How do you like living up here going from house to house?"

"It's not what we like but we don't know what's out there. Have most people turned into what those guys were?"

"No, we'll tell you about a place where people live peacefully. And we have an offer for you and your wife. I'll tell you about it while we eat." John said.

"Eat? Jasmine blurted out. "You mean you two have food?"

"We sure do, and you and your husband are welcome to some of it." Ralph said.

John and Ralph lowered the tailgate and slid coolers to the back of the truck bed and opened them. They pulled out cold fried chicken and peanut butter and jelly sandwiches and offered them to the couple.

Jasmine's eyes opened wide as she took the food.

"Oh, wow," Derrek said. "Our first meal in two days."

"You guys eat while we tell you our community and. We have some hot coffee in a thermos we made a couple of hours ago." John said.

"Coffee." Derrek blurted out "Wow, you guys are great."

Ralph handed them a cup each and poured coffee in them, next he filled his and John cups.

As they ate John told them what he knew to be out there, which was very little. Ralph told them about their community. And they had run across a lot of bad people before going to the town they live in.

John took a sip of coffee from a tin cup. "This is our first time away from the town in six months." So, we didn't know what to expect. There are a lot of people living in the town, but we need more so we can survive. There is sufficient food to support a lot more. I would like to invite you to go look at the community."

Derrek eyes widened and he smiled. "That sounded like what we are looking for."

"Well, it's there for you two if you feel that way," John said. "The truth is we are trying to increase the population of the town with young folks. Everything is working fine for now, but it will require young people to make it grow."

"Especially young people who want to have babies," Jasmine said.

"And smart folks like you two," Ralph said.

John drank the last of the coffee and turned his cup up. "Grounds. You can't get coffee without them now days." He slapped the cup against his hand. "Where are you guys from and how did you end up here in North Georgia?"

Derrek spoke. "I wouldn't say we are from any one place. We are from everywhere."

Jasmine chimed in when confused looks came across John and Ralph's faces. "Our parents were circus performers. My birth certificate says I entered the world in Florida. It was during one of the shows' stops. My mother said she got out of the hospital two days after I popped out and she and my father left with the show."

Derrek told them, "I arrived three months before Jasmine, in Louisiana under the same circumstances."

"Derrek and I were acrobats in the show since we were ten years old. We started training at three." Jasmine said.

That explains how you came off the hill and the flip off the rock," John said. "That is interesting."

"Only now we are out of work," Jasmine said. "Unless either of you know of a traveling circus around."

"Haven't seen one lately," Ralph said.

Jasmine looked at her husband. "We didn't want that for our children anyway. If we have kids, we want a stable life for them. Somewhere like the town you are talking about. And you need babies for your town to grow."

John and Ralph told the couple more about their town and asked if they had transportation. Derrek and Jasmine nodded and told them they had a car and plenty of gas.

You folks have adapted well to the new world and

made the best of it, John said.

"The hunting is good and the folks who had lived around here had put up plenty of canned vegetables and fruit. But someday the food will run out. And I worry about when that day comes," Derrek said.

"But because of one incident all our worries are put to rest if we choose to accept your offer. The misfortune of some brought us to our fortune. Your community is a life saver," Jasmen told them.

John showed the town's location on the map. "Let's hit the road gentlemen. Where is your car?"

Derrek pointed. "Behind that building over there."

The couple disappeared and a minute later a new Ford Explorer appeared from the rear of the building. Two arms waved from the windows, and they were gone.

Ralph and Jonn loaded into the pickup and took off for another town.

Ralph scanned the trees outside. "You know, I believe that couple could make it on their own if they had to."

John tapped the brakes to get around a curve, then hit the gas after the road straightened. He glanced at Ralph. "I guess that comes with the intense training they put in to get where they are."

CHAPTER 22

The Rangers

The Rangers left the college and drove to the town to search for fuel to fill their cans. The extra running around had depleted their supply to the point that they couldn't make it to their destinations. The gas the community had was still good. It was lasting longer than they thought it would, but they had no diesel fuel.

There were plenty of cars parked downtown but they were all gas burners. The people in the community told them they had emptied most of the cars.

Lindsay spoke up. "I have a better idea. There is a hand pump with a long piece of hose attached to it at my house. We can use it to pump fuel from the tanks. Most service stations sold diesel."

"Best idea I have heard all day," Dawson said.

"Ah, you turd knocker. You wouldn't know a good idea if it hit you in the head," Mike blabbered out.

West slapped Dawson on his belly with the back of his hand. "Don't you two jack asses get started."

Jes looked at the girl he had developed feelings for. You are as sharp as you are pretty, he thought. "Let's go get that pump."

"Heee haw, let's go," Dawson said.

"Wilcox and Walker you two look after things

here," Jes said.

It turned out that not all the stations had diesel pumps, but most did. The second one they stopped at had green rubber covers on some of their handles indicating that the pump was diesel. West pulled in and stopped the hammer.

After a visual search of the area Jes stepped out and walked around the building and back to the vehicle. "Dawson get out and give me a hand getting the fuel. The rest of you sit tight."

"Look for the opening in the ground. They should be marked, gas or diesel. Grab the bolt cutters. I'm sure they will have locks on them."

After checking two fillers marked gas they found the one marked diesel.

Jes lifted the cover off revealing a lock on a smaller cover. "Cut this lock off."

Dawson made child's play of the lock with the large bolt cutters. He reached into the hole, pulled the now useless lock off and tossed it over on the grass. He opened the lid and sniffed. "It's diesel."

Jes told Dawson. "Go get the hummer and pull it over here."

Dawson fast walked to the waiting vehicle, got in and fired it up. "We have us some fuel."

"Why didn't you guys' motion for us to drive over to where you were?" Lindsay said.

"If anyone is watching us and they want to rob us we don't want them to know that there is anyone in the hummer fixing to shoot them. And that is what we will do if we have to." West told her.

Lindsay looked at the men, tightened her lips and rubbed her hands together. "I know. I should have known that."

"Information to live by," West said.

Jes and Dawson stood by the filler hole turning the handle on the pump handle filling the drum on the trailer.

"Don't look now but we are being watched," Jes said.

"Yeah, I saw them too," Dawson said.

Jes put himself between the hummer and the men, turned and faced his men. He put his fist on his chest with two fingers out. He put his hand on his left shoulder.

"Two bodies across the road in the bushes," West said.

Two men headed across the road with their rifles pointed at the two Rangers.

"Just hold it right their fellows and nobody gets hurt," one of the men said.

"What do you want? We don't have any food or anything of any value," Jes said.

The men looked at the two soldiers' shirts. "Look what we got. Two of those Rangers that samson and us ran into at the school." The man looked at the M60 on top of the hummer. "No body working that gun now."

"How did you like that demonstration," Jes asked.

"Mighty impressive. Where is the other big fellow that was with you?"

"He's around somewhere.

The man looked around. "I don't see him. I guess we will just have to take that vehicle with us. Samson is going to thank us for this."

West walked from behind the Hummer. "Oh, I am

sure he would be very pleased. If you could take it that is."

"What do you mean if we could take it. No one to stop us."

Mike Hand raised up from inside the hummer, placed himself behind the M60 and turned it on the two men.

"That fellow up there will stop you," Dawson said.

The two men looked at the machine gun.

Jes smiled. "Drop the rifles and put your hands up, dick heads."

Two weapons hit the ground and four arms went skyward. The men stood straight as boards.

"We weren't going to take the thang. Neither one of us know how to drive it anyway," one of the men said.

"I knew you wasn't going to get it," Jes said. "Get on your knees."

"You can't make us. We know the Army won't kill us."

Jes and Dawson walked behind the men and stopped.

"In the back of the head?" Jes said to Dawson.

"Sure, why not. Then we have two less to worry about." Dawson answered.

Jes pulled the bolt back on his pistol. "Let's do it then."

"Oh, they're going to kill us," one of the men said.

The two Rangers hit the men in the back of their knee with the butt of their rifles. The men went down falling on their sides.

"I told you men to get on your knees."

The men grumbling about the hard concrete.

"We're down, just please don't kill us," one of the men said.

"Tell me something if you want to live. When will Samsom have his men hit the community?" Jes asked.

The two men looked at each other.

"You are not going to answer my question?"

The men smiled and one spoke. "You'll know."

Jes quickly pulled his forty-five and shoot the men in their heads. Unhook the trailer. Leave the pump here. They are hitting the community now."

The two Rangers jumped into the Hummer and Jes ordered. "West to ger to the college. They might under attack."

It took only a few minutes before the college came into view. They could hear gunshots. What they did not hear was the M60s firing.

"What is wrong with the M60s, I wonder." Dawson said.

Jes drove to a building next to the gym and stopped. Everyone jumped out and scrambled down alongside the side of the building, leaving Hand to control of the gun on the hummer. They saw two men on the hummers, but they were not Rangers.

Jes and Dawson fired causing the two men to fall off the hummers.

Jes saw the back door open. Seeing it was Walker he stepped from behind the building and waved his arm. When Walker saw him he waved and Jes and the others took off toward the building stepping over two bodies getting to the door.

West looked at the men on ground not moving. One's arm was twisted behind and bent backwards at the elbow. The other man's legs were bent out in an odd way. Both men's heads were twisted around.

Inside Jes leaned on the wall. "Give me a run down, guys."

"The two guys outside were up on the roof keeping a watch." Walker said.

Wilcox spoke up. "We asked a few people if they knew them when they showed up. A few said they live in their houses and show up occasionally and bring some food to swap. They were sure they were okay. After a couple of hours, we replaced them with two other guys. They mingled for a while and asked if they could see the hummers. I opened the door, and they shoved guns in our backs."

Then gunshots came from the guys out front. That is when we took those two out. Then we took fire from two men on the hummers.

The men were doing a good job holding them off out front. I believe they are waiting on their men to get the M60s working. That will never happen.

Walker you and Wilcox took aim and fired at two more men climbing on the hummer. Both men went down.

"Walker you and Wilcox keep watching here. The rest of you follow me," Jes said.

When they reached the front, they saw the rest of the gang piling onto the pickups and leaving.

"When they realized their men couldn't get the machine guns working, they decided it was time to go," Jes said.

The next morning Jes and West was standing outside the gym.

Jes's thoughts were on the green-eyed dark-haired

girl that had his attention. What she thought about marriage. He asked West, "Has Joy ever been married?"

West thought for a moment. "No, she has not."

"You two are close to the same age and both of you are still single."

West asked, "What are you getting at."

"Just you two are in your thirties and still single."

"As you are too."

Jes thought for a moment and said, "Lindsay has never been hitched either. Don't you think that's strange? The four of us our age, meeting those girls here and neither of us have ever been married."

"It is amazing how things can change," West said. "Think about it. For a year we were part of a six-man team guarding weapons. Now we are here talking about two girls we met just days ago. There's not that many people left in the world, and we end up with those two women."

Jes pressed his palms together and pushed, tightening his muscles in his arms. He relaxed his arms and said, "And they are not married. I wonder if fate did it. You know like it was meant to happen."

"You think it was pre-determined?"

"I don't know. What is your reason for never getting married?"

"Just like you, I have been to busy keeping alive the past few years. There is another reason. I wouldn't put a woman through the worry of will I make it home or not."

"That's part of my reason. The biggest reason is I am a selfish person."

"I haven't noticed that about you," West said.

"I'm talking about I never wanted to take care of or worry about anybody or answer to another person."

Their conversation was interrupted by a pickup roaring down the street.

Jes and West walked to the curb with their M4s at the ready position. The truck came into view and moving at a slow pace. Jes and West pointed their weapons at the driver and the passenger. The driver's hand went up holding a white piece of cloth.

"Would you just look at that," West said.

"They give up easy," Jes said and waved his arm for them to come to them.

The truck approached slowly, the cloth waiving. The driver stopped next to the two Rangers. The window on the passenger's side came down. The man spoke. "Are you the boss of those army guys?"

Jes looked the men over. Both were thin and under nourished. The driver had long unkept dark hair and a beard the color of his hair. The other man had greasy blond hair and a light-colored beard. Both men had yellow nicotine-stained teeth. "I am the sergeant in charge what can I do for you?"

"Sampson wants to see you. He wants to have a cease fire. So, you two can talk."

West leaned on the truck. "That is a pretty hefty request after you men bugged out yesterday empty handed."

"I don't think that has nothing to do with him wanted to talk," the driver said.

"What makes you say that?" Jes asked.

"The boss hasn't been himself the past few days. He isn't the same man he was when I met him. I'll say that."

The passenger nodded. "That's right. He is just not the same person he used to be. I think is Delilah that is the cause of it."

"Why do you say that?" West asked.

"He and Delilah was up all last night reading. I don't know what they are reading but the more they read the weird he gets."

"Tell him we'll honor a cease fire. Where does he want to have this parley?

"What is a parley."

"It's a negotiation that goes on between enemies. Usually between the top officials." Jes said.

"Well, that is what he wants to do. You can bring your weapons if you want to." The man put his arm out the window and handed Jes a note. His fingers were stained by cigarette smoke. This is the directions on how to get there, oh, and bring that preacher fellow you got with you. He said to come early cause what he wants to talk to you, about might take a while."

"He wants he reverend Ball there. What on earth for?"

"I am only privy to so, much information. And that isn't it." The man said.

"Tell your boss we'll see him shortly. With our weapons." Jes said.

The pickup took off without another word from the men.

The two Rangers walked back to the Gym. Jes went one way looking for Lindsay and West went looking for Ball.

Jes found the girl he thought he was falling in love with and showed her the note with the directions on it.

"It's a summer camp is on a lake about twenty

minutes north of town," she told him.

"Do you know where the reverend is?" Jes asked.

"Yes, he is in the break area."

"He wants the reverend to come with us. Maby somebody died and he wants a funeral service."

"By all means take the reverend," Lindsay said.

Jes found Ball sitting at a table talking to West and drinking coffee.

Ball got up and he and West met Jes and Lindsay.

"Are you dressed for a trip?" Crier asked. "We will be gone for the better part of the day."

"I guess so, but I want to tell Laura I will be gone for a while."

"Do it and meet me at the hummers out back."

CHAPTER 23

The men reached the place on the map and Jes stopped on the road to scope the place out. A man got out of a pickup parked on a side road and motioned for them to follow him."

Ball was scanning the area. "Are you sure those guys are on the up and up. They look desperate. They might just want some hostages."

"I believe they are. Their man sounded desperate when we talked to Samson. I believe they are on the edge of starvation."

"Maybe they figured the only way they can get food now is to negotiate for it," Ball said. "You know Samson is not the sharpest knife in the drawer."

The pickup stopped in front of the largest building in the camp and the driver got out. He motioned for Jes and Ball to get out. "This way gentlemen."

The two men followed the man into the building. Sampnon and Delilah were standing at the far wall behind what looked like an altar. Samson was reading from a book while his girlfriend listened to the words so, intense they didn't notice that Jes and Ball had entered the room.

Ball put a hand on Jes's arm stopping him and they listened for a moment. "He is reading scripture from the bible. The Old Testament."

Sampson closed the book and began praying. He

stopped when he noticed the two men. "Our guest are her Delilah. Welcome please join us," he told them.

Ball followed Jes across the floor. Is this a cult these men have started, Jes thought? He looked around to see if there were any dead animals that had been used for a sacrifice. He looked for cups they might drink blood from. But there was nothing to indicate there had been any kind of ritual killing going on. The men stopped at the altar that was made from pieces of scrap wood. Jes looked around again for any of Samson's men. The room was empty of everything except for several small chairs. There was a curtain hanging from the ceiling about twelve feet wide. Jes made a step toward to the curtain.

Samson answered his curiosity. "We are alone. I have no doubt that we could not withstand what your men would bring down on us if we were to do harm to you. But that is not the reason for us being alone."

"So, what are we here to talk about? Is it going to be some kind of work together agreement after what happened yesterday?" Jes asked.

"In one way yes but not for that reason." Samson said.

"You are not even close Sergeant," Deliah said. "Just listen to what Samson has to say."

Jes nodded. "Well, we are here at your request, so talk."

Samson looked at the two men moving from one to the other smiling. "Deliah and I desire to be baptized."

Jes and Ball stood frozen staring at the two. "You want what?" Jes said.

Samsom stood tall. "You heard correctly, we both

wish for the reverend Ball to baptize us. After that he will perform our marriage ceremony."

Ball thought, this leader of this ruthless gang suddenly wants to repent. "Are you going to atone for his sins, Samson?"

"Let's not get into that right yet. Let's just do one thing at a time. I'll need some time to adjust."

"You do realize if I marry you two it will not be legal in the eyes of the law." Ball said.

"It will be a marriage in the eyes of God." Samson said. "I never could see why the government had to give their permission anyway for people to marry."

Jes rubbed his neck. "Samson damned you are right. What did you do before the virus hit."

Samson looked at the floor. "I was a." He looked at the two men. "I was a men's underwear model. Not a sleezy model. High-end magazines. Delilah was a runway model. High fashion clothes."

"What brought this change over you two?" Ball asked.

The man who had come to a sudden change held the bible up. "We have been reading this. It has some heavy stuff in it."

"It has cool things in too," Delilah said. "Like those two people who lived in that garden with all the fruit. The girl was a bit—not a good person. She tricked that guy Adam into eating the apple that they were not supposed to eat. She was the cause of all the evil in the world. Isn't that just like a woman?"

"Some of them, yes." Ball said.

"I believe a lot are that way," the girl said.

"That man built a boat big enough for his family and all those animals. That could have been the line in the sand for me. I might have given up," Samson said. "But that man didn't."

Ball said, "Yes, that was Noah, and the boat was an Ark. God spared him, his family and two of all the animals in the world so everything could start over."

Samson looked up at the ceiling. "It must have been a big boat." He looked at the reverend. "I want to be able to walk through the valley of the shadow of death and fear no evil."

"Amen. You got the idea, brother. Palms 23:4," Ball said.

"I feel that is where we are right now. The valley of death," The soon to be Christian said.

Ball stretched his arms out in front of him, bent his elbows with his fist closed. "We had better get this done. Let us pray," he said.

After the prayer Jes looked around. "Where are we going to do this? That lake is ice cold."

"I have that covered." Samson walked to a curtain hanging across the room and pulled it back exposing a large vat and a large potbellied stove. "Been heating water all night. I have some robes I lifted from a church, so we don't get our clothes wet. I will get the fire going in the stove."

Reverand Ball focused on the tub filled with water.

"How many baptisms will I be doing." He walked over and put his hand in the water. "Feels just right.

"Not everyone has seen the light. Twelve of my men and us two," Samson said.

"Praise the Lord. Bring on the sinners," Ball said.

Samson walked to the door, opened it, and motioned for his group to come in. After the last person entered the building samson turned to Ball. "It appears that all my group has had a change of heart. There will be twelve men and six women to take the plunge, Reverand Ball."

Ball put his hands together. "The more the better."

Because there were only ten robes the ones going first went behind two sheets hanging across the opposite side of the room from the vats. After they had their dip the last eight had to change into wet robes for their turn.

When Samson and Delilah's turn rolled around, they came out in dry white robes trimmed in gold lace.

"I saved these for us," the groom to be said and stepped into the vat. Delilah stepped in behind him and they stood facing Reverand Ball.

"Which shall go first?" Ball asked.

"I shall go first," Samson said. "I will be the start of my family doing as I do."

When the baptisms were over, Ball raised his hands in the air. "Praise the lord. I have saved a community."

The last ceremony of the day was the marring of Samson and Delilah. After that was over, they had a feast of vegetables and a deer meat from buck that one of the men had bagged the day before.

"Fresh meat. The Lord in providing today," Ball said. "I'll have a slice of those ribs."

Jes grabbed up a plate and headed to the meat line. "I would like to have a cut off of the rump."

The Ranger and Ball stayed for an hour enjoying the food and the conversation.

"No one will believe this." Jes said. On their back to the community. "You know every damn—sorry reverend. That entire deer was devoured."

"I am not surprised. That group resembled a hoard of heathens while they were eating."

"They were before you gave them the dip," Jes said.

"I am not sure I believe it happened myself." Ball said. "But I feel it inside me, therefore it had to have happened. I believe I will take the act of preaching up again."

"You have a congregation waiting on you. Tomorrow is Sunday. There is a chapel on campus."

As Jes piloted the hummer back toward the college he thought about the wedding Ball had performed. Marriage wasn't something he had thought much about. He had valued his freedom to come and do whatever came to his mind without having to tell anyone. The main reason was that he did not want to have to worry about anyone. And he didn't.

That was until he met the green-eyed, dark-haired beauty who had moved into his head and assumed free residence. He had never thought about renting out space in his head. But he had no notion of evicting her. Yep, she slipped up, moved in, and closed herself in as tightly as a tick.

The Town

Dean sat at one end of a bench in the town square with a cup of coffee in his hand. He was wearing a red parka. On his head was a ball cap with a sheriff's badge sewn on it. Jerry sat at the opposite end bundled in a blue coat of the same make. He was holding a coffee cup.

They were discussing the group they sent out three days earlier. The conversation turned to John and Ralph, a couple of men who decided to leave town for a while to scout for other people.

Dean took a sip of coffee and lowered the cup. "I wonder what those two are doing. They have sent people here so there are folks out there."

Jerry was looking at two men across the street talking. "Think about it," he said. "What are the odds that they would run across that young couple John's family knew."

"Lucky for that couple," Dean said and motioned across the street. "You see that fellow over there with the blond hair."

Jerry looked at the blonde-haired kid who was sitting on a bench across the square. "Yeah, he's a sneaky, conniving, cuss."

Dean lifted his cap, ran a hand through his hair and put his cap back on his head. "Oh, well, it's a little cool are you ready to go in and tackle those reports."

Jerry stood. "Yeah, they are not going to write themselves,"

The boy across the park was named James Luther. The girls eighteen and above call him cutie pie because he has a smooth complexion like a girl, curly hair, and blue eyes.

The younger teen girls adore him. He is seventeen years old, not what one would call good-looking; he is a pretty boy. To the older teen girls, he is not girlish, he just lacks masculinity. But he is a liar and a con.

A seventeen-year-old boy asked one of the girls his age why she didn't go for him like the younger girls did?

Her answer. Would you go with a girl who looked like a man.

A 1965 Red Chevrolet SS pulled to the curb and parks. The car belongs to Miles Simmons. Miles's daddy drove the car off the showroom floor when it was brand new.

Angela Simmons, the granddaughter of Miles Simmons, got out and closed the door of the Chevrolet. She was a pretty girl of sixteen. Her parents didn't make it through the virus. She has a sister who is twenty years old and a twenty-two-year-old brother. Miles and the three kids live in a house four blocks from the town. Even though Angela is young she teaches elementary kids at school.

Angela knows James Luther, but she is not taken to him like some of the younger girls. She didn't see James when she stopped and went into the clothing store.

The blonde boy sat and watched as she went into the store and waited for her to come out.

When she got to her car James approached her and began talking. "You want to ride around for a little while? Maybe get out of town for a spell. I haven't been away from here in six months."

"Wow, now that you mentioned it neither have I. Where is your car?" she asked.

"Oh, it's at home. I needed some exercise, so I walked to town."

"I would like to, but I can't burn my papa's gas. He needs it to last a week for him to get to work at the stables and back home. It's a mile from our house."

James smiled. "Don't worry about it, I'll fill it up from what I have in my car when we get back home."

"You will? I'd love to get out of town and ride around. But only if you're sure You can replace my gas."

"No problem, let's go." James jumped into the passenger's seat and rubbed his hands together. He looked at the gas gauge when Angela started the car. "Oh, boy, it's full we can go all day."

"I can't be gone that long," Angela said.

"Let's drive over to the meeting place?"

Angela looked at James. "Where is that?"

"Just drive I'll show you where to go."

After driving for ten miles James directed her onto an unpaved road that led to a large clearing where several cars were parked. Looking around she knew most of the kids there.

James and Angela got out and mingled with the others. After an hour a few suggested they go to another place.

Angela protested but James told her that they would not stay long.

Three miles later they stopped at another place where there were trails in the woods they followed for an hour before going back to the car and driving home.

When they got back to town James told Angela. "Just drop me off where you picked me up."

Angela parked in the same spot they left from. "Oh, there is my granddad. He can go with me to your house and get the gas. That way he won't be upset with me for being gone so long."

Miles Simmons opened the driver's door. "Where have you been young lady, I have been worried sick?"

"We wanted to get out of town for a while, and we

went for a ride." She looked at the boy. "Where do you live?"

James smiled. "Why do you want to know where I live?"

"James, you owe me."

James looked at the gas gauge. "A half of a tank. That is not bad."

"It not enough."

"Yeah, but I can't let you have mine. I need it."

"You said that you would replace what I burned, and we started with a full tank and now I have a half tank. It won't last my grandaddy a week and he'll have to walk to work and back. Don't you remember I told you that."

"I remember you telling me, but I still can't give mine up."

"James, you promised, and we need it."

"Sorry pretty thing."

Miles was six feet four inches tall and two hundred and forty pounds. He was seventy-five years old. That should have made him an easy fellow to get over on. "You told my granddaughter that you would put gas in my car if she rode you around?"

James got out of the car. "Yeah, but I'm not going to give my gas away."

"That's all you have to say?" Miles said.

"Yep," James said and started to walk off. "See you. I enjoyed the free ride."

Miles grabbed James by the shoulder and spun him around. "I want what you promised my granddaughter boy."

James put his face out at Miles. "Want in one hand and piss in the other and see which one gets full first."

Miles drew back and came down on James's face with a fist that was hard as a rock.

The blonde-haired smart ass hit the ground. "Oh, you have almost killed me."

Dean and Jerry were standing across the street and hurried over.

"What's going on here, Miles?" Dean said.

Angela and Miles told Dean what caused the ruckus.

Dean pulled the boy to his feet. "Did you promise this young lady you would fill her tank up if she rode you around?"

"Yes, but I need what I have. At least she got to spend time with me."

Dean took the boy by the collar and led him to his car. Follow us to this boy's house. We'll get what he owes you."

Miles and Angela got in their car and follow the police car.

At the boy's house Dean made James transfer enough gas to fill Mile's tank.

"That's not the first time I have had trouble out of that boy," Dean said.

"Thank you, a lot," Miles said.

CHAPTER 24

The Mission

Natalie took over for Les, and helped Ruth clean and put everything away after breakfast was over.

After devouring their meal, their five guests had fallen asleep or passed out. It was difficult to tell which. After packing, instead of waking the people up, Les, Billy and Bentley left to scout around and see what the area had to offer.

A couple of hours later they were back. Les wanted to ask his company about other people in the area. He walked over and squatted beside the man and shook him until he opened his eyes.

The man jerked back startled to see everyone. "I'm sorry, I had forgotten where I was. Thank you for the food and water. We would not have made it through the day if we had not come across you and your friends. It's not easy knowing who you can trust. I took a chance with you all, and I am glad I did." He looked at his family. "I don't know what we are going to do."

Les held out a cup of coffee. "You're right you all could die. How long have you had your family roaming around?"

The man took the cup. "Several days. I lost count."

"Where did you come from?"

"Up the road a piece. Our community was doing good. We planted crops in the spring, and they had produced well. There was enough food to feed all of us through the winter."

"Wait, you mean you had a community with other people and a farm?"

"Yes and still do. Things were going good until a gang of thugs showed up."

"Hold on a minute," Les told the man and called for the others to come over. "I want everybody to hear what you have to say. What is your name?"

"Jason." He pointed to the others. "My wife, Rita, my daughter Francis. This is Wonda and her daughter Lily. Wonda's husband is locked up back at the town we all live in. It's a town called Haynesville."

"I know where that town is." Jerry said. "It's just South of here about seventeen miles. How many people are there?"

"There are seventy-five of us. Now they are slaves doing what ever those men and the women they brought with them want them to do."

Les, let the man settle down. "Okay, Jason, how many men and women are holding your people."

"Twenty-two men and twelve women. One day they just rolled up on us while we were working the crops. They broke into our houses the first night they were there while we were asleep. They took our weapons and dragged the kids and women out and threatened to kill them if we retaliated."

"What kind of weapons did you people have?" Les asked.

"We just had rifles, shotguns, and handguns. Even if they don't kill everyone, they will keep all the food for themselves, and the people will starve."

Les looked at Jerry. "What do you think? Should we have a look at the situation?"

"Twenty-two men and I'm sure the women will fight along with them. That's five to one odd," Jerry said.

Richard perked up. "Too bad for them." He held his hands up like he was holding a weapon and moved back and forth like he was spraying bullets while making a shooting sound. He put his hands down. "We have that M60 I told you about. I hid it in the back. There's plenty of ammo for it."

"What are our chances?" Jerry asked.

"If we catch them in a bunch and by surprise, we can cut the odds down to where we have an advantage."

Jerry stared at the man and his family. "If we don't those people in that town they will die. I don't want that on my hands."

"It's settled. Let's have a look at the community those people left from," Les said.

Jason told Les. "I recommend we exit off the 75 onto Highway 224 and go down to Highway 341. That will take us to the center of the community. They all are staying in some houses two blocks from where we'll hit town. During the day they keep guard on us and make the women wash their clothes and prepare food for them."

"Do they bunch up in a group," Les asked.

"At night they party," Jason said. "They broke into a liquor and beer warehouse somewhere and stole more whiskey than they could ever drink. They congregate around several fires they build in drums. In the early evening and get drunk. Most of them will be together."

"We'll hold up here until almost dark." Les said.

Richard rubbed his hands together. "Haw, haw. I'll get the M60 ready. I have been waiting for the chance to use that baby."

At dusk they loaded up and headed to the town Jason and his family called home.

Jason, his family, and friends were in the pickup with Billy driving and Richard, standing in the bed leaning on the cab.

A few miles from town they cut off their lights and slowed to a safe speed of twenty miles per hour. Richard had the M60 loaded and ready. He had brought several blankets from the motel they spent the night in and placed them on top of the truck to rest the bipod and gun on.

When they rounded the last curve before reaching town, they could see the glow of the fires the gang built in the drums to keep warm.

Jason told them. "The first street we will come to is 3rd Street. If we go left, we will come out one block North of where they stage themselves and party every night."

They took the rout Jason suggested and stopped the trucks behind a building one block from the fires.

Les got out, walked to the corner, and spotted the gang where Jason said they would be. After getting the best count he could he went back to the pickup. "How can we be sure none of the town's people are not in the crowd?" he asked Jason.

"They lock everybody in a building at night. That

way they don't have to keep watch on them."

"They're scattered out. We need them grouped up," Richard said.

Jason said, "See those tables between the drums of fire. That is where they have the food, and they all line up to pile it on plates. Just give them a little while and they will be pushing and shoving each other like animals to get to the food."

Ruth stared down the street toward the fires. "It's hard to believe what this virus has turned some people into."

Les said. "It turned some people. Others it just brought out what was always in them."

After waiting twenty minutes the gang began to gather in two lines at the tables.

A big man stepped up on a table and yelled. "Bring him over."

Two gang members pulled one of the town's men by a rope around his neck. They stopped at the table the big man was standing on.

"This is what happens when one of you leave." He raised a pistol and shot the man in the head.

"Oh, my God," Jason said, "I caused that. I need to go back before he shoots somebody else."

"No, the damage is done. We are going to do what we came to do and unleashed our damage on them."

The gang began to gather at the tables pushing each other like the animals they are.

Billy pulled the pickup to the middle of the intersection, turned toward the men, and stopped.

After a few minutes they stopped shoving each other lined up on both sides of the tables.

"That's what I'm talking about, you scumbags,"

Richard said and without warning Richard cut loose on them with the machine gun.

Les on one side of the road let loose with the M16. Billy on the other side began firing. Bentley in the middle of the road sent a volley of bullets toward the gang. Men were dropping like flies. Within a minute the gang had been reduced to seven men and two women. The thugs returned fire hitting Bentley in the shoulder. Richard cut loose again with the machine gun, and they took off running in different directions.

"Let them go. It will be too dangerous to go after them in the dark. We'll get them in the morning," Les said.

Four minutes later three pickups entered the street three blocks South of where the gang members lay on the ground. The trucks headed South at a high rate of speed.

"What a better way to clear a town than have the bad guys turn tail and run."

"They killed ten people in our community," Jason said. "They're getting away and they'll be back."

Les said, "They are not going anywhere."

"Let's go get them," Richard yelled.

Les, Richard, and Billy took off after the trucks. When they caught the truck Billy pulled alongside one of the trucks. Richard and Les began firing until they were sure all the passengers were dead. Billy caught the second truck and made short work on the occupants. The third truck was to far ahead for them to catch.

Billy stopped at the to get a count. Between the two trucks there were five men and. The two women escaped with two men.

"I can live with those four getting away," Les said.

"At least we got the bastard that shot the guy.

"It's over guys. Billy, help me get these weapons out of the trucks," Richard said.

Back in the town they gather up all the weapons and ammo. After that they went to where the gang was living and cleaned it of all the ammo.

"Stack those weapons on the sidewalk. Everyone can grab what they want. There is plenty of ammo. That way the community can protect themselves," Les said.

When they were finished stacking the rifles Jerry commented. "This area looks like a war zone."

Richard, still standing in the bed of the truck leaning on the cab, looked around. "We left five bodies down the road."

Les stepped out onto the ground. "Count the bodies here. We want to be sure they are all accounted for.

After getting count Richard told Les. "All dead and accounted for."

"Jason, round up all the folks and tell them what happened. And they are free again. Make sure each person who in able gets a weapon. Is there someone here that can look at our man's shoulder?"

Jason's wife said, "I'll take care of him. I'm a nurse. We need to get him to our infirmary."

"You guys have got a health facility, food, and homes. I would say you folks are in pretty good shape," Ruth said.

Jerry said to Jason, "I'll go with you. I want to run something by you."

"Sure, I am open for suggestions. What's on your mind?"

"We are looking for a town to move to from North Georgia. We are also looking for people to join us. You have things going well here. So, I'll not ask you to leave what you have. I believe we will make good neighbors."

"That sounds like a good idea, and we would feel safe with you guys close by," Jason said.

"We will help you as much as we can. And it might be better if you didn't take your people to where all those bodies are," jerry said.

"I believe you are right."

"Any chance our injured man can stay here, and we will pick him up on our way back through," Jerry asked.

"Sure, thing but you and your friends should stay a few days to rest up."

CHAPTER 25

John and Ralph

John and Ralph had spent the night in a house on a hill overlooking the road. They rotated between sleep and guard duty.

After a sandwich and coffee, they heated some and both shaved before heading North.

It wasn't long before they came upon a crossroad with a couple of buildings. There was a sign that let them know there had been a Bar B Q stand there before. They slowed and took in the scene.

Ralph pointed. "Piece of paper on that door of that building over there."

John pulled up to the front of the building and stopped.

Ralph eased out and looked around. Satisfied, they were alone; he walked over and read the note. "Well, I'll be damned," he said loud enough for John to hear. He walked back to the truck.

"What was the be damned about," John asked.

"The note said all the residents of the town left looking for more people to build a settlement. It named a few towns they would go to." He reached in and pulled the map off the dash, walked to the front of the truck, and unfolded it on the hood. His index finger traced the lines representing roads. He looked up and pointed. "Thirty miles that way to the next town that had more than two stores."

"Don't worry, you fellows are not going anywhere." A man stepped through the door the note was attached to and walked out a few feet pointing a shotgun at them. He wore a red winter shirt. "I got double aught buck in this thing. Do you know what it'll do to a man? Dumb question, you know what it'll do don't you?"

"You guys have just donated your truck." Came from another man who stepped out wearing a camouflage shirt pointing a revolver. He went over and looked in the bed of the pickup. "Looks like we got plenty of gas too. What's in this?" He raised the lid on the cooler, reached in and uncovered the food. "Fried chicken. You fellows are too well supplied to be just roaming around."

The man held the pistol out as he walked to the cab and looked in. Got an AR15 and an M4 in here. I bet we could persuade them to tell us where they live. Could be we might get everything we need from there."

"We bought that stuff from a couple living on a farm in Dawsonville," John said.

"I don't think you did that. We were in that town two days ago and the people there are not hospitable." I would say you are from a town somewhere around here. That chicken fried nicely as it is, I bet you got some women there too."

"The man with the red shirt said, "We want to shoot them here or in one of the buildings?"

"Not here or in the building," green shirt said. "We'll walk them off in the woods. They might have some friends that decide to come looking for them. Not bad putting that note on that door to get people to stop and read it."

"Enough talking let's get this over with. I want a piece of that chicken. Okay, guys, that way." The man with the pistol pointed.

Ralph was behind the man wearing the green shirt leading them into the woods. John was behind him, and red shirt was bringing up the rear. The terrain was steep, rocky, and loaded with trees with low limbs.

"A little piece more and we'll be over the hill," Red shirt said.

Green shirt and Ralph ducked under a low limb.

"This is as good a place as any," Red shirt said.

John looked back and saw him pull the hammer back on the revolver. John pushed a low limb with his hands and thought, the oldest trick in the book. He ducked, let the limb go and yelled as it caught the man in the face knocking him to the ground. John was on him before he knew what was going on. Green shirt turned to see what was going on. Ralph grabbed him around the waist, picked him up and slammed him to the ground, his head hitting a rock sending the shotgun to the ground. In a few seconds, the situation had changed in John and Ralph's favor.

They got the men on their feet and motioned them down the hill.

Being in charge posed a question for them. The men just a minute earlier were going to kill them. That begged for a decision as to what to do with them now. Let the men go and someone else would fall victim to them. Even if they tied them up, they would get loose.

The decision was made for them when the men

slipped on the wet leaves. They came up each with a rock the size of a baseball. They drew back and threw them. One caught John on his right shoulder causing him to drop the gun. The other one got Ralph by the shirt. But it didn't do the man any good. Because it knocked Ralph back and his hand jerked causing the shotgun, he had taken from the man to go off. The buckshot turned the man's face into hamburger meat. This startled red shirt, and he bent and picked up another rock, but he didn't see John pick up the gun. He was two feet away with the rock raised when the gun went off and the bullet hit him in his chest.

They left the men where they fell and went back to their pickup, got in and drove off.

"I guess we were a bit careless back there," Ralph said.

"Yes, we were but we are wiser now. Damn is there anyone left that can be trusted?" John said.

"Yes," Ralph said, "You and I."

John slowed the truck and eased along. "The best place to start would be in the middle of town. When we see a house look for smoke coming from the chimney."

They found the doors open in most of the buildings in the next town. They looked as though the stores and found nothing. The last dwelling looked like it hadn't been visited in months.

In the next town John stopped in a gravel parking lot, got out and walked to a building with a closed door and pushed on it. The door wouldn't move. He yelled to Ralph, "Somebody had a reason to lock it."

Ralph got out, holding a blanket folded several times. He wrapped it around his shoulders and took off running. When he got to the door, he stopped. "On second thought." He lifted a leg and thrust his foot against the door. It opened with such force it slammed against the wall on the inside. "That's how you get in a locked building."

John stood looking at the open door. "You get no argument from me. What was the blanket for?"

"I was going to run into it at first. But I didn't want to break my shoulder." Ralph went inside and examined the lock "It was locked from the inside. There must be a reason it was. All the shelves are empty except for turned over empty cans."

They eased down the rows of shelves eying the empty cans that were left.

They stopped and looked at a closed door in the back.

"It smells like someone has been cooking Polk Salad," John whispered. He eased to the door, pushed it open and looked inside. A finger went to his lips as he looked back at Ralph. He curled his finger a couple of times.

Ralph advanced to the door, stepped around John, and stuck his head inside. He looked back at John and whispered, "They look to be in their late teens. Hold on a second?" He removed two candy bars from his pocket. "This might take some of the fright out of them." He tossed the bars next to two girls lying on the floor.

One of the girls opened her eyes and looked at the candy next to her. She saw the other bar and shook the girl next to her. "Amy, look."

Amy opened her eyes. Without hesitation she grabbed the bar. Both girls tore the wrappers off and shoved the candy in their mouths, bit off a piece, chewed and swallowed. They scoffed the bars down before looking at the men standing in the door.

Amy looked up. "Reba, the door."

The girls, both with frightened looks on their faces stared at the men looking at them.

"Reba and Amy are your names?"

The girls stared at the men for a moment.

"Yes, who are you and you?" the one the other called Amy said.

"Just two fellows passing by."

"Please don't hurt us," the one named Reba pleaded.

"If I did my wife would do far more damage to me than I could do to you girls," John said. "And my daughters would too."

"And my future wife would shoot me if I did. I can't run fast enough to dodge a bullet from Betty," Ralph said.

"You have a family?" Amy asked John.

"Yes, I sure do. I gather you girls haven't eaten anything lately."

Reba pointed to the smelly greens on the wood stove. "That is all we can find."

The girls threw their covers off and got to their feet, looking at the two men like shy children. Each had stringy hair, dirty faces and their clothes were ragged. They both were tall, maybe five-nine and slim like most people now days. Amy had dark hair; Reba was a blonde. They were sure the girls would be nice looking when cleaned up.

"You girls hold tight I'll be right back." Ralph turned, walked to the front and out the busted door and proceeded to the truck. After collecting a few items from a cooler and putting them in a bag. He reversed his route back to the store and sat the bag on a table. He called out for the girls to come out of and get it.

"Breast or thigh?" he said.

The girls looked at him, mouths open. "I thought you were nice men."

"We have fried chicken thighs and breasts. I am sorry for the way I presented them. That's what my wife would ask our girls when they were young."

The girls looked at each other, then ran to the bag.

"Who gives a damn how you say it. Breasts and thighs please for each of us," Reba said.

Ralph pulled food from the bag. "Coming up." He prepared paper plates of chicken, corn, potato cakes and corn bread.

The girls wasted no time sitting down and digging into the food. After a few bites, Amy stopped eating long enough to look up. "I guess we are acting like animals."

"That's alright, hungry animals," Ralph said.

"Reba said, Hungry isn't the word for it, Mister. Our asses are reaching starvation."

Ralph handed them a cup of water. "We can make some coffee if you two want it."

"Coffee, I love coffee," Amy said.

Reba looked up. "Oh, hell yes, me too, I need something to energize my butt. Wait a minute. Are we dead and gone to, uh, up there?"

"Not hardly," Ralph said and filled the percolator with water and put a few scoops of coffee in the strainer. "I'm going outside for some wood to start a fire." He came back in with two hands full of small twigs and put them in a portable stove. Next, he used a long stem butane lighter to start a fire. He put the coffee pot on one of the eyes. "It doesn't take long to make. We'll walk around and keep an eye on the area just in case somebody shows up here while you girls finish eating."

After five minutes the men came back to the store.

"Boy, that coffee smells good," John said.

"It has never smelled better," Reba said.

John filled their cups with the mesmerizing liquid. "What are your girls last names?"

Amy spoke up. "Amy Blevins."

"My name is Reba Atkins."

"Okay, my name is John Carstairs, and his name is Ralph Bishop. How did you two get up here?"

"We were damn idiots. That's how," Reba said.

Ralph smiled. "Not why you are here. How did you get here?"

Amy looked up from her cup. "We trusted the wrong people."

Reba blurted out, "You can say that shit again. The bastards thought they could play us."

Ralph, now used to her language, offered them a piece of jerky. "Play you? As in how?"

Amy took the food from Ralph. "They are boys from our neighborhood. Our parents died and they said we should leave the city and go to the mountains where we can raid some of the smaller stores."

Reba spoke up. "Yeah, that's what they said, they wanted to do. After we got up here, they said to put out or get out. By God here we are. Out of their car and hungry as Hell. But we are still virgins. And going to stay that way until we get a husband."

Amy sat holding her cup close to her mouth with both hands trying to cover her blushing. "Reba is telling the truth. This coffee is, so good."

John poured himself a cup of coffee, filled Ralph's cup and stared at the girls. "Couldn't get any plainer than that." He thought poor things, they have been through Hell, and they still have their sanity. He gave them time to finish their drink and asked them. "More coffee?"

Both girls held their cups up and John filled them. "How old are you girls?"

"Eighteen and the sad thing is. We didn't get to graduate high school. We were seniors. My mom and I went shopping, and I had bought a pretty dress to wear. She was proud of me for committing to Georgia Tech." Tears filled Amy's eyes when she finished.

"Damn, I was all set to put on my new dress and shake my butt across that stage," Reba said. "Then I was on my way to drama school. I was going to move to Hollywood and become an actor."

Amy, holding her cup close to her mouth said. "She would have made it too. I have seen her in some of our high school plays. She can sing and dance."

"You girls have bigger things to think about now than graduation," Ralph said.

"You're right. Like where are those two assholes that left us here?" Reba said. "Can we borrow a gun to shoot them with?"

John nodded his head. "Yeah, we have a few. How much damage do you want to inflict on them?"

"As much as I can," Reba said.

"You could kill them with our guns," John said.

"Oh, no I couldn't do that," Amy said.

Reba said, "I could shoot them in their legs."

John puckered his lips. "Oh, well, let's find them and you can cripple them."

Reba stood. "I am ready. I got some of my energy back. I might shoot that thing between their legs off." When she took Amy's arm and pulled her up, her friend swayed and put her hand on her head. "Whoo, I'm not as strong as I thought I was."

"We should let your food settle. You need to get your strength back first. After that we'll concentrate on the boys." Ralph said. "Before we go off looking to avenge your girl's reputation let us tell you two something that just might make you forget about shooting those boys."

"I doubt you can tell me anything that will change my mind about that but go ahead it must be good."

"Well," Ralph said. "There are not a lot of people left in the world. Any time someone is killed that is one less. Some people are mean, and the only choice might be to kill them or be killed."

John told the girls. "We live in a town you girls will be welcomed to live in. And it would be better than staying here and starving and looking for those boys. Or worse things could happen. You could be killed by an animal or someone." John told them about the age breakdown, and they needed young people to keep the town going in the future.

Reba spoke up. "Or some men might come by and give us the options to put out or die. If it's not a cult or slave camp for young girls, used to populate the town I think we should go with you."

"Your mind is always thinking. And about the

worst-case scenario," Amy said.

Reba smiled. "Well, I wonder if I'll meet a boy there and get married? My kids and my grandkids will grow up there."

Amy pointed at her friend. "You overthink everything, too, Reba."

"It's the future I'm thinking about. I can see it now. My grandmother helped start this town, fifty years ago."

"Amy laughed. "Oh, yes, and how about this. My great grandmother and great grandfather were two of the original settlers of Amy and Reba Ville."

"Are they some young boys there? Nice ones that know how to treat girls?"

"Might be one or two running around town," Ralph said.

"Really there are several? Just running around town all day like ants? I can see it now; we just grab one by the arm. I love it," Reba said, and they all laughed.

"It's up to you girls. First, we need to find you two some clothes."

They look down at their tattered garments.

Amy pulled the dress out. "We do look a mess, don't we."

"Where are you girls from," Ralph asked.

"Alpharetta," Amy said, "And we had gathered up enough food to last for a few months before it was all taken from the stores. It got to where we were afraid to go out of our house. Things got worse and it was dangerous just to stay in our home in town. The boys would come by to check on us every day."

"On one if those days when they came by," Reba

said. "They said they had witnessed a person being beaten to death by four guys. They thought the man was pulled out of his house."

"When it got dark, we loaded everything in the trunk and a pull trailer and piled into Randy's car and headed north."

Amy told them. "A store had left canned food and sodas in them. We had coffee for the first two months. We have been in North Georgia for three months sleeping in houses and buildings. Living off the food we had brought with us and finding some here and there. The boys were with us up until a week ago. Then they pull their stunt."

Reba said, "We found a map and luckily for us Amy's dad had taught her how to read and follow the lines on one. Which she said represent roads."

"It was difficult being left alone and walking from town to town. This store we were in had a few cans of beans and greens left in it," Amy said.

"We have no idea why the boys turned on us the way they did." Reba said. "I knew their hormones raged at that age, but not to the point that it caused them to go bat shit crazy," Reba said.

Amy scratched her head. "One boy's name is Randy; he came to our school two years before the virus hit. We had known the other boy since the first year of high school. His name is Allen. Both had played football for high school."

Reba leaned on one of the shelves. "We believe the put out or get out thing was Randy's idea. It started one day when he just up and said he thought we should have sex. I told him he was full of shit. He could go off and do himself."

Amy, looking embarrassed, said. "Every day it was the same thing. Randy making suggestions and Allen not saying much. Then one day Randy cursed and threatened us. I told him he would get a knee between the legs if he laid a hand on me. Then he told us there were two choices. The boys threw two sets of clothes at us when we got out."

Ralph and John noticed on a few occasions while Reba talked Amy's face turned a light shade of red.

They stepped outside the building and stood in front of it looking around.

"I believe I'll check in the rest of these buildings for anything useful," Ralph said after loading their equipment in the truck.

"You go one way, I'll go the other," John said.

"Oh, you can forget about finding anything worth having. We have gone through all these buildings," Amy said.

Reba leaned on the door frame. "Amy is telling you the truth. There isn't anything worth a damn in any of them."

John took a step toward the door. "Well, you know what they say. One man's junk is another man's treasure. We won't be long."

"Hold on, you can't leave us standing here. You never know who will come up," Amy said.

"That is true, wait on us." Reba agreed.

Amy went with John. At first, it seemed all the buildings were left unlocked. Ralph and Reba found the same thing the way they went. When they met at the last building at the back of a parking lot John tried the door, and it was locked.

Reba looked at Amy and back at the men. "We

didn't try this one. I think I saw it, but we were scared to come back here."

Ralph held up a scabbard and pulled a bowie knife from it. "I found this in a drawer behind a counter. I think the man who owned the place put the handle on it. It has a fourteen-inch blade."

"That is a big knife," Reba said. "I wish I had seen it. But it doesn't matter now."

"Oh, it will prove to be handy," Ralph said.

"Well, I guess we didn't look good enough."

John eyed the knife in Ralph's hand. "You were looking for food. Which you did not find."

Ralph slid the blade of the knife between the door jam and the door and pressed the blade on top of the slide that keeps the door closed. He twisted the knife, moving the slide in just a little and pulled on the door trapping the slide, he rested the knife on the slide again and pushed the door in to ease the tension and twisted the blade again, moving the cylinder in. He pulled the door toward him to hold the slide in place while he placed the blade on it. He repeated the maneuver until the slide was free. The last time he pushed the door it opened.

"Wow, magic," Reba said. "Are you one of those guys that does tricks?"

"No, it's simple thuggery. I can also open it with a credit card or a driver's license." Ralph said, stepped through the door and turned his flashlight on. "Take a look at this."

John eased through the door and pressed the button on his flashlight. "If this is what I think it is we have struck pay dirt. Take a gander at all those new batteries."

"And those new automobile parts. We have some vehicles that need parts. There are some books over there. Most likely reference books to match pares to a car or truck."

"Wasn't all that on computer?" John said.

It was but maybe they had it on books too, just in case something like a virus hit." Ralph said. "Nothing we can do with it, except send a crew out to gather all they want." Ralph walked over and picked up one of the books and thumbed through it. He left the book and walked down one of the isles. He reappeared two boxes in his hands. One small and one larger. I need a starter for my car." He held out the other box. A set of spark plugs for that old truck you found."

"And is that what is in that box?" John said.

"Yeah, that is what they are. We are in luck. There are plug wires back there too. We should get them."

"I believe I will, where are they."

Ralph handed John the sparkplugs. "I'll get them for you."

John slid the box in his back pocket. "We'll make a list of the parts we need and send some guys back to get them."

"Damn we would have passed this up," Reba said.

When they left the building Ralph made sure the door was locked. "Let's drive up the road and see if we can find you girls some clothes," he said.

"I want jeans and a warm flannel shirt," Reba said.

After they were seated in the truck Amy looked at the building they came out of. "You know, all this stuff we are finding will be gone someday. My children will never know what we had and lost."

"It will be the wild ass west all over again," Reba

said. "I have heard, history does repeat itself."

"Oh, I can see us now talking with our kids. The conversation will be. Come on dear, we are going to the museum. What is it called mommy? Atlanta."

In the next town, they found a general store. Even though the shelves were empty the store provided a couple of dresses. The clothes were two sizes too big. They also found a winter shirt and a pair of pants for each that were big for them, but they welcomed them.

"Nothing like North Georgia fashion," Reba said.

"If those boys threw our clothes away, they better not let me get my hands on them," Amy said.

By the time they finished searching for another town for anything of value it was getting dark. Ralph suggested they stay in one of the houses for the night.

CHAPTER 26

The Rangers

Jes and West Helped their four partners load their trailers for their journeys' home. It had been two years since either had seen their families. Dawson had no family left. So, he is going home with Mike and his family who lived in South Alabama. The only contact Mike had from his family was just before the cell service went out. His father told him that everyone had taken the shot, and they were fine. He had no idea if they were still okay. He told the group that being on the road with them was an adventure and he was enjoying it, but he had to see about his family.

Carl Wilcox said his feelings were the same. It is exciting exploring the land now, but he wanted to know his family was safe. He had heard from them while the cell service was working, and all of his family had taken the shot. Clyde Walker said the last time he heard from his family his father told him that Houston had become too dangerous, and they were going to find a less populated area to live in. That was before the cell phones stopped working. He has not heard from them since. He had no idea where to look so he was going to stay with Carl and his family.

West shook the guy's hands. "I wish you fellows a safe trip home. These past few years have been a part of my life I will cherish from now on. I hope to see you all again."

Jes leaning on one of the trailers. "Guys we have been through a lot together over the past years. I will sure miss you. Stay connected with those satellite phones."

Dawson looked up. "Well, sarge, I hate to leave you behind, but you have a good reason to staying."

"Yeah these folks need someone to look out for them," Jes said. "And we will help them to move back to their homes."

Dawson nodded a couple of times. "And most definitely you need to help the one with dark hair and green eyes." Dawson turned to Reverand Ball who was eating a peanut butter and grape jelly sandwich. "I believe it is something in the water around here that is causing these ceremonies."

"You had better hit the road. You have been drinking the same water," Ball said.

"Who will marry you and Laura," Dawson asked.

Lindsay showed up. "You guys didn't think you could sneak off with out me seeing you off did you."

"Not on your life. Take care of the big goon okay," Carl said.

The four Rangers climbed in their Hummers loaded with food fuel and ammo bid their friends farewell and drove off ending a chapter in their lives that bonded the men together like glue.

"We had better get busy with this moving if you want to get settled in so you can spend the night in your homes again," West told the group who had gathered to tell the four rangers by and thank them for what they had done for them.

The move was not as time very consuming because the only things most had brought was clothes and a few personal items. They left all of their furniture at their houses. By the end of the day almost everything was back in the homes it had left from not long ago.

Everyone commented on how happy they were to be back home again.

For the past few days West had been spending a lot of time with a cute blonde named Joy Ingles who was good friends with Lindsay, and she lived three houses from her. Right after they met she told West she and her boyfriend broke up a year before the virus hit. That evening she West, Jes and Lindsay were visiting at a park in the neighborhood.

A pickup stopped and a man got out with two packages of white butcher paper and walked toward the four were sitting. "I got you girls something." He put the wrappings on the table.

"Would you care to join us," Joy said.

"I want to finish making my rounds before it gets to late." He walked to his truck, got in and drove off.

This being the first time they had really talked about anything other than surviving Jes wanted to get to know more about the girl he had fallen for. He started out by asking her where she was living before the virus and what she did.

Lindsay told him she was living in Roswell. She moved to where she lives ten years ago. She had been a personal trainer for the last seven years. Before that she was a fitness instructor.

Luck have it West was not shy with women. "Joy did you lose anyone close to you to the virus?"

She reached down and rubbed the calf on her right

leg. "Muscle tightening up." As she rubbed it she said. "I lost my parents."

"I am sorry to hear that," West said.

"It has been a difficult go dealing with their loss and having to survive too. But I am making do."

Jes asked Lindsay. "Did you lose anyone."

"Not in the virus but my sister died in a car wreck a year before it hit. It would have been easier going through this with her. My parents I lost ten years ago."

"How about you all? Did either of you lose anyone?"

"We don't know. We haven't heard from our families. Neither of us are married," Jes said.

When Joy made a comment about how cold it was getting no one said a word. The men stood, took the women by a hand, and walked each of them to their house up on the porch, went inside and closed the door.

The next morning Lindsay and Jes were sitting at the kitchen table, having a cup of coffee.

Lindsay looked at the floor, the walls, and the ceiling. "It is so great to be back in my home. Why did we all think it was a good idea to take up residence in that collage?"

"You were scared and at times like that people look for safety. And being in a large group seemed safer. People just have a difficult time getting along living together," Jes said.

They were interrupted by a knock on the door.

"I know who that is. I'll be right back." Lindsay got out of her chair and walked to the door. When she opened it Joy walked in carrying a brown bag. West walked in behind her.

"What do you have?" Jes asked.

"A big surprise for you two men," Lindsay said.

Joy began emptying pulling the contents and placing them on the table.

"Oh, wow, you girls are something else.

In no time both men were feasting on a breakfast consisting of eggs pancakes, oatmeal and a big surprise, bacon. All was cooked on a two-burner propane stove.

"Where did the bacon come from?" Jes asked.

"What is that man's name that stopped by yesterday." Lindsay said. "Oh, dumb me, Mister Vest raises hogs, and he butchered a couple the day before you folks got here. That is what he gave us last night. He has a lot put up in salt and the rest he spreads around."

"He said in a couple of days he is going to Bar B Q a whole hog. He said he has enough meat to go with it that he can feed the entire community," Lindsay said. "He said he has the ingredients to make some fantastic sauce. That will be worth staying around for, right."

The men smiled. "You bet it will," Jes said.

"I wouldn't miss it for the world," West said.

With breakfast over and the dishes cleaned and put away the four set out on a scavenger hunt for nothing particular just anything they could use. Really the hunt was to get out for a while and check out the town. They wanted to see if any looters have paid a visit to the area. If anyone had been there they would be on the lookout for them. Better to find them than they find you.

The first store was a drug store in the downtown area. It had been gone through and wiped clean of the medicines. All they found was a few tubes of lipstick.

They strolled down the sidewalk looking in windows as they passed by.

At an intersection when they reached the end of a building two guys stepped in front of them. Each had knives with twelve-inch blades. One had dirty blond bushy hair and a four-inch beard. The other had slicked back dark hair and was clean shaved. Despite a food shortage neither suffered from malnutrition. The new jeans and shirts they wore gave the impression they had found a clothing store. Both men were over six feet tall and maybe two hundred and thirty pounds.

The men held their knives up.

Slick hair said, "We want those guns."

West said, "They are not guns. They are rifles."

"What damn difference does it make?"

"Makes a lot of differences. It means you don't know much about weapons. You might shoot yourself," Jes said.

"Just give us the damn things." Slick hair said sounding aggravated.

"I don't know if we should," West said.

"Man, we can have these blades in your guts before you can get those rifle off of your shoulders."

"Given the distance between us you probably can," Jes said and stood looking at the man.

Slick hair stared at the two soldiers.

Bushy hair sounded nervous. "Well, are you guys going to give us the damn things?"

"No, we are not," Jes said.

"Why not," Slick hair said nervously.

Jes put his finger up. "If you come at us with those knives we will take them from you, twist you around, wrap our arms around your heads and twist them until your necks break. You'll not hear the snapping of the bone. That is how fast you'll die."

Slick hair stomped his foot. "I knew they were for real Rangers. Look man we are sorry. There is no way we could have hurt you all. Look." He held his hand up and jabbed it. The blade sunk back into the handle. "It's not even a real knife."

Blond Hair spoke up. "We are part time actors, and these were prop from a play."

Jes asked grinned. "Part time actors. If you had gotten our guns what would you have used them for?"

Slick Hair said, "Protection, if you showed us how to use them."

"Oh, hell are you two for real. What did you do with your time when you were not acting?" West asked.

"We were Chip N Dale Dancers," Blond Hair said.

"I don't believe this," Jes said. "First we have an underwear model and his model girlfriend. Now we have Chip N Dales. Where did you people come from?"

Slick Hair looked at his friend and back at Jes. This underwear model, is his name Samson and the model is Delilah?"

"That would be them," West said. "You guys know them?"

"Yes, we used the same agent in Atlanta." Blond Hair said. "Do you know where they are?"

Jes, West and the girls laughed.

Jes said. "Do we know where they are. You bet we do. How would you two like to join Samson's flock?"

"You mean Samson and Delilah have goats?" Dark

Hair said.

"Not goats. The people kind of flock," Jes said.

"Oh, you mean he has taken on some Religion."

Jes nodded. "Both of them Baptized and married. We will take you to them if you will tell us where you came across those new clothes."

"You have a deal. We found them in the stockroom of a clothing store three blocks down. We'll show you. The room is hidden in the back. I didn't pay much attention, but I don't know if they have anything to fit you folks," Bush hair said.

Sansom and Delilah didn't recognize their two friends when they first stepped out of the Hummer. It took slick hair calling their name for them to realize who it was. When they recognized them they were excited to see them.

Jes West and the girls didn't stay long they wanted to get back and rummage through the clothing store the men had told them about.

They did catch the part of the conversation where the guys were excited to join Samson and his community. There was talk about being baptized as a requirement to live there.

The next day the Bar B Q kicked off in the park in the neighborhood. Mister Vest pitched in two hogs and sauce he swore it would make you slap your mother-in-law. But he did not recommend doing that.

The community pitched in vegetables and tea someone had pulled off of a shelf of a grocery store a few months back. It needed to be served while it still had flavor.

Jes and West sat at a table watching Lindsay and Joy taking food out of baskets and placing it on a table. Both men had been to many picnics and family gatherings with plenty of food and refreshments. But the feast unfolding in front of them was something they had thought they would never see again. The smell of Bar B Q on a large grill filled the air bringing back memories of home in Louisiana.

Jes thought about how his uncle cooked a hog. He had a hole in the ground at farm. He would burn hickory wood on a fire next to it and shoveled the hot smoldering wood in the hole. He would place half of a hog on a rack above the wood. It was a slow process, but the meat was tender and delicious.

The reverend Allen Ball appeared and took a seat across the table. "What do you men think of this?"

"It is something the community needs to take their minds away from what their situation," West said.

"What do you think, Jes. Jes," Ball said after not getting an answer. "What do you think about this?"

Jes not looking a Ball said. "About what."

"About all of this. The food—."

Ball gave up when he realizing he wasn't going to get an answer.

Jes's attention was on Lindsay. The way her jeans fit her body, the way she moved and interacted, her smile that lit up his day. He thought about the twist in her walk. Today there was a smile on her face that had been there all morning. He looked around and realized that everyone acted as if this were a family picnic. Or a company gathering. It was the first time since the virus he had seen people happy. He looked at West and noticed a smile on his face. He wondered if he was thinking about Joy.

West Couldn't take his eyes off of Joy. Her slim body moving about helping set up for the feast. The way she interacted with the people you wouldn't know there was a virus that wiped out most of the people in the world.

The two women broke off from the crowd and headed toward the men, each with a plat in one hand and a cup in the other. When the girls reached the men the sat the plates and cups on the table.

"Lindsay said, "We will right back with our plates. So, don't start without us."

The Rangers didn't take their eyes off the girls as they walked to the food table, fixed themselves a plate and walked back.

The four sat, eat and enjoyed themselves more than they had in a year. For a time in a year, they went about the day not thinking about the virus.

Jes had given it to the fact that his renter was going to be a permanent resident in his head but not rent free. Every time he looked at her, touched her, held her, and every time he kissed her and thought about her would be her payment. His free-wheeling lifestyle was gone, replaced with this lovely woman.

After finishing a second helping of Bar B Q the four went for a walk around the park.

Before they made it back to their table Jes stopped West long enough for the girls to get ahead. After a brief conversation, the men caught up.

After they finished their walk Joy told them. "You guys have a seat; Lindsay and I will pack these dishes so we can take them home and clean them."

After the dishes were packed Lindsay took a seat

next to Jes.

He put a hand on her knee. "West and I am going to find a house and stay here. For a while anyway. What do you think."

"Oh, that is a good idea, isn't it Joy. I second it."

Joy smiled. "The best news I have heard in a long time."

"We have so much to do at our houses, I think tomorrow, or the next day will be a good time for you guys to start looking," Lindsay said.

"We can each take a house and get started. Do you have a list," West asked Joy.

"I just happen to have one on my kitchen table."

Lindsay stood and picked up the dishes. "Mine is on the coffee table at my house. The first thing on my list is easy access to water."

"Same here," Joy said. And we have to put up an outside toilet somewhere in the yard."

After an inspection of the houses and checking the list the girls had written up they put their thoughts together and produced a solution for the water.

"I have an idea," Jes said. If we go a mile out of town I'll bet we can find houses with wells. And some of those wells might be close to the house."

They used what daylight was left to search for houses outside the city water reach. There were some houses that were only a few years old that had wells in the yard.

"These houses are perfect for us," Lindsay said, referring five houses at an intersection. Jes passed the last house and turned right on the cross street. One house sat on the corner and one next to it. The houses were only a hundred feet apart.

Lindsay said, "If you come out of the back door it's only a hop, skip and a jump to either of the houses.

"I remember these houses being built," Joy said. "Yes they are just what we need."

West parked the Hummer. "Let's get out and look for the wells."

"Surly the sewer system does not run out this far, so they are on a septic tank," Jes said.

It didn't take long to find the wells. "It appears that one well supplies two houses. And the last house has its own well. There must be a lot of water under us," West said and looked at the pumps used to pull the water from the ground. "What we need are generators that run off of gas and solar. Let's go inspect the houses then we will go to town."

The girls liked the open floor plan in each house even if they were all identical. Three bedrooms, two bath, kitchen, Livingroom, fireplace room and a deck.

"Same builder built all of these houses." Joy said.

"And he didn't spend much on the floor plan, since he used the same layout for all the houses." Jes said.

The girls chose a house each of the three on the main road. Jes and West chose the one next to them.

"Cheaper two people living in one house," Jes said.

"That is true. And men can live together but women can't. Unless it is an emergency," Joy said.

"Like a virus right," Jes said.

"The virus was an urgency for a while. Now it is a way of life," Lindsay said.

"West stretched his arms out and bent his elbows a couple of times. "Let's make this more of a way of life and go find some generators."

"We can get some from the college," Lindsay said. "I believe we had six that ran off of solar and gas. I want to bring my pickup out here."

Joy spoke up. "Oh, good idea, I'll bring my car."

"After we have everything we need here. We should go by that gym we worked found and bring some of the weights and equipment out here. It will save us going to town so often. It only takes one lucky shot to put one of us down," West said.

"Well thought out.," Jes said. "Our luck might run out one day. Anything you girls want or need we should get it."

Lindsay looked around. "Why are we not finding any bodies?"

"A friend of mine who subs for the CIA told me that most people died in the hospital."

"There were not that many hospitals," Joy said.

"They put large tents up in the parking lots."

"Tents? People died in tents," Lindsay said. "Those tents must have been huge."

"They were very large, and a lot of them. Enough to hold two thousand beds. Bodies were moved out as soon as people died which was often. The average stay in one of those was a few hours and rotated then in and out that quickly." Jes said.

"Who is this friend, I have heard you talk about him before?"

"His name is Carter Logan?"

"I know him West said. "He is a resourceful guy."

The End

Look for the third and final book in the series.

ABOUT THE AUTHOR

Ron lives in Georgia.